dreams and being true to yourself." **BookTrus**

"Sensational and unforgettable, falling in love with this book came as naturally as breathing. The best book I've read all year." **Blog of a Bookaholic**

"It has been what I can only describe as a transformative experience." **New Zealand bookseller**

"A promising first novel with no lack of heart and soul." **School Library Association**

"A heart-warming story told from the point of view of four girls who feel they don't fit in. An inspirational story about friendship, life and finding your place in the world. A story that will have significance for many teenagers." *Carousel*

"In her moving and inspiring story Siobhan Curham addresses the needs of teenagers today through the wonderful power of dreams and the imagination." *The School Librarian*

"I liked all the characters, and although they were all different, I could relate to them and I started to know, like and worry about them, just like friends. I was kept reading right to the end and I would definitely recommend this book to my fr

Tell It to the Moon

SIOBHAN CURHAM

WALKER
BOOKS

This is a work of fiction. Names, characters, places and incidents are either the product of the author's imagination or, if real, used fictitiously. All statements, activities, stunts, descriptions, information and material of any other kind contained herein are included for entertainment purposes only and should not be relied on for accuracy or replicated as they may result in injury.

First published 2017 by Walker Books Ltd
87 Vauxhall Walk, London SE11 5HJ

2 4 6 8 10 9 7 5 3 1

Text © 2017 Siobhan Curham
Cover illustration © 2017 Kate Forrester

The right of Siobhan Curham to be identified as author of this work has been asserted by her in accordance with the Copyright, Designs and Patents Act 1988

This book has been typeset in Berolina

Printed and bound in Great Britain by Clays Ltd, St Ives plc

British Library Cataloguing in Publication Data:
a catalogue record for this book is available from the British Library

ISBN 978-1-4063-6615-0

www.walker.co.uk

This book is dedicated to the dreamers. I hope it inspires you to live a life beyond your wildest dreams.

"With freedom, books, flowers and the moon, who could not be happy?" Oscar Wilde

Chapter One

Although it was only Christmas Eve, Rose had already made a New Year's resolution. A resolution she swore she was going to live by for the rest of her days … even if it killed her. It was to never again let the so-called adults in her life make her do something she didn't want to do. And being brought to this crappy interpretive dance class by her dad's girlfriend, Rachel, was only strengthening her resolve.

"Feel the music inside your body," the instructor, Harmony, cried from the front of the studio. "Feel it take you over. Feel yourself *become* the music!"

Rose stared at Harmony. She was all blonde hair and white teeth and muscles – like a Barbie doll on steroids. DANCE LIKE NOBODY'S WATCHING said the gold lettering on her top. Well, she was certainly living the logo, Rose thought, as Harmony flailed about to the cheesy theme tune from *Titanic*. She looked like she'd drunk a bottle of Jack Daniels and was about to keel over any minute.

"Become the music!" Harmony cried again, flinging her arms in the air.

Rose looked around the studio. Surely the others could see what a fruit loop she was. But all the other women had their eyes closed and were flailing in unison. It was like being at a zombie cheerleader convention and Rose didn't know whether to laugh or cry. What the hell was she doing here? Ah, yes, that's right, she was supposed to be "bonding" with Rachel. When her dad had suggested they go out to get to know each other better, Rose had assumed they'd go for coffee, but no – Rachel had brought her to Deranged Dancers Anonymous.

"Feel your heart opening!" Harmony cried once more. "Feel it grow as big as the cosmos!"

Rose glanced at the door. She could slip out now, while they all had their eyes shut, and wait for Rachel in the foyer. She could tell her she'd been feeling sick. It wouldn't be a lie. She *was* feeling sick – sick of being in New York – something she'd never, ever imagined she'd feel. The whole point of this trip was to spend some quality time with her dad, but in the week since she'd got here he'd been wrapped up in rehearsals for his next movie and she'd been stuck with doe-eyed Californian beach babe Rachel instead.

"Close your eyes and let yourself go!" Harmony called. But her eyes were open now and she was looking straight at Rose.

Against all of her better judgement, Rose closed her eyes and flung her arms in the air. Celine Dion's warbling reached a crescendo.

"Feel your heart going on and on for an eternity," Harmony said breathlessly.

Rose frowned. What did that even mean? How could your heart go on and on for an eternity? She hated all this New Age bullshit that women like Rachel lapped up like eager puppies. She wanted to storm to the front of the class and put on "Welcome to the Jungle" by Guns N' Roses. That would give them all a reality check.

"Feel your heart expand beyond this planet, up past the stars and the moon and into infinity."

At Harmony's mention of the moon, Rose softened slightly. What would the Moonlight Dreamers think if they could see her now? She bit down on her bottom lip to stop herself from laughing.

Amber looked at her blank computer screen and sighed. She walked over to her bedroom window and sighed. She stared at her reflection in the mirror on the wall and sighed. But it was no good. She still couldn't think of anything to write about. Amber had been suffering from an acute case of "blogger's block" for weeks now. Before, she'd had no problem coming up with things to write about – everywhere she'd looked she'd seen the seed of an idea. But now her brain felt as gloopy as porridge and the world seemed to be sucked dry of all new ideas. Then a thought occurred to her. Maybe she should write a blog about not being able to write a blog. Yes! Finally she had something to write about. She hurried back to her laptop and typed the words BLOGGER'S BLOCK across the top of the page. Then she sat and stared into the blankness of the screen until she started seeing dots.

"What am I going to do?" Amber gazed at the black-and-white print of Oscar Wilde that hung on the wall above her bed. "Help me, Oscar. I need some wordspiration!" She reached for the well-worn book of Oscar Wilde quotes on her desk, flicked to a random page and began to read.

"Most people are other people. Their thoughts are someone else's opinions, their lives a mimicry, their passions a quotation."

Amber sighed. Usually she loved the fact that Oscar always knew exactly what to say about her situation but today it felt uncomfortably close to the truth. Over the past couple of months a creeping fog of self-doubt had snuck up on Amber, paralyzing her with indecision. It wasn't just her blog she was blocked on, it was her dreams, too. And, as the founding member of the Moonlight Dreamers, this was hugely worrying. She hadn't told the others how she'd been feeling – she'd been way too embarrassed. So, every time they met she'd make up a dream – something she felt she ought to want to do – but there was no passion behind it. Not like the other Moonlight Dreamers. When Rose talked about her cake-making or Maali her photography or Sky her poetry they'd glow with excitement. Their dreams lit them up from inside. But when Amber talked about building her blog or visiting another of Oscar Wilde's London haunts she felt dull inside. As Oscar so rightly said, currently, her passions were nothing more than "a quotation".

Amber opened her desk drawer and looked at the pencil sketch she kept inside. The sketch she didn't feel able to openly display but that she'd looked at every day since her dad Gerald had given it to her. It was a sketch of her mum – her surrogate mum. Gerald had drawn it in the hospital, just before Amber was born. The heavily pregnant woman – her mum – was gazing off into the distance, a look of sadness etched on her face. But why was she sad? Amber slammed the drawer shut. Then she highlighted BLOGGER'S BLOCK – and pressed DELETE.

Maali turned on her fairy lights and lit a stick of incense, then she sat cross-legged in front of her shrine, shut her eyes and took a deep breath. She had some serious praying to do.

"Dear Lakshmi, thank you so much for all that you've blessed me with," she began. "I really am truly grateful. I've been trying so hard to let go of my selfish needs and focus on helping other people but I was just wondering..." Maali opened her eyes and looked at the Lakshmi statue. She was so beautiful, standing there on her lotus flower, so serene. Why couldn't she be like that? *Because you're not a goddess*, her inner voice chirped. Maali blushed. "I'm sorry, Lakshmi, it's just that I ... I really want to meet my soulmate and it's especially hard at this time of year. Everywhere I look all I see are couples cuddling in their Christmas jumpers and kissing under the mistletoe."

This wasn't strictly true. She'd seen only one couple kissing under the mistletoe and that had been in an advert for breath-freshening mints, and yesterday she'd seen a couple in Christmas jumpers having a huge argument in the middle of Brick Lane. Apparently he was a "selfish pig" for not wanting to spend Christmas Day with her family. But still…

"I wish there was some way you could give me a sign," Maali continued, looking straight into Lakshmi's painted brown eyes. "Just to let me know that my soulmate's on his way. Or if he's not; if I'm supposed to be on my own for this lifetime and dedicate myself to God." Maali shuddered inwardly at the prospect. "Please, Lakshmi. Please give me a sign. Please let me know that my soulmate's on his way. Please let me know who he is." She took a deep breath to try to compose herself. Downstairs she could hear her parents and brother chatting with her Auntie Sita and Uncle Dev. They came over every Christmas Eve for dinner. "Thank you for my family, Lakshmi. Even my brother. Please help him to grow out of his annoying 'I'm bored' phase soon. And thank you for the food we're about to eat and all of the fun we're about to have. Thank you for this house and our shop and all our riches. And please take care of the Moonlight Dreamers and shower your blessings upon them."

Maali opened her eyes and looked at the photo of her friends on the shrine. She'd put it there a week ago, when Rose went off to New York and Sky had gone away with her dad, to bring them protection. They'd taken the photo at the end of their last meeting. They were all leaning against the wall of Amber's roof garden, trying to look cool and mysterious but then, just before the timer on Maali's camera had gone off, a pigeon had dive-bombed the terrace and they'd all started laughing. Maali loved the picture. She loved the way the candlelight threw shadows on their faces. She loved how happy and vibrant they all looked. "Thank you so much for the Moonlight Dreamers and for bringing them into my life," she whispered to Lakshmi.

"Maali!"

She jumped at the sound of her mum's voice from the hallway below. "Yes?"

"Could you pop to the store for me, please? We've run out of ghee."

"Sure." Maali stood up. "Thank you, Lakshmi," she whispered to the goddess as she turned off the fairy lights. Then she grabbed her coat and headed down from her attic room. Her mum was waiting for her at the foot of the stairs, holding her purse. She was wearing her favourite emerald-green sari and her arms were covered with intricate henna tattoos. She looked beautiful. Beautiful and stressed. Two deep frown lines had formed between her eyebrows.

"Are you OK?"

Her mum nodded and forced a smile. "Could you get some matches, too?" She handed Maali some money.

"Of course." Maali followed her along the narrow corridor that ran the length of their flat. It smelled of cooked tomatoes and coriander and cumin. Maali's stomach rumbled. As they reached the living room door she looked inside. It had all gone quiet. Her brother, Namir, was playing Lego on the floor but her Auntie Sita and Uncle Dev were sitting in silence looking at her dad, who was in his armchair next to the family shrine. He was rubbing his eyes.

"Are you OK, Dad?" Maali asked from the doorway.

He looked at her and blinked, like he couldn't see her for a moment. "What? Oh – yes, yes, I'm fine." He smiled but, like her mum's, his smile seemed forced.

"He just had a bit of a dizzy spell," her mum whispered. "Off you go."

Outside, the air was crisp and cool. Maali instinctively looked up at the moon, a thin, silver crescent over the nearby mosque. At the last Moonlight Dreamers meeting Amber had suggested that, as they wouldn't be together for a while, if they had a problem they should try telling it to the moon instead. But for once Maali wasn't comforted by its silvery light. Something was up with her dad. He'd seemed exhausted the past couple of weeks. True, the sweet shop had been packed in the run-up to Christmas, but he was used to it being busy. Maali hoped he wasn't coming down with something – it was a horrible time of year to get ill.

As she walked past a vintage clothes shop the door opened and a woman walked out, bringing with her the burst of a song from the shop stereo.

"*Ashes to ashes. . .*" the singer crooned.

Maali caught her breath. She'd been trying so hard not to think of Ash in the weeks since their last encounter. When she'd asked Lakshmi for a sign this was definitely not the kind she was looking for. Ash couldn't be her soulmate, tragically; he belonged to another, the glamorous Sage – or Sage and Onion, as Rose liked to call her. Maali hurried up the road. *Lakshmi, please help me find out who my real soulmate is*, she prayed. A group of men and women were weaving their way along the pavement towards her, singing a Christmas song. The women wobbled on their high heels like they were walking on a rocking ship and the men were red-faced and swigging from bottles of beer. Maali quickly looked down at the pavement. In her experience drunk people were always the most likely to be racist. It was as if the hatred they kept stored inside of them when they were sober oozed out with the stale beer fumes. She moved over to the edge of the pavement and quickened her pace.

"Merry Christmas!" one of the women cried as Maali drew level. She looked up nervously. The woman was smiling at her. Her red lipstick was smeared around her lips, making her look like a clown.

"Merry Christmas," Maali mumbled.

One of the men staggered over. His tie was half undone and a cigarette hung from his mouth. "Merry Christmas!" he said to Maali, although his eyes seemed to be having trouble focusing on her. The ash from the end of his cigarette fell off, landing on Maali's coat.

"Thank you. Merry Christmas," she said, hurrying along. It was only when she went to brush the ash off that she realized the significance of what had just happened. Twice this evening she'd asked Lakshmi for a sign and both times she'd been given Ash.

As the sound from the huge brass gong reverberated around the meditation room Sky glanced at her dad. He sat cross-legged, spine straight, messy blond hair tied back, eyes closed. Was he happy? She couldn't tell. His face was completely expressionless. Ever since her mum died, Christmas had been one of the hardest times of the year. And this year Liam had seemed even sadder – his break-up with Savannah was still so fresh. The official reason they'd come to Glastonbury on retreat was for a holiday, but Sky knew that the real reason was because Liam wanted to get away from London and the memories of his break-up with Rose's mum. Ever since they'd moved back into their houseboat there'd been an aura of sadness about him. It had been his first relationship in five years, and when it ended in such spectacular style he'd seen it as a personal failing. Sky had appreciated Liam feeling bad about moving them into Savannah's house so soon but she didn't want him to feel guilty. Despite their terrible start she'd ended up becoming close friends with Rose and they'd both become Moonlight Dreamers, which was without doubt one of the best things that had ever happened to Sky. As she thought of Rose she smiled. She wondered how she was getting on in New York. Even though Rose had been playing it cool, Sky could tell she'd been really excited to see her dad.

The gong rang out again. Sky took a deep, incense-filled breath and tried to centre herself into her meditation. But her monkey mind, as the Buddhists called it, kept leaping about. She wondered how the other Moonlight Dreamers were doing. She thought of Amber and Maali at home in London. She thought of the moon, shining down on all of them – apart from Rose, of course, as it would still be daytime in New York. It was comforting to know that, no matter where they were, they could always look up at the moon and feel connected. Sky couldn't wait for their next meeting. But then a feeling of dread started seeping into her. When they got back to London something horrible was going to happen, something she'd been trying to block out for weeks. But now, in the silence of the meditation room, it echoed through her mind like a crashing gong: *when she got back to London she would have to start going to school.*

Chapter Two

Something strange was happening. Rose wasn't sure if it was the heat of the dance studio or the scent of the aromatherapy oil burner, or the hypnotic quality of Harmony's voice, but she was actually starting to get into this interpretive dance baloney.

"Feel your power rising inside of you!" Harmony cried as she stalked around the studio, her face gleaming with sweat. All the other women, who'd looked so polished and immaculate at the start of the class, were now dripping with sweat too and several of them even had a hair out of place. "Think of all the things you want to achieve in the New Year – all of the dreams burning away inside of you."

Rose thought of her dream of becoming a patissier and pictured it as a flame burning brightly inside of her.

"Dance your dreams into being!" Harmony yelled.

Rose felt her whole being light up. She no longer had to think about how to move her body, it was as if the music had worked its way into her and was moving her from the inside out. As she danced wildly she imagined being back at work at the cake shop in Camden. Then she thought of Francesca, the cake shop's owner. She thought of her glossy dark hair and ruby-red lips and she felt a tingling deep in the pit of her stomach.

"Dance through any fears!" Harmony yelled. "Unleash your inner tiger! Hear her roar!"

Rose had felt pretty fearless since weathering the internet storm over her topless photo. There was only one thing she could think of that still made her afraid.

"You are a tiger!" Harmony yelled. "You fear nothing."

Rose began spinning round and round the studio until her edges blurred. She felt wild and unstoppable. And she was going to face up to this final fear once and for all.

After the class was over, Rose and Rachel spilled out of the studio and onto Broadway, cheeks glowing. It was freezing out. The steam billowing from the vents in the street looked like giant puffs of icy breath. New York City was so full of life that it wasn't hard for Rose to imagine it as a living, breathing creature in its own right.

"So, what did you think? Wasn't it awesome?" Rachel said, gazing at Rose.

Normally, Rose hated when people asked your opinion and then gave you the answer they wanted all in the same breath, but the dance class had left her feeling so mellow she couldn't summon the energy to be pissed off.

"Yeah, it was all right," she said, pulling her woolly hat down against the cold breeze. The truth was, the class had ended up being way more than all right. Harmony had worked some kind of hocus pocus dance magic and helped her get really clear on what she needed to do.

"Isn't it, like, amazing how freeing it is to just lose yourself in the music?" Rachel mused. "Shall we go get a green juice?"

Although Rose would have much preferred a hot chocolate, she nodded and followed Rachel into a hipster health-food joint named The Raw Deal. The whole place had been constructed from bleached wood, from the rows of bench-style tables to the beams running across the ceiling and the scuffed floorboards.

"What would you like?" Rachel asked, gesturing at a huge blackboard on the wall behind the counter.

Rose cringed as she read the names of the juices: Enlightenment, Peace, Tranquillity, Zen. "I'll have a Namaste," she said hesitantly.

"Cool choice!" Rachel exclaimed.

After they'd got their juices they slipped into one of the booths at the back.

"I guess your mom must live off green juice to keep that amazing figure of hers," Rachel said, before taking a sip of her Inner Child.

Rose fought the urge to snort with laughter. The last meal she'd seen Savannah having was half a pack of Marlboro Reds and a glass of champagne – and that had been for breakfast. Savannah had come off the wagon big time since she and Liam had split up. It was yet another reason Rose wished they were still together – the main reason being that she'd still be living with Sky. It was so weird to think how much she'd hated Sky's guts when she first moved in. Now she missed her like crazy.

"Yeah, sometimes," she muttered, before taking a gulp of her own drink and almost gagging. It was gross. Like toothpaste mixed with pond water.

"It must be so much fun having her as a mom," Rachel continued.

Rose sighed. Why all the questions about her mom all of a sudden? "Yeah, it is," she said defensively, although fun was one of the last adjectives she'd have picked to describe her life with Savannah.

"She's so beautiful." Rachel sighed.

And then Rose got it. Rachel was insecure. And who wouldn't be, hooking up with the ex-husband of one of the world's most beautiful women (according to the likes of *Vogue*, anyways)? When Rose's dad had left them for Rachel, Rose had been furious. And she couldn't figure out why he'd rather be with someone so vacuous. But, having stayed with them for the past week, she'd begun to work it out. Rachel was much more low maintenance than Savannah – an adoring fan-girl who hung on Jason's every word. And although she hated to admit it, Rose could see that he was happier with Rachel – and way calmer.

Rose felt jealousy nipping at her insides but she ignored it and leaned across the table. "A very wise person once said that no object is so beautiful that, under certain circumstances, it will not look ugly."

Rachel blinked her huge eyes slowly. "Wow, that's really profound. Oprah, right?"

Rose frowned. "What?"

"The person who said that. Was it Oprah Winfrey?"

Rose shook her head. "No. Oscar Wilde."

"Far out." Rachel took another sip of her juice. "Is he, like, a fashion designer?"

"No. He's, like, dead. He was a really famous writer, back in Victorian times."

"Oh!" Rachel gazed into space.

Rose tried to imagine how her dad ever managed to have an interesting conversation with Rachel. And then something occurred to her. People seemed to have relationships for several reasons. There were the people who chose their partners because they wanted an easy life. They picked people who would say and do anything to please them, like her dad had picked Rachel, or they picked people who fitted in with what was expected of them, like Rose had picked Matt before. But then there were the people who chose the third, dangerous option. The people who followed their hearts, who chased love with the bravery of a tiger – even if it meant shocking or disappointing others. People like Oscar Wilde, who had gone to jail for love. People like Rose.

* * *

Amber looked at her pocket watch. She'd been sitting in front of her blank screen for one hour, forty-eight minutes – a new personal best. She decided to check the spam folder in her email to break up the monotony. Among the usual "lottery wins" she spotted a comment notification from her *Wilde at Heart* blog – probably someone else asking when she was going to post again – and an email from … her heart almost stopped beating … from the Happy Families Surrogacy Agency. Finally, she had a reply! Gerald and Daniel had given her the agency details when she'd told them she wanted to try to contact her surrogate mum. They'd warned Amber not to get her hopes up, that her surrogate mum might not want to be contacted. And when Amber hadn't heard anything back she'd assumed they were right, but now… She looked at the unopened email. It had been sent three days ago. Three days ago! There'd been an email about her birth mother on her computer for three whole days and she'd been completely unaware! Her skin prickled with goosebumps. What if it was a message from her mum? There'd been something about the sadness Gerald had captured in his sketch of her that had lodged in Amber's mind. Was she sad because she regretted having a baby for money? Had she wished she could keep Amber, having carried her for nine months? It was questions like these that had given Amber the confidence to email the agency to see if they would forward a message. She'd spent days crafting the email, making sure it was just the right balance of reaching out without appearing needy. It was the last piece of writing she'd done that she felt proud of. She took a deep breath and clicked the email open.

From: happyfamiliessurrogacy@gworld.com
To: wildeatheart@googlepost.com
Date: 21st December 17:30
Subject: Your recent enquiry

Dear Amber,

Thank you very much for your recent enquiry.

Unfortunately, your surrogate mother has stipulated that she does not wish to be contacted. I'm afraid this is most often the case with surrogacy.

I do hope you understand and I'm so sorry not to be able to help you further.

Warm regards,

Maria Holland
Administration Officer
Happy Families Surrogacy Agency

Amber felt a bitter blend of hurt and disappointment building at the back of her throat. She hadn't realized until now how badly she'd wanted to hear from her mother. She hadn't realized how strongly she'd believed she *would* hear. She didn't know how to process this latest development. There was a knock on her door and she slammed her laptop shut.

"Can I come in?" Daniel called.

"Yes." Amber sat up straight and tried to compose herself.

Daniel was wearing a Santa hat, Rudolph the Reindeer jumper and dark jeans. With his short golden hair and beard he looked like a really handsome Father Christmas. "Dinner's almost ready," he said with a grin. "Gerald isn't happy with how the rice turned out, though — he thinks it's too sticky. It's actually fine. But I just wanted to warn you. You know how temperamental he gets when he's chef-ing."

"OK." Amber tried to act normal but she felt really disorientated — all she could think of was the email; the words "unfortunately" and "sorry" stinging like nettles.

"Are you all right, honey?" Daniel sat down on the edge of the bed. He might not be her biological dad but he could still read her better than anyone, able to detect the slightest change in her mood without her saying a thing. Normally she loved this, as it made it so much easier to talk to him about stuff, but not tonight. She couldn't bear the thought of having to tell him what had happened. Speaking those words out loud would make them real. She wasn't ready for that yet.

"I'm fine," she said, getting to her feet and forcing a smile. "Come on then, let's get Christmas started."

Down in the kitchen Gerald was standing hands on hips,

red-faced and frowning at the oven. "It's a total disaster!" he declared as Amber and Daniel came into the room. "Christmas is ruined!"

"Calm down, darling." Daniel gave Gerald a hug, raising his eyebrows at Amber over his shoulder.

Ever since she'd found out that Gerald was her biological dad and they'd started getting along better, Amber had found his theatrics amusing, but tonight she couldn't find anything remotely funny. All she felt was a growing anger. Although she wasn't a head-in-the-clouds romantic like Maali, she'd been excited at the prospect of finding out about her mother, and hopeful at what she might discover. The email from the surrogacy agency was like having a door slammed in her face.

Amber sat down at the table. Gerald had laid it with their fanciest cutlery and each place setting had a napkin intricately folded into the shape of a flower. But they could have been eating from paper plates with plastic knives and forks for all Amber cared. How could her mother not want to know her? Amber was her flesh and blood. Made from one of her eggs. How could she not feel any curiosity about who her daughter had become? Normally Amber liked the questions that frequently filled her mind but these felt like an enemy invasion; all they brought was more hurt. Daniel sat down next to her and Gerald brought them two plates piled high with paella.

"Disaster is served!" he said, plonking the plates down in front of them.

"It looks lovely," Daniel said.

"Yes," Amber muttered. "Anyway, I like rice sticky."

"I told you it was too sticky!" Gerald exclaimed to Daniel. "She didn't even taste it. She could tell just by looking at it!"

"No – I – he..." Amber looked at Daniel helplessly. She didn't want to get him into trouble.

"He what?" Gerald glared down at them both.

"My surrogate mum doesn't want to know me!" The words burst from Amber's mouth, seemingly of their own accord.

The room fell silent. Daniel and Gerald looked at each other.

Amber looked into her lap. "I got a reply from the agency," she muttered. "Apparently she stipulated that she doesn't want any contact with me. So that's that." She picked up a forkful of paella. "Happy Christmas."

From: roselnyc@hotpost.com

To: wildeatheart@googlepost.com; halopoet@hotpost.co.uk; lakshmigirl@googlepost.com

Date: 25th December 10:30

Subject: Happy Christmas! I miss you guys so bad!

Greetings from NYC, my fellow Moonlight Dreamers!
OMG I miss you guys SO BAD! Life back in my beloved home city hasn't been nearly as much fun as I'd hoped. Mainly because my dumbass father is obsessing over his next movie role and his doe-eyed girlfriend is about as

frustrating as watching coffee percolate. Please tell me your news before I shrivel up and die from boredom. The good news is, I'll be home real soon – and in time for our meeting on New Year's Eve. I changed my flight – yay! I cannot wait to see you all again. I hope you're having an awesome Christmas Day. I'm spending it with my dad and the sappy Rachel. We're having raw courgette noodles with avocado salsa for dinner (!!!) and raw brownies made with beetroot (!!!) for dessert. Rachel is a surfer babe from California. She doesn't do anything without first consulting her Angel cards and she says "like", like, every second word. Amber, you would HATE her. Oh, Amber, how I miss your dry sense of humour and your serious face. Please can you send me a selfie of you frowning for me to use as a screensaver? And, Maali, can you pray to that goddess chick of yours that I make it home without totally losing my mind? And, Sky, please could you write me one of your awesome poems about the evils of step-moms? I don't mind if you use my mom as inspiration – even though her role as your step-mom was sadly short-lived. Oh shoot, my dad's calling me – my raw dinner must be un-cooked.

Love you guys so much!

Rose xoxo

PS: There's something I need to tell you all and I'm afraid I might chicken out when I see you so I'm letting you know ahead of time, so you can force me to spill. Sky, you have

my full permission to chant your hippy mantras in my face
until I crack ☺

From: lakshmigirl@googlepost.com
To: wildeatheart@googlepost.com; halopoet@hotpost.co.uk;
roselnyc@hotpost.com
Date: 25th December 11:05
Subject: Re: Happy Christmas! I miss you guys so bad!

Dear Rose – and fellow Moonlight Dreamers,
It was so lovely to hear from you and I will add you to my
prayer list. All is OK here – at least I think it is. My dad's
been very tired, which isn't like him at all, so I've been a bit
worried about him. I can't wait to see you on New Year's
Eve – I can't think of a better way to start a fresh new year.
I hope you've all got some really cool new dreams to share.
Lots of love,
Maali xxxx

PS: Rose, the important thing you've got to tell us better not
be that you're moving back to America!

From: wildeatheart@googlepost.com
To: halopoet@hotpost.co.uk; roselnyc@hotpost.com;
lakshmigirl@googlepost.com
Date: 25th December 11:22
Subject: Re: Re: Happy Christmas! I miss you guys so bad!

Dear Moonlight Dreamers,

I really miss you all too. Things have been tough here. I just had some bad news. This quote from my beloved Oscar sums it up: "When the gods wish to punish us they answer our prayers." I'll tell you all about it when I see you. I hope the rest of your stay in New York goes well, Rose. Did you mean it about the photo? I can never tell when you're joking! My Christmas Day is going to consist of dinner COOKED by Daniel – sorry to rub it in, Rose! And then, after Gerald makes us watch the Queen's speech, we'll have our annual family Scrabble contest (we only play it once a year because Gerald takes it SO seriously and sulks for ever if he loses). Sorry to hear about your dad, Maali – I hope he feels better soon.

Love,

Amber

From: halopoet@hotpost.co.uk

To: roselnyc@hotpost.com; lakshmigirl@googlepost.com; wildeatheart@googlepost.com

Date: 25th December 19:27

Subject: Re: Re: Re: Happy Christmas! I miss you guys so bad!

Dearest Dreamers!

I'm so sorry it's taken me so long to get back to you – the retreat I'm staying in barely has any internet reception.

You wouldn't believe the lengths I've gone to just to get the slightest signal on my phone – I practically had to climb onto the roof! Sorry you've had some bad news, Amber. Hope you're OK? And hope your dad's OK too, Maali. Rose, I feel your pain. My Christmas dinner consisted of a nut roast, which should really have been renamed a nut sog, and just about every vegetable that has ever existed. It's been OK being here, though, as my dad's been a lot happier. I think he's been enjoying being the yoga student for once instead of the teacher. Rose, I wrote you a step-mum haiku. (I've done so much meditation over the past few days my brain's gone to sleep and it's all I could manage!)

STEP-MUM HAIKU

Always a step off,

never able to replace

the one we love most.

Chapter Three

Rose stared across the table at her dad as he did a set of press-ups on the dining-room floor. His head was freshly shaven and he was wearing sweats and a vest top – all part of his preparation for the role of a down-and-out boxer from the Bronx. Only he would be anal enough to insist on staying in character on Christmas freakin' Day.

"Seriously?" Rose glared at him. "Can I please just spend Christmas Day with my dad instead of Rocky Balboa?"

Jason frowned and got to his feet. "My role is not a reprisal of Rocky Balboa," he said in a thick New York drawl. "Donny Delaney is a complex, multifaceted character with a very troubled past. Yo, Rachel," he yelled, "where's the dinner?"

Rose sighed. How did Rachel put up with this bullshit twenty-four seven? But Rachel came bounding into the room, wearing a grin as wide as San Francisco Bay. "Here you go, hon," she trilled, placing two serving dishes in the middle of the table. One was full of courgette noodles garnished with fresh basil. The other contained some kind of avocado-based mush. Rose had never seen so much green food. It made her want to run to the nearest burger joint and stuff her face full of warm, greasy meat.

She turned to Rachel. "Doesn't it annoy you when Dad's in character all the time?"

Rachel continued smiling sweetly and shook her head. "No, not at all." She looked at Jason and blushed. "I guess it's the price you pay for living with one of the world's greatest actors."

Oh purlease! Rose's gagging reflex had never seen so much action since she'd got to New York.

Jason reached across the table and took hold of Rose's hand. "Don't be angry. You know the sacrifices us thespians have to make for our craft." Finally he was talking in his normal British accent – even if what he was saying was utter garbage.

"Yeah, and what about the sacrifices your families have to make?"

Jason's eyes widened in shock. He genuinely didn't seem to get how selfish he could be. He glanced around the luxury apartment. "Hmm, some sacrifice," he muttered.

Rose thought about telling him a few home truths. But she stuffed her anger back down. What was the point? He was as wrapped up in his life as her mom was in hers. Rose could shout and scream all she liked but it wouldn't make a difference. It was time for her to make something of her own life. She had to give up on her parents being in any way remotely normal. They came from Planet Celebrity – a place fuelled by green juice and social media mentions, where self-obsession reigned.

"Let's not argue, darling." Jason smiled that sparkly eyed smile that always sent female movie-goers into a frenzy. "We hardly get to spend any time together as it is."

Yeah, and whose fault is that? Rose thought, helping herself to a plate of shrubbery. When she'd first arrived in New York her dad had been all over her – it was the first time he'd seen her since the whole internet storm and it had felt so nice to feel his concern. But all too quickly he'd gotten wrapped up in rehearsals and she'd been left spending most of her time with Rachel – or escaping Rachel and riding the subway to her old favourite haunts alone. She had met up with a few of her old crowd from school but all that had done was show her that they'd never been true friends. Those guys never had her back the way the Moonlight Dreamers did. They only wanted to talk about the infamous Instagram photo and what her mom was up to. They were gossip junkies, not friends.

"So," Jason said, putting down his knife and fork and staring at her intently. She couldn't help thinking he was acting even now – playing the part of the doting parent. "What have you got planned for next year?"

Rose watched as he helped himself to some courgette noodles. She got the distinct vibe that he was just going through the motions – saying what he thought he ought to. She was overwhelmed by the urge to do something to make him sit up straight and pay attention to her for once. Yes, why didn't she see if he was really listening? "Next year? Well, I'd like to train as a patissier and – I've decided to come out." She sat back and waited for his reaction.

Rachel let out a little gasp. Jason kept putting food on his plate. "Really? That's nice, darling…" Then he froze. "You've decided to what?"

"To come out."

He stared at her. A clump of courgette noodles dropped from his fork. "To come out? What, as in sexually?"

"Er, yes, Father, that is what coming out tends to mean." As Rose looked at him her bravado started to morph into fear. She hadn't wanted him to be the first person she told. She'd wanted it to be the Moonlight Dreamers. What if he was a dick about it? She wasn't sure she'd be able to take it. Why had she said it? Why had she let him get to her? Why hadn't she just bitten her lip?

"So, you're saying that you're gay?" Jason ran his hand across his shaven head. He looked genuinely shocked.

Rose nodded.

"But after the…"

"After the what?"

"The Instagram photo. You said the guy who posted it was your ex-boyfriend."

"He was."

Jason frowned. "But why did you go out with him if you're gay?"

"It was an experiment. I was testing myself." Rose's skin was starting to crawl with embarrassment. She didn't dare look at Rachel.

"So, you're not into guys?"

"No." Geez, what did he want her to do? Write an explanation on the tablecloth in her blood?

"I think this is so cool!" Rachel exclaimed, breaking the awkward silence.

"You do?" Rose glanced at her. She was nodding and smiling. But it wasn't one of her usual, slightly vacuous smiles. This one reached her eyes. This one had meaning.

"Uh-huh. I think it's great that you've taken ownership of your sexuality and that you've been brave enough to share it with us, isn't it, honey?" Rachel looked at Jason and nodded, as if willing him to agree.

Rose looked at her dad. He still looked shell-shocked. "Yes. Yes, thank you for sharing something so personal with us, Rose. For feeling that you could open up in such a personal way." He got to his feet. "I don't know about you, but I feel the need for a hug."

Relief rushed through her. She walked round the table to Jason and he held her tightly. She closed her eyes and pressed her head against his chest and for a moment she was taken back to a time when her parents weren't that well known, back to a time before she had to think about things like fame or sexuality, when life was simple and anything could be solved by one of her dad's hugs.

"Are you sure this isn't – I don't know – some kind of phase? Or some kind of reaction to what happened with the photo?"

"Dad! I do know my own sexual desires." OK, now this was getting seriously cringe-worthy. She broke away from him. "Could we just get back to our Christmas courgettes and talk about something else?"

"Of course."

They sat back down at the table.

"So, go on then – tell me all about this Donny Delaney character," Rose said, eager to shift the spotlight from her "sexual desires", even if it meant listening to her dad drone on about himself yet again.

Jason's face lit up. "Well, as I said, he's a very complex character and…"

As Rose listened to Jason ramble on about tragic flaws and story arcs she felt a warm glow inside of her. After years of carrying her secret like a ticking time bomb she'd finally told someone, and guess what? The world hadn't ended. If anything it had made her feel closer to Jason and Rachel, which was a miracle in itself. Now she just had to tell the Moonlight Dreamers. Oh, and her mom. But how hard could that be?

WHIRLPOOL

BY Sky Cassidy

Fear grips me by the wrist,
pulling me into its swirling depths.
I try to breathe but my lungs fill with ice,
I try to cry but the words freeze in my throat.
Is this what it feels like to be dead?
Suspended in time and space,
mummified by dread.

I search for bravery
but all I see is a darkening whirlpool
and the ghostly spectres of terrible outcomes
whispering *"what if. . ."* over and over and over again,
pulling me deeper and deeper
and deeper
down.

Chapter Four

Sky pulled the door of the houseboat shut behind her and stepped onto the bank of the canal. Coming back home had been a bittersweet experience. Sweet in that there was no place she loved more in the world than their cosy little boat, but bitter because coming home meant she was now just days away from starting school. As she strode along the tow-path the question that had been haunting her all week filled her mind again: why, when she'd been home-schooled for years, did Liam have to send her to school now? She understood that he needed to earn more money and not having to teach her would leave him with loads more time to run yoga classes, but still… She only had a few months to go before her GCSEs. Could he not have just held out until then and spared her the torture? The only good thing was that she'd be going to the same school as Amber. But this was only vaguely reassuring because it also happened to be the school where Amber had been plagued by bullies who couldn't seem to accept the fact that she had two dads and liked dressing in men's clothes. What would those girls make of Sky and the free-spirited life she'd been living? Would she get bullied for being home-schooled and living on a boat? Or for the pink strands in her hair or the clothes she wore? It seemed like anyone who was in any way different to the OMGs, as Amber called them, was persecuted just for breathing.

Sky followed the footpath up some steps and away from the canal. The rain-slicked road glimmered in the lights of the passing cars and the pavement was crowded with girls in high heels and guys in tight jeans and buttoned-up shirts making their way to their New Year's Eve parties. Sky was so glad she was going to a Moonlight Dreamers meeting. She was so excited to see the other girls again. She couldn't think of a better way to welcome in a New Year – especially a year that threatened to be so challenging.

Her phone vibrated in her pocket. She took it out and looked at the screen. It was a text from Rose.

Yo! The eagle has landed! I'm in a cab on my way to Brick Lane. DO NOT, I repeat, DO NOT start without me! Xoxo

Sky ducked into the doorway of a betting shop and sent a quick reply.

Yay! SO pleased you made it back in time. Can't wait to see you and HEAR YOUR NEWS. I haven't forgotten by the way and I will MAKE you tell me. I've

Sky put her phone back in her pocket and carried on her way feeling slightly lighter. She might have to start school soon but first she had a Moonlight Dreamers meeting – and that was guaranteed to make her feel a whole lot stronger.

Maali tightened her sari and looked in her bedroom mirror. She'd never worn a sari to a Moonlight Dreamers meeting before, but it was New Year's Eve and she felt the urge to wear something special. Her ruby-coloured sari was her favourite outfit by far. The colour was rich and vibrant. It reminded her of rose petals. She looked at her Lakshmi figurine and sighed. Ever since her heartfelt prayer on Christmas Eve for a sign about her soulmate she'd seen references to Ash everywhere. Ashtrays, cigarette ash, her dad looking *ashen*-faced. She'd even come across an article on the Huff Post about Ash Wednesday – in the middle of Christmas. If that wasn't a sign she didn't know what was. But a sign of what? Maali grabbed her coat and bag and made her way downstairs. Her parents were in the living room with Namir watching Harry Potter for the millionth time.

"I'm just off to Amber's!" she called from the hallway. It was great that her parents knew her friends now and she didn't have to lie when she wanted to meet them, like she had in the early days of the Moonlight Dreamers.

"Maali, could you come here for a moment, please?" her

mum called. She sounded really panicked.

Maali opened the door. The living room was dark, with only the flickering light from the TV. "Is everything OK? Dad!"

Her dad was on the floor, lying on his side, with her mum crouching over him. Namir was hugging a cushion on the sofa and looked frightened.

"Could you get a glass of water, please?" her mum asked.

"What's happened? Is Dad OK?" Maali stood rooted to the spot.

"Yes, he just fell getting up to reach the remote control. Please could you get some water?"

"Of course." Maali raced to the kitchen, her heart pounding. How had her dad fallen over just getting the remote? It didn't make sense. She filled a glass with water and hurried back to the living room. Her parents were sitting on the sofa now but her dad still looked really spaced out.

"Are you OK?" Maali said, handing him the glass.

Her mum took it and gently raised it to his lips. "Take a sip," she said softly.

"Is he OK?" Maali looked at her mum.

She looked as anxious as Maali felt. "Yes. He tripped. I think it's too hot in here. Do you think it's too hot in here?"

Maali shrugged. What did that have to do with anything? "Not really."

Her mum's face fell. Her dad blinked hard and forced a smile. "It's OK. I'm fine." He reached out for the water but his hand was trembling and he spilt it all over his lap.

"He keeps having these dizzy spells," her mum said. "I told him he needs to get his eyes tested."

Maali looked at her dad. He was pale and drawn. Surely whatever was causing his dizzy spells was more than just poor eyesight.

"Can we watch the movie now?" Namir asked in a quiet voice.

"Oh pet, of course we can." Her mum turned to hug him. Then she looked up at Maali. "You go see your friends. Everything's fine."

Maali frowned. It felt wrong to leave them when her dad was so poorly.

"Go on. Have fun," her mum said in a fake-jolly voice.

Maali looked at her dad. "Go on," he said with a weak smile. "Enjoy yourself."

"OK, if you're sure?" Maali kissed him gently on top of his head.

Please help my dad, Lakshmi, she prayed as she made her way from the flat. *Heal him from whatever is causing this.* Normally, when Maali asked for the gods' and goddesses' help with something, she felt an instant sense of relief. But not this time. This time she felt an uneasy churning deep inside.

Chapter Five

Amber lit the last of the candles dotted around the room and sat down at her desk. It hadn't stopped raining all day so they were having the meeting in her bedroom rather than up on the roof terrace. Rose and Sky were sprawled across her bed, legs entwined. Amber felt a warm glow of satisfaction as she thought back to the very first Moonlight Dreamers meeting. The tension between Sky and Rose had threatened to derail the whole thing before it even began, but thankfully they'd somehow ended up as close as sisters.

"I wonder where Maali is," Amber said, taking the Moonlight Dreamers artefacts from her desk drawer and arranging them in a circle on the floor.

"Yeah, she's got no excuse being late," Rose said with a grin. "She only lives round the corner. I came halfway across the world and I got here on time. Anyone want some duty-free Toblerone?" She reached down to her backpack beside the bed and pulled out a huge bar of chocolate. Even after a transatlantic flight Rose looked stunning. Her cropped golden hair made her cheekbones look even more pronounced and her make-up-free eyes sparkled like emeralds. "Man, it's so good to be here," she sighed, offering Sky the chocolate.

"It's so good to have you here," Sky said. "I'd had this horrible feeling you were going to have such a great time in New York you wouldn't want to come back."

"Ha! No danger of that." Rose snorted. "Not with my dad. He is seriously high maintenance. I've come to realize," she said, sitting upright, "that you guys are more like my family now. It was the one thing that kept me sane over Christmas – knowing I had you to come back to."

Sky broke off a chunk of chocolate and passed the bar to Amber. "Same here. I mean, I love my dad but I can't talk to him the same way I can talk to all of you."

"Huh, try having two of them," Amber retorted. She put on the deep and serious voice she reserved for Oscar Wilde quotes. "'Fathers should be neither seen nor heard. That is the only proper basis for family life.'"

"Amen, sister!" Rose exclaimed, leaning back on the huge bank of cushions at the head of the bed.

"Oscar?" Sky asked.

Amber nodded. "Of course." She took her pocket-watch from her waistcoat pocket and flipped it open. "I hope Maali's OK."

Sky checked her phone. "I haven't heard from her. Have you?"

Amber was about to check when the doorbell rang.

"Don't worry, darling!" Gerald called up the stairs. "I'll let her in. Just think of me as the butler."

"I think your dads are awesome," Rose said.

Amber shrugged as she placed the moonstone in the centre of the circle, but she couldn't help feeling a burst of pride.

The sound of footsteps on the stairs was followed by a gentle knock on the door.

"Come in!" the three girls yelled in unison.

Maali stepped into the room.

"Wow! Maals, you look amazing!" Rose leapt up from the bed and grabbed her in a hug. Sky followed hot on her heels. Amber hung back awkwardly. Since getting to know the other Moonlight Dreamers her social skills had definitely improved, but she still found public displays of affection slightly awkward. Although they were in her bedroom, so it was hardly public.

"Happy New Year," she muttered, patting Maali on the shoulder.

"Thank you." Maali looked at them and her eyes filled with tears.

"What is it? What's wrong?" Sky said, grabbing her hands.

"Has someone hurt you?" Rose's face was suddenly serious.

"Do you want a mint?" Amber asked, her eyes falling on a packet of Polos on her desk. OK, why had she done that? Who asks someone in tears if they want a mint?

Maali shook her head. "No, thank you. I'm so sorry. It's nothing. Well, it's something but I don't exactly know what.

There's something wrong with my dad. My mum says he needs his eyes tested but I know it's more than that. It's not just that he keeps getting dizzy, he looks so pale and haggard too. And people don't look pale and haggard when they need their eyes tested, do they?" She looked at the others questioningly.

"OK, rewind!" Rose took Maali by the hand and led her over to the bed. "Sit."

Maali sat on the edge of the bed and started biting her bottom lip.

"Now start again from the beginning in sentences we can understand," Rose instructed.

The other girls sat on the bed around Maali. "My dad's been acting really weird over Christmas—"

"Join the club!" Rose exclaimed. "Sorry, go ahead."

"How do you mean, weird?" Sky asked.

"He keeps getting dizzy and he looks so tired all the time. And then tonight…" Maali started fiddling with the gold trim on her sari. "He fell over in the living room—"

Rose grinned. "Too much Christmas sherry?"

"No. He doesn't drink."

Rose nodded. "I'm sorry. Carry on."

"My mum said he'd fallen getting the remote control, but it was like he'd fainted. He was acting all spaced out. And when I got him some water he spilled it all over himself."

Rose frowned. "Are you sure he hadn't been drinking? My mom does stuff like that all the time when she's been hitting the champagne."

"No, I told you – he doesn't drink."

"Maybe he's coming down with the flu," Sky said gently. "There's a lot of it about this time of year." She quickly looked something up on her phone. "Yes, it says on Doctors Direct that flu can cause dizziness and exhaustion … and weight loss."

"Really?" Maali looked at her hopefully.

"For sure." Rose nodded. "My mom had the flu a couple years ago and she was like a zombie. She could barely stand. And she lost a ton of weight – which of course she loved, as she had a lingerie shoot coming up. My mom must be the only person alive who actually likes getting sick!"

"I'm sure it's the flu," Amber said. "Gerald had it really badly a few years ago and he's had the vaccination every year since. He said at the time that he thought he'd never paint again. He thought the virus had killed his artistic streak – but then he is prone to over-exaggeration!"

Maali gave a relieved smile. "Thanks, guys."

They sat in silence for a moment. Amber looked at the others, feeling the sudden urge to form the circle. "Should we begin the meeting and say the quote?"

"Yes!" Rose got to her feet. "Let's do it." She took hold of Maali's hand and helped her up. Then she held her other hand out to Amber. Sky came and stood between Amber and Maali to complete the circle. As Amber felt the warmth from Rose and Sky's hands seeping into hers she began to feel a glimmer of hope for the first time since Christmas Eve.

"'Yes: I am a dreamer…'" she began.

"'For a dreamer is one who can only find her way by moonlight,'" the others all joined in, "'and her punishment is that she sees the dawn before the rest of the world.'"

They stood there for a while, holding hands in the flickering candlelight, staring down at the moonstone in the centre of the circle.

Amber tightened her grip on Sky and Rose's hands. She didn't want to let go. She didn't want to go back to the loneliness and hurt she'd been feeling since she discovered that her surrogate mum wanted nothing to do with her; she wanted to stay in the warmth and safety of the Moonlight Dreamers. She wished she could talk as easily as the others. She wished she could spill out her troubles the way Maali had done so she could get their advice and support.

"Could I..." She broke off and looked down at the floor.

"Could you what?" Sky asked softly.

"Could I tell you guys something?"

"Er, hello!" Rose raised her eyebrows. "What's rule number six?"

Amber blushed.

Rose squeezed her hand. "Go on, say it."

"Moonlight Dreamers tell each other everything – even the bad stuff. Especially the bad stuff," Amber mumbled. But how could she tell them? How could she tell them that the email from the surrogacy agency had left her feeling completely unsure of herself and her place in the world?

MOONLIGHT DREAMERS ~ THE RULES

1. *The Moonlight Dreamers is a secret society — members must never speak a word of its existence, or what happens at the meetings, to others.*

2. *Meetings will begin with members reciting the "moonlight" quote from Oscar Wilde.*

3. *This quote is the Moonlight Dreamers motto and must be memorized by members — and NEVER forgotten.*

4. *All members must vow to support the other Moonlight Dreamers in the pursuit of their dreams — always.*

5. *Moonlight Dreamers are proud of being different. Being the same as everyone else is a crime against originality, the human equivalent of magnolia paint.*

6. *Moonlight Dreamers tell each other everything — even the bad stuff. Especially the bad stuff.*

7. *Moonlight Dreamers never, ever give up.*

Chapter Six

Sky looked at Amber. Her gaze was fixed on the moonstone. Clearly she was finding it difficult to make a start. "I have an idea," Sky said. "It seems like we all have stuff we need to talk about. Personal stuff." She shot Rose a look. Rose immediately turned away. Whatever she had to tell them must be really personal; it was unlike her to look so bashful. "Why don't we tell it to the moon, but all together, instead of on our own?"

"But it's still pouring outside," Amber said as the rain lashed against her bedroom window.

"We don't have to go outside to do it," Sky said. "I just thought it might make it easier if we're not talking directly to each other." She thought about having to tell the others that she was scared of going to school. It felt so pitiful. At least if she didn't have to look at them and see their reactions it would make it slightly easier. She looked at the moonstone. "I know. Why don't we take it in turns to tell it to the moonstone while the others just listen?" Her face began to burn. Was what she was saying making her seem like a total idiot? She glanced up. To her relief, she saw that Amber was nodding. And now Rose was too.

"So, where do the others go while we tell it to the moonstone?" Amber asked.

"We could sit behind you or beside you," Sky said. "The main thing is we're not facing you, so you won't feel so self-conscious."

"OK." Amber let go of Sky's and Rose's hands and crouched down to pick up the moonstone. The others arranged themselves on the floor behind her.

Sky relaxed. She could imagine telling them about her school fears like this. She watched as Amber sat cross-legged, holding the moonstone in front of her. Her jet-black quiff gleamed in the candlelight.

"So, it's like this," she began. "Ever since I found out that Gerald is my biological dad, I've kept thinking about my surrogate mum – wondering who she is and why she had me the way she did. I mean, I know she had me for the money. But *why* did she have me for the money? It seems like such a massive thing to do – to sell your own baby. And did she ever regret it? And did she – did she ever think about me?"

Amber's shoulders slumped. Sky shot Rose a worried glance. Rose shook her head, as if to say, *Let her continue.*

"Anyway, as you know, I made it my dream to try and get to know her and about a month ago I emailed the surrogacy agency. I didn't tell you at the time because I wanted it to be a surprise." Amber gave a bitter laugh.

Rose went to say something but Sky quickly placed her hand on her arm. It was so hard getting Amber to open up, if any of them said anything now she might stop talking. She glanced at Maali. Maali was watching Amber, mesmerized.

"Anyway, they emailed me back the other day to say that my surrogate mum had stipulated that she didn't want me to contact her."

Rose was opening and closing her mouth like a goldfish, clearly desperate to say something. Sky tried not to think of the expressions they'd be pulling behind her back when she told them how she'd been feeling about starting school. She looked at Amber, wondering if she'd finished and if she ought to put her hand on her shoulder to offer her some comfort. Amber wasn't exactly a huggy person. But then she started speaking again.

"The thing is — ever since I found this out I've been feeling really weird. Like I don't know who I am or what I'm supposed to be doing. I haven't said anything to you guys, but I've been having doubts about my blogging dream for weeks now and this has made it a million times worse. How can I know what I ought to be doing with my life if I don't know who I truly am? If I'll never know who I truly am?"

"Sounds like you're having an existential crisis," Rose said.

"Shh!" Sky said, scared Amber would clam up.

"What?" Rose frowned. "She is."

"A what crisis?" Maali asked.

"An existential crisis," Rose replied. "It's when you start questioning the whole reason for your existence. Apparently my dad had one right before leaving me and my mom for Rachel. At least that's what he told *Vanity Fair*."

"It's all right for you," Amber said, turning to face the others. "You all know who both your biological parents are, but imagine if you didn't. Imagine if you had a massive question mark hanging over one half of your identity."

Rose frowned. "Hmm, sometimes I think I'd prefer a couple of question marks to the pair of exclamation marks I was dealt."

Sky felt a twinge of sadness as she thought of her own mum. But at least she had had her for the first eleven years of her life. At least she could remember what she was like. At least she knew exactly where she came from. She reached out her hand and took hold of Amber's. "It must be horrible."

Amber gave her a grateful smile. "It is."

Sky looked at Maali and Rose and they all gathered around Amber.

"I know you don't believe in God," Maali said.

"No, I don't," Amber said abruptly.

"But I really do believe that there's a loving force within all of us and the whole universe."

Amber frowned.

"And that loving force can be like a mother to you, if you let it," Maali continued, smiling sweetly.

"It's not so much that I want a mother," Amber said. "I have Gerald and Daniel. I *love* Gerald and Daniel. It's more that I want to know who I am."

"Maybe you're better off not knowing," Rose said.

"How do you mean?"

"Well, she might have some really gross personal habits, like picking her teeth … or voting Republican. At least this way you're a blank slate – or half of you is. You can be whoever you want to be." Rose crouched on the floor in front of her. "And let me tell you, the Amber I know is awesomeness in a pin-striped suit!"

Amber laughed. "I've never been called that before."

"Yeah well, get used to it because it's true."

Amber smiled. "Thank you."

"It is true," Sky said, putting her arm round Amber's shoulders. "You're an amazing person. You don't have to know who your birth mum is to know yourself."

"Yes," Maali said, taking hold of Amber's hand. "You're such a strong person in your own right. You're so interesting and so much fun to be around."

"I am?" Amber stared at Maali.

"Of course," Maali said. "You started the Moonlight Dreamers. This is the most interesting and fun thing I've ever done. I'd be proud to have you as a daughter."

"Preach it, Mamma Maali!" Rose said, giving Maali a high-five.

There was a moment's silence, then they all started to laugh.

"Thank you for being so kind. I really appreciate it. Hopefully this feeling will wear off soon." Amber shifted back and offered the moonstone to Sky. "Would you like to go next?"

Sky felt a stab of panic. "Oh, I don't know."

Amber placed the stone in her hand. "Go on."

Sky turned away from the others. She took a deep breath. If Amber could do it, then so could she. The moonstone was glowing white, blue and gold in the candlelight. She pretended she was alone and closed her eyes. "What I'm about to say is going to sound really stupid—"

"No, it's not," Rose said.

Sky swallowed hard. She had to come straight out with it, get this torture over with. "In four days I'll be going to secondary school for the very first time and I'm dreading it." She sat in silence for a moment, listening to the tapping of the rain against the window. She sounded pathetic but there was no way she could get out of it now. "I'm dreading that I won't fit in and that I'll hate it and that the teachers won't be anywhere near as fun or interesting as my dad. But most of all … I'm dreading the other students. I know this sounds ridiculous but I'm scared."

She stopped talking. The silence was excruciating, broken only by the low rumble of thunder outside.

"Are you done?" Rose whispered in her ear.

Sky nodded.

"You aren't pathetic!" Rose exclaimed, moving round to

face her. "You're – you're awesomeness in DM boots! You'll make new friends no problem … just be sure to remember who your best friends are, though."

Sky started to laugh. "Thanks."

"Rose is right. They're all going to love you," Maali added, placing her hand on top of Sky's. "You're one of the kindest people ever."

"Really?" Sky had always thought of Maali as one of the kindest people ever so this was praise indeed.

Maali nodded and looked at her solemnly. "They're all going to love you at your new school."

Amber patted Sky on the back. "And don't forget you'll have me there, so you've already got one school friend."

Sky nodded. "That's the only good thing about it!"

"Thanks," Amber said gruffly.

"I'm sorry," Sky said. "I feel like such a baby. It's just that it's been building up inside me all over Christmas and I can't tell my dad because I know he needs me to go to school so he's free to work and make more money. I feel better already just for telling you – or telling the moonstone – or whatever."

"You're gonna be fine," Rose said.

Sky felt herself relax. It was so good to be back with her fellow Moonlight Dreamers. A problem shared was a problem quartered with them. She held the moonstone out to Rose. "OK, your turn."

Rose's face fell. "Oh, I don't know. Maybe we've had enough emotional outpourings for one night."

"Oh no you don't," Sky said firmly. "Don't make me chant mantras at you."

Rose shifted onto her knees. "Seriously though, I don't know if I'm ready. I don't know if I should. What I've got to say, well, it might affect this – us."

Sky's heart skipped a beat. What did Rose have to tell them? Was she thinking of moving back to New York after all? What else could affect the Moonlight Dreamers?

"Are you moving away?" Maali said, her eyes wide with alarm.

A flash of lightning lit up the room.

Rose shook her head. "No! No way. It's nothing like that. It's – it's something about me. All right, give me the damned stone." She grabbed the moonstone from Sky and clutched it tightly. She looked at them defiantly, then bowed her head and closed her eyes. "I'm gay."

Chapter Seven

Rose kept her eyes shut tight, willing someone, *anyone* to say something, *anything*. When she'd run through this scenario in her mind – at least five thousand times – it had been Maali's reaction she'd worried about the most. She was fairly certain that, with two gay dads, Amber wouldn't be the slightest bit fazed at her news and Sky was such a *peace-out-one-love* hippy that she was fairly certain she'd be chilled about it, but Maali … Maali was so into her religion. What if the Hindu gods and goddesses frowned on people being gay? What if it was seen as being a sin? How would it affect their friendship? Would Maali stop being a Moonlight Dreamer because of it? Would Rose be responsible for the break-up of the group?

"You're gay?" Sky finally broke the silence.

Rose half-opened her eyes and squinted at her. She looked totally shocked. "Uh-huh."

"What, gay as in you like girls?"

Geez, what was up with people? Why did they suddenly forget what gay meant the second you came out to them?

"Yep." Rose snuck a glance at Maali. Her mouth was actually hanging open. She looked at Amber, hoping that she at least wouldn't look so fazed. Amber was nodding her head slowly, looking deep in thought, like she'd just worked out a particularly complicated puzzle.

"But what about that guy you were going out with – Matt?" Sky asked.

"Matt's a dick," Rose muttered. She was starting to feel defensive now. One of them better hurry up and say something supportive. She felt like reminding them all of rule number four: *All members must vow to support the other Moonlight Dreamers in the pursuit of their dreams – always.* She wasn't exactly sure if she could define being gay as a dream but she definitely dreamed of being happy.

"This is so amazing!" Maali exclaimed with a grin.

Rose stared at her. "It is?"

Maali nodded. "To have the courage to declare your true path to love and devotion."

"Right," Rose said slowly, not entirely sure what Maali was going on about but liking the sound of it.

"And now it all makes sense," Maali continued, her eyes shining brightly.

Rose crinkled her eyebrows. "It does? What does?"

"The way you're so down on guys."

"I'm not down on guys. Well, only the idiot ones – like Matt."

"Yeah, but remember that time in the coffee shop, when

you were supposed to be helping me find the confidence to talk to boys?"

Rose thought back to that day when she'd shown Maali how to flirt with the sleazy barista. Then she remembered how disparaging she'd been of Maali's dream. "OK, so maybe I was a bit hard on guys in the past, but that was only because I was feeling so frustrated – because I was living a lie."

Sky was still looking really confused. "But why did you send that photo to Matt if you weren't into him?"

Rose felt a mixture of anger and disappointment building inside of her. Why was Sky being so difficult? "I told you – because I was pissed at my mom for telling me what to do all the time. I was only going out with him as an experiment."

"An experiment in what – seeing how high your imbecile tolerance levels were?" Amber said with a wry smile.

Rose felt a burst of relief. "Yes! And to see if I really was gay."

"How do you mean?" Maali asked.

"Well, it's been kind of confusing, you know. Like, I kept getting these feelings for girls – not any of you, by the way, just want to put that out there right up front. Not that you're not attractive but you guys are like family to me and..." Rose took a moment to compose herself. "This is going to sound really dumb but Matt was the best-looking guy in the school. I figured that if I was ever going to be into a guy it would be him."

"You're right," Amber said, raising her eyebrows. "That is really dumb."

"I know! I know! I sent the guy a topless photo, which he then shared with the world on Instagram, so I fully accept that where that boy is concerned I was dumbness squared, but I just needed to be certain. And he sure helped me do that! Sky, can you please stop staring at me like I just fell out of an alien spaceship and say something supportive? Rule number four, remember?"

Sky blushed. "I'm so sorry. Of course I support you – it's just a lot to take in."

"I think it's great," said Maali, and Amber nodded her head in agreement. "It's like you finally make sense."

Rose laughed. "Yes, I guess I do. But – but what about your religion?"

Maali frowned. "What about my religion?"

"Doesn't it say that all gay people must be thrown off tall buildings or burnt at the stake?"

"No!" Maali gave a deep sigh. "For your information, homosexuality isn't mentioned a single time in the Hindu texts. For Hindus it's all about the importance of love and devotion between two people – it doesn't say who those two people have to be or what sex they have to be."

Rose felt overwhelmed with relief. "Well, thank Oscar for that." She leaned back against the bed. "Now can we please change the subject? Isn't it time we got on to our New Year dreams?"

"Yes!" Amber went over to her desk and took a notepad from one of the drawers.

"How are we going to give our dreams to the moon with a massive storm going on outside?" Maali asked.

"Don't worry, I have an alternative plan," Amber said mysteriously.

Rose hugged her knees to her chest. She'd done it. She'd told the Moonlight Dreamers and it had all gone OK – better than OK in Maali's case. Sky was the only one she was still a little unsure of. She gave her a sideways glance. Sky quickly looked away.

Amber handed each of them a piece of paper. "Apparently we're coming into a Capricorn new moon."

"What does that mean?" Rose rummaged in her bag for a pen, pulling out her boarding pass, a baking magazine and a year's supply of key-lime-pie-flavoured gum.

Amber sat back down. "It means it's a great time to set intentions for the year ahead because Capricorn's the sign of hard work … or something."

"OK, cool." Rose offered the gum around.

Sky took a piece and smiled. A proper smile. Rose nudged her in the ribs. "You OK?" she whispered as Maali and Amber got their pens out. "You know, with me…?"

Sky nodded. "Of course."

"Who wants to go first?" Amber asked.

"Can I?" Sky sat forward. "My dream for this year is to perform more poetry in public – but with my eyes open and actually breathing this time!"

Rose grinned as she thought back to Sky's first ever poetry slam, where her nerves had gotten the better of her. "You were great."

Maali nodded. "Yeah, that judge was a fool."

Sky grinned. "Thanks, guys, but I do think they had a point. Looking at the audience and remembering to breathe are important skills when you're trying to perform a poem!"

"Anything else?" Amber asked.

Sky shook her head. "No, that's it really. Just that poetry becomes a bigger part of my life so it'll take my mind off school and give me something positive to focus on."

"Sounds like a plan to me," Rose said, nodding.

"How about you, Rose?" Amber asked. "What are your dreams for the year?"

"To learn more about cake-making and to work more in the shop and…" Rose felt her cheeks start to burn. What was up with her? She never blushed. "To kiss a girl," she muttered.

"To what?" Maali said.

"To kiss a girl – like, properly." An image of Francesca popped into Rose's mind. This happened a lot when she thought about kissing a girl, even though it was highly inappropriate because Francesca was her boss and way older than her. But she was so beautiful. Rose thought of her shiny dark hair and her dimpled smile and the way she spoke in her lilting French accent. OK, enough already, coming out seemed to be turning her into a gay version of Maali.

"That's so lovely," Maali sighed.

"Yeah well, let's not get carried away," Rose said. "How about you then, Maals? What are your dreams for the year?"

Maali's face clouded over. "Well, I suppose my main dream is for my dad to be OK."

"Of course," Amber said. "But what's your dream for *you*?"

"Promise you won't laugh at me?" Maali said, looking at the others anxiously.

"Of course," Sky said.

"Or call me stupidness in a sari?" Maali said, looking at Rose.

"As if!" Rose replied.

"Well, I'd still really like to meet my soulmate and…" She looked down into her lap. "I'd like to forget all about Ash," she muttered.

"Say what?" Rose said. "As in cigarette ash?"

"No! As in Ash – the boy I thought was my soulmate but who belongs to someone else!"

"Ah, right." Rose grinned. "Sorry, in my mind he'll always be Old MacDonald."

"He's not an actual farmer!" Maali said with a frown. "He just works at the City Farm part-time while he's at college."

Rose sighed. Maali was clearly still one smitten kitten when it came to Ash. "Well, you never know," she said. "He might have broken up with Sage and Onion over Christmas. Maybe he got sick of going out with someone who reminded him of turkey stuffing."

Maali gave her a weak smile. "I doubt it. But thank you."

Rose put her arm round her shoulders. "Don't worry. Your prince will come." She turned to Amber. "So, Amber, what's your dream for the New Year?"

Amber thought about the dream she'd made up for this moment – to get more readers for her blog – and she could practically hear Oscar Wilde moaning that it was nothing but a quotation. She cleared her throat. "My dream is to find out who I truly am and what I should be dreaming," she said, hoping that she didn't sound like too much of a loser.

"Cool!" Rose said.

"Is it?" Amber looked at her. "I was worried it might sound lame – a Moonlight Dreamer without a dream."

"But you do have a dream," Rose said. "A massive dream. And we're all here to help you achieve it, OK?"

Amber nodded and gave a relieved smile. A huge crash of thunder reverberated around the room. "Wow! That was a real sockdolager!" she exclaimed as Maali shrieked and cowered next to the bed.

"A sock-what-er?" said Rose.

"Sockdolager. It was my word of the day yesterday from Dictionary.com," Amber explained. "It means an almighty crash or loud noise."

"And that, right there, is why you're awesomeness in a pin-striped suit," Rose said with a laugh.

Amber's cheeks flushed. "Thank you." She took a pen from the breast-pocket of her suit. "OK, let's write our dreams down and then we're going to burn them."

"Burn them?" Maali's eyes widened in alarm.

"Yes. As we can't release our dreams into the wind tonight we're going to release them into fire."

"Cool!" Rose repeated and quickly jotted down her dreams on her piece of paper. She loved this part of the Moonlight Dreamers meetings. Seeing her dreams either in pictures or in words really helped make them seem more achievable somehow. PROPERLY KISS A GIRL she wrote, followed by a heart and three kisses. Geez, she really was turning into gay Maali!

When they'd finished they turned to Amber, who produced a large bowl and a box of matches from beside her bed. "I think it should be safe to do it in here," she said, putting her dream into the bottom of the bowl. The others followed suit.

"Dear Moon, please help us to achieve our dreams this coming year," Amber said, taking a match from the box. "And please help us to be the kind of Moonlight Dreamers that Oscar Wilde would be proud of."

"Yes," Rose muttered.

Amber lit the match and dropped it into the bowl. The paper started glowing red and then a huge flame shot up.

"Yikes!" Maali exclaimed. "Are you sure this is safe?"

As the flame grew higher the girls leapt to their feet.

"I'll get some water!" Amber cried.

But before she could move they heard footsteps on the landing. "Girls, would you care to join us for a New Year's toast?" Gerald called through the door.

"Shit!" Amber looked at them frantically, then back at the burning bowl. "Shall I throw it out the window?"

"No!" Sky exclaimed. "The curtains might catch fire or you might kill a passer-by. Has anyone got a drink?"

"Girls?" Gerald called. The flames leapt even higher.

Rose tipped the contents of her bag onto the floor. "I've got a can of Coke."

"Quick!" Amber grabbed the can, snapped it open and poured it on to the flames. With a horrible hiss, they spluttered and died. Amber shoved the smouldering bowl into her cupboard. Rose bit down hard on her lip to stop herself from laughing.

"Amber!" Gerald called. "Is everything OK in there?"

"Yes, Dad. Everything's fine." Amber shot them all a warning look before opening the door.

Gerald looked dapper as ever in a three-piece suit and scarlet silk cravat. Rose had no idea how Amber could have been so convinced that Daniel was her biological dad: she was Gerald's daughter through and through.

"Good God, what's that smell?" he said, sniffing the air.

"Sky was burning some incense she brought back from her hippy retreat," Rose said quickly. "It's called Burnt Dreams."

Maali spluttered.

"Hmm." Gerald looked at them suspiciously. "More like burnt entrails. Anyway, Daniel's made some of his delicious

70

mulled wine and we were wondering if you'd care to join us for a toast." He looked at Maali. "We have some non-alcoholic fizz too, although it really is a poor substitute."

"Of course," Amber said. "We'll be down in just a minute." She shut the door behind him and they all sat in silence as they listened to his footsteps creaking off down the stairs. Then they dissolved into a laughing heap on the bed.

"Burnt Dreams!" Maali gasped. "Oh wow, that was so funny!"

"Yeah, thanks for blaming it on me," Sky said, before dissolving into laughter again.

"It was all I could think of." Rose snorted.

"That was way too close," Amber said. "Imagine if we'd burnt the house down."

"Yeah, great start to the year that would have been," Rose said.

"I love you guys," Maali said.

"Me too," Sky said.

"Me three," Rose added.

"Me too," Amber said.

"No – you're supposed to say me four," Maali said.

"Oh – right – yes – me four," Amber said awkwardly and they all started laughing again.

As Rose hugged her aching sides she felt happier than she'd done in the longest time. She'd spent so much of last year unsure of things – unsure of where she wanted to live. Unsure of who she wanted sexually. Unsure of who she truly was. But now, as the New Year ticked its way towards her, she'd never felt more certain of where she wanted to be and who she wanted to be with – and it was a great feeling.

Chapter Eight

As soon as her alarm clock went off, Maali's eyes shot open.
Today was the first day back at school after the Christmas
break and that nervous first-day-of-term feeling was
bubbling inside her. She got up and turned on her fairy
lights and knelt before her shrine. But before she could start
to pray she heard hurried footsteps from the landing below
and the bathroom door banging shut. Maali hurried down
from her attic bedroom and found Namir standing outside
the bathroom hugging his toy dinosaur.

"What's going on, Nam?" Maali asked.

"Daddy's being sick. I think he must have eaten too many
sweets," Namir replied.

Their mum opened the bathroom door and came out on
to the landing. Maali just glimpsed her dad hunched over the
toilet before her mum closed the door.

"What's wrong with Dad?" Maali asked.

"I think he has the winter vomiting virus," their mum
replied.

"Gross!" Namir exclaimed.

She looked at him and smiled. "Come on, let's get you ready for school."

"Do you think that's what's been causing the dizzy spells?" Maali asked.

Her mum nodded and Maali felt a wave of relief. At least they now knew what was wrong, and once her dad was over the virus, things could go back to normal.

"Thank you, Lakshmi," she whispered as she made her way back up to her bedroom.

Sky lay in her bunk, staring up at the low ceiling. This was it – the day she'd been dreading for months. The day she started school. She hadn't been feeling too bad about it yesterday. She and her dad had gone to a really cool exhibition about Tibetan Buddhism and she'd left it feeling all Zen. But it felt as if her fears had been doing press-ups on the floor beside her bunk while she slept and now they were bigger and stronger than ever. She reached for her phone and started scanning through the texts from the other Moonlight Dreamers. Amber had sent her an Oscar Wilde quote:

"Be yourself ... everyone else is already taken" and YOURself is more than good enough.

Maali had also sent her a quote, which she assumed was from a Hindu text:

"Desire nothing, give up all desires and be happy." xxxxx

Sky thought about this for a moment. How was it possible to give up all of your dreams and desires and be happy? Wasn't it your desires and achieving them that *made* you happy? She knew that if her desire not to go to school was somehow magically granted she'd be extremely happy. She made a mental note to ask Maali what she meant the next time she saw her. She clicked on Rose's text.

School is for fools
Cos it's full of rules
But you have the tools
To make them all drools (?!!)

OK, so clearly I don't have your poet skills BUT I am a
great judge of character (apart from when it comes to
certain guys obvs) and I can tell you now that you rock!
So don't be scared be awesome. Love ya xoxo

Sky grinned. Trust Rose to be able to make her laugh on what was possibly going to be the worst day of her life – apart from when her mum died, of course.

When Rose had come out to them at the New Year's Eve meeting, Sky had been shocked and a little hurt that Rose hadn't felt able to say anything to her before. But she realized now that this was selfish and silly. It must have been a really confusing time for Rose and it made what happened with Matt and the photo seem even worse in a way. Sky thought about how Rose had dealt with the internet storm and how she'd found the strength to come out of it more fearless than ever. That was how Sky needed to be now – more like Rose. She got out of her bunk and looked at herself in the mirror. So what if her new schoolmates thought she was weird for being home-schooled and living on a boat? So what if they hated the pink strands in her hair? She was a Moonlight Dreamer – she didn't need anyone else's approval.

Rose hesitated outside her mom's bedroom door. Ever since she'd got back to London, Rose had wanted to tell Savannah that she was gay, but there hadn't been the opportunity. When she'd arrived home on New Year's Eve the house had been full of Savannah's usual party posse of models and make-up artists and a handful of aging rockstars. Since she'd broken up with Liam, Savannah had been see-sawing between partying and detoxing. The break-up and last year's media witch-hunt about her age had left her pretty fragile and Rose didn't want to do anything to rock the boat. The one good thing to have come out of the incident with the photo was that it had brought her and Savannah closer than they'd been in years. Rose wanted to keep it that way, so she'd made her dad promise he wouldn't breathe a word about her sexuality and said she'd tell Savannah when the time was right.

Rose heard a loud whirring sound coming from the kitchen and made her way downstairs. Savannah was up – and juicing. This was great. If she was juicing it meant she was in the detox phase of the drink-and-detox cycle, when she was always more positive and clear-headed. Rose could come out to her now and, if it did go badly, at least she'd have the excuse of having to leave to go to school. She could just tell her and go – coming out hit-and-run style.

"Hey."

Savannah was standing by the juicer, holding a glass of what looked like frothy blood but what Rose guessed was beetroot. Her long golden hair was tied into a high ponytail and she was wearing her yoga gear.

"Where'd you get the blood, Vampira?"

Savannah frowned. "It's not blood, honey, it's beetroot juice."

"I know, I was joking." Rose stared at her – she seemed a little tense. "You OK?"

"Yeah. I guess." Savannah sat down at the breakfast bar and took a sip of her juice. Despite it only being seven in the morning, she was wearing a full face of make-up. It made Rose mad and sad in equal parts how she'd become increasingly paranoid about her looks. After her own mini internet storm she'd realized that the only way to be free from the craziness of the online world was truly not to care. As Oscar Wilde said: "Always forgive your enemies; nothing annoys them so much."

Rose went over to Savannah and placed a hand on her shoulder. "What's up?"

Savannah sighed. "I've got a meeting with the perfume company today."

Rose sat down on a stool next to her. "What about?"

Savannah made a pair of air quotes with her hands. "'Moving forward', apparently."

Rose's heart sank. One of the worst by-products of last year's witch-hunt was Savannah getting dropped from a couple of her biggest contracts. "You don't know it's going to be bad news, though."

"I've got a bad feeling, honey. And so does Roxanne."

Roxanne was Savannah's new manager – a straight-talking Londoner with snowy-white hair cut into a fierce bob. She was a massive improvement on Savannah's last manager, the perma-tanned sleazebag Antonio.

"You know, Mom, maybe you need to stop caring so much."

Savannah's perfectly plucked eyebrows practically shot up to her hair line. "Stop caring?"

"Yes. There's more to life than modelling contracts, you know."

"Oh, really?" Savannah looked around the state-of-the-art kitchen. "Tell that to the bank manager."

Rose inwardly sighed. Today was clearly not going to be the day she came out to her mom. She was starting to wonder if that day would ever arrive.

"I'd better get to school," she said.

"OK." Savannah forced a smile. "Have a great day, hon. I'll let you know how the meeting goes."

Rose hugged Savannah tight. She felt so small and thin. "Don't let the bastards get you down, Mom, OK?"

"OK." Savannah pulled her pack of cigarettes from the fruit bowl.

"Can everyone get out their text books and turn to page fifty-seven, please."

As the History teacher, Mr Collier, tapped something into his laptop, Sky flicked through the pages of her book. It was the third lesson of the day. She felt as if she was being cooked alive by the sweltering central heating and her skin prickled from the constant stares of her classmates. She was exhausted from the sheer pressure of having to take so much in and not put a foot wrong. Her first three hours, four minutes of school had taught her two things. One: secondary schools were really noisy, especially between lessons, when the chatter and the chair-scraping reached eardrum-shattering proportions, and two: schools were like military-style boot-camps. The way the students all had to say "yes sir, no sir, three bags full sir" at every turn. The way they all had to keep to the left-hand side of the corridor when they were walking between lessons. The way some of the teachers would yell if anyone said the wrong thing in class. She didn't get how this was supposed to make them want to learn. When she'd been home-schooled Liam always encouraged her to think for herself and question things. But here it seemed more about cramming as much information into their minds as possible, with no time for debate.

Sky loosened her tie a fraction. She'd never had to wear a tie before and it felt as if she was being strangled. Cooked alive and strangled. It wasn't a great combination. She looked at the clock on the wall. Forty-seven minutes until lunch break and then she'd finally be able to see Amber. They were doing quite a few of the same subjects but, because the school had no idea of Sky's ability, she'd been put in lower sets. She thought about Amber in another classroom somewhere in this huge rabbit warren of harshly lit corridors. It was vaguely comforting to know that somewhere in this alien world there was another Moonlight Dreamer.

Sky glanced at the girl sitting next to her. She was tall and thin with short black hair. Her skin was so pale it had a pale blue tinge.

"I'm Vanessa," the girl muttered, picking at a shred of loose skin by her fingernail.

"Hi, I'm Sky."

"Cool name." Vanessa continued picking at her finger.

"Thank you." When Sky's tutor had introduced her to her form at the beginning of the day, her name had been greeted with a couple of raised eyebrows and a few sniggers. It had not been the best of starts. Sky tried to think of something else to say to Vanessa but it was as if the heat had melted all the sentences in her brain into one big word-soup. She had to say something. Vanessa was the first person who'd spoken to her all morning. This could be her chance to make a friend.

"Do you like History?" Sky inwardly groaned. What a lame question.

"No." Vanessa started picking at the skin on a different finger.

"What subjects do you like?"

"None." *Pick. Pick.*

"Oh." Sky scanned the classroom. The other kids were in pairs or groups of friends. Vanessa was the only one who'd come and sat next to her. Maybe she didn't have any friends. Well, that was fine. They could be friends. She needed to ask her another question, try and get some kind of conversation going. "Where do you live?"

"Why?" Vanessa finally stopped picking at her fingers and looked at her. Her eyes were a pale, watery blue, matching her skin.

"Oh, no reason, just – just trying to make conversation."

Vanessa nodded. "Off Old Street."

She went back to her fingers. Sky looked at the clock. Only one minute had passed since she last looked. This was starting to feel like torture.

Mr Collier snapped his laptop shut and came to stand at the front of the class. His gaze fell upon Sky. "Aha, the new girl."

Sky squirmed.

"Sky, isn't it?"

Sky nodded.

She heard someone mutter something at the back of the class and laughter rippled towards her. She was so hot now that even the tips of her ears were burning.

"Welcome to History, Sky. I hope you're going to be very happy here."

Vanessa muttered something unintelligible.

Sky nodded to Mr Collier. "Thank you." She looked down at the table, dread weighing heavy in the pit of her stomach. She had a feeling that school was not going to make her "very happy" any time soon.

Chapter Nine

Amber stood by the door of the canteen scanning the sea of faces for Sky. All morning she'd been thinking about her, wondering how she was getting on. Hordes of students pushed past and then finally, there she was. Amber's heart sank. Sky looked really stressed. Her normally porcelain skin was flushed bright pink and her curly blonde hair looked frizzy and dry. She scanned the corridor anxiously.

"Sky!" Amber called, making her way up the corridor towards her.

Sky's face lit up with relief. "Amber! Thank God you're here. I can't seem to find my way anywhere in this place. Every corridor looks exactly the same." She grabbed her in a hug.

Amber patted her on the back. "How's it been?"

"OK ... ish. Is there any way we could go outside? Get some fresh air? And some peace and quiet?"

"Of course. Come with me." Amber led Sky away from the canteen to the fire exit at the other end of the corridor.

"Ah, look, Amber's got a friend." Amber froze at the sound

of Chloe's voice. Ever since Rose had been a guest on Amber's blog a few months earlier, Chloe and her cronies had laid off her a bit. When the blog post went viral it became the talk of the school and knowing a celebrity's daughter seemed to trump having two gay dads and the PE lesson from hell incident. Amber turned and stared at Chloe. As usual, Chloe's face was caked with make-up, as if she painted on the same mask of cool indifference every day. Amber wondered if there was actually a nice, smiley version of Chloe beneath all the make-up and she grinned.

"What's funny?" Chloe said, taking a step towards her.

There was a time when Chloe used to scare Amber but not any more. "You are," Amber said. "You're hilarious."

Chloe's mascara-ed eyes widened. "What – but..."

"Come on." Amber grabbed Sky's arm and pulled her towards the door.

"Who was *that*?" Sky asked as soon as they were outside.

"*That* is my nemesis," Amber said, pulling her blazer collar up against the cold. "Or at least she was. She doesn't really bother me now."

Sky looked back at the door. "Please tell me there are some nice people in this place. Apart from you, of course."

"Oh, I'm sure there are." Amber rooted in her bag for her sandwiches. "I just haven't found them yet."

"Seriously?" Sky looked really dejected.

"I'm sorry. I didn't mean to put you off. You don't need to worry. You won't be considered a 'weirdo' like me. You don't dress like a so-called man. You don't have two gay dads."

Sky sighed. "No, I have one hippy dad who home-schooled me and I live on a boat and I have a name that everyone seems to find hilarious."

Amber felt sorry for Sky. She was normally so bright and bubbly. It was horrible seeing her like this. "Oh well, on the plus side, at least we have a year-group assembly next period so we'll be together."

"Yeah. I just wish..." Sky broke off and looked at the trees lining the end of the playground. Their leafless limbs flailed about in the cold breeze.

"What?"

Sky took a deep breath. "Nothing. Let's talk about something else. How's your dream going?"

After spending the rest of lunch break talking about possible ways in which Amber could get clearer on who she was and what she wanted to do with her life, the girls went back into school. Sky seemed a lot brighter now, her skin glowing from the cold.

"So, what happens in assemblies?" she said as Amber led her to the school hall. "Do you all sing songs and stuff?"

"What? No! It's normally just the head of year telling us some boring information about parents' evenings or performance targets. I tend to use it for daydreaming time."

Sky laughed. "Good idea."

They went into the hall and sat down. Amber glanced around, trying to see the hall through Sky's eyes. It must be so weird having never been to secondary school. Sky was slumped down in her seat like she was trying to make herself smaller. Amber hoped she'd settle in soon. From her point of view, the prospect of the next two years at school with Sky was a great one. She would finally get to experience secondary school life with a real friend. But was that selfish of her if Sky was so unhappy to be here?

The Year Head, a short man called Mr Jenkins, came onto the stage and gradually the hall fell silent. "Welcome back, Year Eleven. I hope you all had a great Christmas." He came and stood right at the edge of the stage and dug his hands deep into his jacket pockets. "Exam time will soon be upon us and I just wanted to reiterate how important these next few months will be for you. The grades you get for your GCSEs will dictate what A levels you'll be able to take. And this in turn will dictate whether or not you go to university…" Amber zoned out. All this talk of exams made her current lack of direction all the more stressful. What if she'd chosen the wrong subjects to study at A level? What if her current writer's block was a sign that she wasn't cut out for English and Creative Writing after all? What if she was actually supposed to be an astrophysicist? She pictured her sad-faced, pencil-sketch of a surrogate mum toiling away over a test-tube in a laboratory. Oh no! What if she was genetically programmed to do science A levels instead of arts? Just as her question attack reached fever-pitch Amber sensed Sky tensing beside her and zoned back in on Mr Jenkins.

"So, if the pressure from the exams starts to feel a bit much, you can always go and see your GP."

Sky leaned towards Amber. "Is he saying it's OK if we end up on medication?" she whispered.

Amber shrugged. They were frequently told about medication in PSHE lessons, whenever they talked about depression or anxiety. It was on the go-to list of solutions: CBT, meditation, meds. Sky frowned and shook her head.

"Are you OK?" Amber whispered.

Sky didn't reply. She just sat there and glared at Mr Jenkins.

Rose burst out of the school door and sprinted towards the gates. There was a bus to Camden at the end of the road in one minute's time. Not that they ever came on time but, knowing her lousy luck, the one time in the history of London Transport that a bus did come on time would be now. As she raced down the road a van driver tooted his horn at her and leaned out the window.

"Nice legs, darling!"

"Oh yeah?" Rose stopped running and pointed to her blazer. "And what part of school uniform don't you understand? Pervert!" Rose flipped him the finger and carried on running. She could see a bright red bus looming over the horizon. She thought of the patisserie and Francesca, and her desire to be there powered her on.

Once on board, Rose collapsed into a seat at the front

of the top deck and took stock of her day. Going back to school after the Christmas break hadn't been nearly as bad as she'd expected. After the photo had gone viral last year Savannah had withdrawn her from her old school and she'd been home-schooled by Liam for a couple of weeks. But that had got all kinds of awkward in the aftermath of Savannah and Liam's break up, so Savannah had enrolled her in a tiny private school in Hampstead. Rose had started at Heathlands School for Girls a few weeks before Christmas and it was proving to be a surprising success. Most of the girls there were heavily into their studies. The daughters of diplomats, business people and bankers – with a high contingent from Asia – they were more into getting A-stars than A-list gossip and that suited Rose just fine. The teachers could be a bit po-faced, in that upper-crust, British way, but Rose found that kind of entertaining, too. It was like being a character in *Downton Abbey* or an Agatha Christie novel – the outrageous American relation. Rose sat back in her seat and watched London roll by, a contented smile on her lips.

It was only when the bus juddered to a halt on Camden High Street that her nerves kicked in. Rose deliberately walked slowly towards the cake shop, trying to get her anxiety in check. It had been almost a month since she'd last seen Francesca. It felt like so much had happened since then, although of course it was only in her mind. Francesca didn't know that Rose had come out. She probably hadn't given Rose a second thought over Christmas. She probably wasn't even gay anyway. This whole crush was entirely pointless, there was no need to get so worked up about it. She gulped as the patisserie came into view. Hard rock was pounding from the souvenir shop next door, the bass line throbbing in time with her pulse. She could do this. She just had to pretend nothing had happened since she'd last been here. Rose pushed the door open and walked in. As usual, there was a French song playing on the old-fashioned juke-box and as usual, the palette of pastel yellows and pinks and blues instantly soothed her.

"Rose!" Francesca exclaimed from behind the counter, throwing her hands up in delight. "You are back!"

"Yep. Sure am." Rose stood there, motionless, feeling awkward.

Francesca came running out to greet her. She was wearing her usual frilly apron over a Fifties-style dress, her shiny chestnut hair tied back with a floral bandana. "We have missed you so much!" she cried, pulling Rose into a hug.

She smelled of a delicious mix of perfume, vanilla and cinnamon. The pit of Rose's stomach started to tingle. "I've missed you too," she said gruffly. "The shop, I mean. Well — and you. You and the shop." Oh geez, this was not a good start at all.

Francesca laughed, showing off her cute dimples. Before, when Rose hadn't allowed herself to admit to her true sexuality, it had been like looking at Francesca through gauze. But now her beauty shone in glorious technicolour and it was doing the weirdest things to Rose's body.

"Take a seat," Francesca said, gesturing to a nearby table. Apart from one elderly couple hunched over coffee and cupcakes in the corner, the shop was empty. "I get you a hot chocolate and your Christmas present."

"You got me a Christmas present?" Rose felt a stab of guilt. She hadn't got Francesca anything. She'd thought about it. Window-shopped her way around Manhattan looking for potential gifts but decided against it in the end in case it gave Francesca the wrong idea. Or the right idea or … oh man.

"But of course!" Francesca cried in her sing-song French accent. "I get all my employees a Christmas present. To say thank you for all your hard work."

"Ah. OK." Rose sat down and pulled off her hat and scarf. She took her phone from her bag. She needed a distraction. Something to focus on to stop her from melting into a love-sick puddle. She had two new texts. One from Amber and one from her mom. She opened Amber's first.

> I need your help! How do you work out what you're supposed to do with your life?

Rose grinned as she typed her reply.

> No worries! Will call you later to arrange a life-coaching session. xoxo

She opened the text from her mom.

Been dropped by the perfume company but it's all good. Will explain when you get home. XO

Rose studied the text. Her mom often said one thing when she actually meant a whole other thing. How could being dropped by another firm be "all good"? Especially when she'd reacted so badly the previous two times. She quickly sent her a reply.

Aw sorry mom. At the patisserie right now but I'll be home soon. Big hugs xoxoxo

Rose sat back in her chair. It was good to get a reality check, to be reminded that there was more to life than Francesca. Rose needed to get a grip on herself before she ended up even more lovestruck than Maali. Shit! Maali. She'd meant to text her today to find out how her dad was.

Hey Maals, how's your dad doing? xoxo

Then she thought of Sky and sent her a quick text too.

Yo! Welcome to the World of School. Hope it wasn't too traumatic. Love ya! Xoxo

Rose breathed in the sweet smell of the cake shop. This was good. Thinking about other people had really helped straighten her head out. Francesca came back to the table holding a hot chocolate in one hand and a small, gift-wrapped box in the other. The reflection of the fairy lights strung all around the shop glittered in her hair.

"Your gift," she said, handing Rose the box. As Rose took it from her their fingertips touched and she swore she actually felt sparks fly.

"Thank you," Rose muttered. She pulled at the wrapping paper but her fingers suddenly felt all fat and clumsy. *Get a frickin' grip!* Finally, she got through the tape and the paper came off. Inside was a jewellery box. She opened it, praying Francesca wouldn't see that her hands were trembling now. Inside, a beautiful silver rose pendant on a chain lay on a bed of inky blue velvet. Each unfurling petal had been carved in intricate detail.

"It is a rose – for Rose!" Francesca said with a laugh. "I get it in Paris. At an antique fair."

"It's beautiful," Rose said, taking the necklace from the box and fumbling with the clasp.

"Here, let me." Francesca took the necklace and went behind her. She was so close Rose could smell her perfume again. Francesca gently placed the necklace around her neck and did up the clasp. "Let me see," she said, coming round to face Rose. *"Ah, très bien!"*

For a moment, their eyes met, and for a moment, time

seemed to freeze-frame right there, inside a tiny cake shop in Camden. Everything just stopped … apart from Rose's beating heart. Then there was the scraping of chairs on the wooden floor and the sound of shuffling and coats being put on as the elderly couple in the corner got up to leave.

"So, I need to talk to you," Francesca said as she went over to clear the couple's table.

"You do?" Rose's brain started shuffling through the possible reasons: *I'm gay and I adore you / I can't fight my feelings any longer / I no longer need your help in the shop / you're fired.* She looked at Francesca anxiously.

"I am expanding the business."

"You are?"

"Uh-huh. I have bought a pitch in a market – starting on Saturdays and if it goes well, then every day." Francesca took the cups and plates over to the counter. "And I was wondering – would you like to run it?"

Rose gripped the edge of the table. "Are you serious?"

"Yes. I think you would be great. The customers love you and it would be such good experience for you. It is how I started out myself back in Paris – selling cakes on a market stall in Montmatre." Francesca smiled wistfully at the memory. What do you say? You could still do work experience here during the week after school but on Saturdays you will take care of the stall. And I will pay you, of course."

Rose could barely believe what she was hearing. This was the best news ever – running a stall could be a crucial step in achieving her dream. "That sounds awesome."

Francesca clasped her hands together excitedly. "*Magnifique!* I will help you there, the first few weeks, until you are ready to do it on your own. And if it gets too busy I get you a helper."

"But – I'd be in charge?"

"Yes." Francesca came back over to the table and sat down. "I see so much of myself in you, Rose. You have the same passion, the same instinct when it comes to baking. I want to help you the same way people helped me when I was starting out."

Completely unexpectedly, Rose's eyes filled with tears. "Shit. I'm sorry." She wiped her eyes but they kept coming. For so long her life had felt like one huge long reaction to her parents and their careers and mistakes and break-ups and other assorted dramas. Now, finally, something was happening that was positive and exciting and all hers, not theirs.

"No apologize for your tears!" Francesca said, shaking her head firmly. "It shows how much you care."

"Thank you so much," Rose murmured, looking down at the table.

"You deserve it. You work so hard for me last year. I know I can trust you with this."

"You can." Rose looked back at her, blinking away her tears. "You really can. I'm gonna be the best goddam cake-stall holder Camden Market has ever seen."

"Oh no – it isn't in Camden Market," Francesca said. "That would be too close to the shop. It is in Spitalfields."

Spitalfields? Rose felt a tingle of excitement. Spitalfields was just around the corner from Brick Lane; just around the corner from Maali and Amber. Spitalfields was Moonlight Dreamers territory. If she was into the same woo-woo stuff as Rachel she would say this was definitely the universe giving her a sign that her dream was meant to come true.

Chapter Ten

All the way home from school, Maali chanted the Gayatri Mantra over and over in her head. *"Aum bhoor bhuvah svah. . ."* Past the retail units in Box Park selling their trendy coffee and designer clothes ... *"tat savitur varenyam, bhargo devasya dheemahi . . ."* Under the graffiti-covered railway bridge ... *"dhiyo yo nah prachodayaat. . ."* On to bustling Brick Lane. The Gayatri Mantra was one of the most powerful Hindu mantras, supposed to bring wisdom and happiness to all who chanted it. It was one of Maali's favourites. *"Aum bhoor bhuvah svah. . ."* She walked past the vintage store Retro-a-go-go, where Amber worked at the weekends. *"Tat savitur varenyam, bhargo devasya dheemahi. . ."* She didn't even think of Ash as she crossed the road leading to the City Farm. *"Dhiyo yo nah prachodayaat. . ."* She walked past the looming red-brick tower of the Old Truman Brewery and her parents' sweetshop came into view. *Please, Lakshmi, let Dad be feeling better now.*

As she drew closer to the shop her heart sank. The lights were out and the CLOSED sign was displayed in the door. Why was it closed so early? She let herself in the side door that led to their flat. Taking the stairs two at a time, she raced into the hall and followed the murmur of her mum's voice coming from the living room.

Her mum was pacing up and down by the window, talking on her mobile. "OK, Sita, Maali's just got home. I'll call you back."

"What's up?" Maali said. "Why's the shop closed? Where's Namir?"

"He's with Auntie Sita," her mum replied. "I had to get her to pick him up from school. Your dad's been very ill. I haven't been able to leave him."

"With the vomiting virus?" Maali asked.

"Yes. I'm going to ring the emergency health line. I'm worried he's dehydrated."

Maali sat down on the sofa. "But he is — he is going to be all right?"

"Oh, of course he is, sweetheart. I just need to get an expert opinion — to put my mind at rest, really."

Maali breathed a sigh of relief. "I'll go and see him."

Her mum shook her head. "He's sleeping at the moment, probably best not to disturb him. Why don't you go and get something to eat and I'll call the doctor."

Maali nodded. But as soon as she got into the hallway she headed straight for her bedroom. She'd completely lost her appetite.

Once she was in her room, Maali lit some incense and

sat down in front of her shrine. She tried to do a simple meditation to calm herself but her fears were way too noisy. She opened her eyes and gazed at the Lakshmi figurine.

"Please help Dad get better," she whispered. "Please don't let him suffer any more." Lakshmi smiled back serenely. "And please help me to stay strong for Mum. I'm trying really hard not to—" She broke off as she heard the sound of footsteps running up the stairs.

"Maali, an ambulance is coming to take Dad to the hospital," her mum said breathlessly, bursting into the room.

"What? But why?"

"They're worried about the fluids he's lost and the fact that he can hardly stand up."

"He can't stand up?"

Her mum shook her head. She looked really scared. "He keeps getting so dizzy. I've called Auntie Sita and let her know what's happening. She's going to bring Namir back here as soon as Uncle Dev gets home from work. But it won't be until about nine o'clock. You're welcome to go round there now and have dinner with them."

"Can't I come with you and Dad to the hospital?"

Her mum shook her head. "No. There's nothing you'll be able to do. It's better that you're here for Namir. And I'll be home as soon as I can." She hugged Maali before rushing back downstairs.

Maali hurried after her, her heart pounding.

* * *

As Sky ran down the steps to the canal tow-path she pictured shedding the events of her first day at school like layers of dead skin. The pressure of being the new girl. The heat and the noise. The regimented lessons. The ever-present tension that polluted the school like a toxic cloud. She pictured it all leaving her body there on the steps. When she got to the tow-path she took off her tie and shoved it in a nearby bin. She undid the top button on her shirt and set off down the path feeling lighter with each step. When she got back to the boat she was going to tell Liam that this whole secondary school thing might have seemed like a good idea at the time – to him at least – but it had actually been a complete and utter disaster. She didn't belong in that world and she never would, so she was going to go back to home-schooling, even if she had to home-school herself. As she marched along the path their houseboat came into view. A thin ribbon of smoke coiled from the chimney. Liam was on the bank beside the boat, chopping wood for the stove.

"Hey, Dad!" she called.

He turned and put down the axe. "Hey, sweetheart. How was it?" He looked at her anxiously.

"Terrible."

Liam's face fell. He put down the axe and ran his hand through his hair the way he always did when he was stressed.

"But it's fine," Sky said breezily. "I know you need to earn more money so I'm going to home-school myself."

Liam shook his head. "No – you can't. You've got your

GCSEs coming up – and then your A levels. You need to have a teacher – *teachers*. Are you sure it's that bad? Maybe you just need to give it more of a chance."

"No. It's horrible, Dad. It's like a prison – with added homework. And it's so noisy and hot and—"

"Ah sure, you'll get used to that."

"But I don't want to get used to it." Sky felt a lump building in her throat. It hadn't occurred to her that Liam would say no. She'd assumed that when he heard how hard it had been for her, he'd be OK with her leaving.

"Sky, I need you to do this for me. I need you to make more of an effort." Liam started pacing up and down on the bank, looking really stressed. "I have to pay the mooring fees for this place. I have to work full-time. I've got no choice but to send you to school … if you want to stay here in London."

Sky's heart sank. It was the worst ultimatum. She either went to school or had to move away from the Moonlight Dreamers. She desperately searched for another reason not to go back.

"But – I've thrown my tie out."

"What? Why? Where?"

"In the bin, back up there."

"Jesus, Sky, go and get it. I'm not made of money."

As Sky stormed back up the path angry thoughts swooped through her mind. This was all Liam's fault. Why couldn't he be a normal dad with a normal job and a normal house? Why did he take her out of school in the first place if he was going to end up sending her back? At least if she'd always gone to secondary school she'd have been brainwashed into always doing what they said and wearing her tie and saying "yes, Miss, no, Miss, three bags full, Miss" every second sentence. Why couldn't she just live in a normal family with a normal name that nobody ever laughed at, like Lucy or Emily or Sarah? Why did Liam have to call her Sky? Why did he go out of his way to make her question the system only to shove her back into it? And then finally, the question she'd hoped she'd stopped asking: why did her mum have to die?

From: lakshmigirl@googlepost.com
To: wildeatheart@googlepost.com; halopoet@hotpost.co.uk; roselnyc@hotpost.com
Date: 4th January 17:58
Subject: EMERGENCY MEETING

Dear Moonlight Dreamers,
Something horrible has happened. Please can we have an emergency meeting? Tonight if possible. Even if only one of you is able to make it. I really need to see someone. Café 1001? 6 pm?
Love,
Maali xx

Chapter Eleven

Amber raced up the café stairs and scanned the tables. Maali was sitting in one of the booths in the gallery overlooking the ground floor, hunched over, still in her coat.

"Maali! Are you OK?" Amber slipped on to the bench opposite her.

"Yes. No. I don't know." Maali blinked really fast, like she was trying not to cry. "Thank you so much for coming."

"Of course. What's happened?"

Maali's bottom lip started to quiver, sending Amber into a tailspin. She was so rubbish when people cried. Crying made her feel awkward in the extreme. "There, there," she said, patting Maali on the hand. For God's sake, why did she have to be so like Gerald? What happened to the nurture part of nature and nurture? Why couldn't she at least have absorbed some of Daniel's natural ability to be affectionate? A terrible thought occurred to her. Maybe her surrogate mum was equally uptight. Maybe she was double-doomed to be socially inadequate.

"It's — it's my dad," Maali stammered. "He—"

"Hey, Dreamers. I come bearing cake!" Rose arrived at the table, her eyes sparkling and her cheeks glowing. She plonked an eggshell-blue cake box in front of them. Amber breathed a sigh of relief. It was no longer just down to her to console Maali. Rose would be way better at this kind of thing.

"Maals! What's up?" Rose sat on the bench and hugged Maali to her. She looked at Amber.

Amber shrugged and mouthed, "I don't know."

"It's my dad," Maali said. "He—"

"Hey, guys." Sky appeared at the table. Her eyes were red and her face was blotchy, like she'd been crying.

Amber's heart sank as she moved along to let her sit down. She must have really hated her first day at school.

"Maali, what's wrong?" Sky leaned across the table and took hold of her hand.

"It's my dad – he's had to go to hospital. In an ambulance."

"What the hell?" Rose stared at her. "Why?"

"He kept being sick. And now he can hardly stand up. The doctors are worried that he's lost too much fluid."

Rose shook her head. "Wow, that winter vomiting virus is a real bitch."

"Do you think that's what it is, then?" Maali looked at her hopefully.

"Well, that's what you said it was in your text to me."

"Yes, but..."

"What?"

"What if it's something more serious?"

Rose shook her head. "I'm sure it isn't. It was on the news the other day that people are dropping like flies from the virus. And at least now your dad's in hospital he'll be able to get all the care and meds he needs. I'm sure he'll be home in no time, you'll see."

Amber watched as the tension faded from Maali's face.

Rose opened the cake box and pushed it towards her. "Eat. Your body needs sugar after a shock. True story."

"Is that actually true?" Maali asked with a half grin.

Rose nodded seriously, but winked at Amber. "For sure. Go on."

Maali took a cake from the box. It was decorated in intricate swirls of icing every colour of the rainbow.

"It looks more like a work of art than a cake," Amber said.

"Uh-huh. My boss, Francesca, made them. She's amazing." Rose's face flushed and she quickly looked back at Maali.

Amber stared at Rose. There was something different about her. She seemed so happy. It was almost as if she was glowing. Amber glanced at Sky. She'd gone very quiet and was staring off into the distance, almost as if she wasn't there. Her traumatic day at school must have really knocked her for six, as Gerald would say.

Maali grinned at Rose through watery eyes. "Thanks for being so lovely, Rose."

Rose coughed. "Yeah well, don't tell anyone. I've still got my hard-as-nails image to protect, yo. Seriously though, you're not on your own, Maals. Is she?" Rose looked across the table at Amber and Sky. "Moonlight Dreamers are always there for each other, right?"

"Right," Amber said firmly.

Sky nodded.

Maali gave them a brave smile. "Thank you. I don't know what I'd have done if you hadn't come to meet me tonight."

Rose frowned. "There was no way we wouldn't have been here tonight. We're always here for you. Got it?"

Maali nodded.

"Good." Rose smiled at her. "Your dad's gonna be just fine. The docs have said it's the winter vomiting virus. They'll know exactly how to treat it. Trust me, he'll be back before you know it."

When Rose finally got home that night she took a moment outside the front door to prepare herself for the various scenarios that might be awaiting her: a) her mom would be at the drunk and morose stage of the Losing a Contract Grieving Process; b) she'd be in bed, sleeping off the drunk and morose stage; c) she'd be working out like a maniac on the running machine while mainlining beetroot juice, stuck in the complete denial stage of the process.

It turned out to be none of the above. When Rose stepped into the huge hallway she heard the sing-song hum of women's voices coming from the living room, then one voice cutting above the others, which wasn't her mum's.

"... and when we play small, we play straight into the patriarchy's hands," the woman said as Rose poked her head around the door. *What the hell?*

Savannah and her manager, Roxanne, were sitting on the white leather sofa gazing at the speaker, who was sitting cross-legged on one of the armchairs, holding a book. She wore a long lilac dress, which would probably be more accurately described as a robe, and her bobbed hair was so shiny, thick and black that it looked like a helmet. Rose cleared her throat. They all turned to look at her.

"Rose, honey, you're home!" Savannah ran over to greet her. She was wearing an old Rolling Stones t-shirt and sweat pants. It was the most dressed-down she'd been in years. Even when she put the trash out she wouldn't be seen in anything less than Givenchy. Rose studied Savannah's face. She wasn't wearing that much make-up either and she looked genuinely happy. Maybe she was stoned. But as Savannah leaned in to hug Rose, her breath smelled of coffee and her eyes were clear. "This is Margot Devine." Savannah gestured to the woman in purple. "She's another of Roxanne's clients. An author and motivational speaker. She's telling us all about her new book."

Rose fought the urge to laugh. In all the possible scenarios she had imagined coming home to tonight, her mom hosting an impromptu book club never came close.

"It's called *The Vagina Vows*," Savannah continued breathlessly.

"Ten ways to unleash the power of your sacred flower," Margot called out.

"I'm sorry?" Rose stared at her.

"That's the strapline," Margot explained. "Ten ways to unleash the power of your sacred flower."

"Wow!" Rose bit down on her bottom lip, not sure whether to laugh or feel totally grossed out.

"You should come listen," Savannah said, tugging on Rose's arm.

"Oh, I don't know." She lowered her voice to a whisper. "It all sounds a bit too gynaecological to me, but you go for it, Mom."

"It's not about sex or anything," Savannah said, way too loud for Rose's liking.

"Good God, no!" Margot exclaimed with a shudder.

"It's all about seeing our femininity as a strength instead of a weakness," Savannah explained. Rose hadn't seen her this wide-eyed with enthusiasm since she got her first NutriBullet.

"Amen, sister!" Roxanne called from the sofa, raising her glass of green juice.

"And not letting the patriarchy suppress us with their lies," Margot said.

"Right on." Rose raised her eyebrows to Savannah. "Seriously, Mom. I think I'm gonna go to bed. It's been a long day what with school and the patisserie and then I just had to go see a friend who's had some bad news. I need an early night. But you guys have fun." She grinned at them and fist-pumped the air. "Flower power!"

As soon as Rose made it to the safety of her bedroom she threw herself onto her bed. She had so much stuff to process from today. Not her mom's latest craze. She hoped to block that from ever entering her mind again. But everything else… She hugged a pillow to her and gazed at the hazy orange glow from the streetlight spilling in through the window. She hoped Maali was OK. When Rose had first met Maali she'd felt slightly irritated by the younger girl, but now she felt nothing but a fierce protection – the way you would for a kid sister, she guessed. She made a silent vow to make sure she was always there for her. Then she thought of what it had been like being back at school – boring but bearable. After how things had gotten last year she could definitely do boring but bearable. Then finally, saving the best till last, she felt for the rose pendant around her neck and thought of Francesca. It had been so awesome to see her again – and the news about the cake stall had been the icing on the cake, excuse the pun. Rose closed her eyes and grinned. This year could not have got off to a better start.

Chapter Twelve

This year could not have got off to a worse start, Sky thought to herself as she walked through the school gates doing up her grease-stained tie. In a final and pitiful act of defiance, she'd left it until the very last minute to put it on. The mood on the boat had been horrible this morning, with her and Liam tiptoeing around each other but neither of them willing to back down. She couldn't remember ever feeling so stressed and she hated it. Being made to go to school was forcing her to become someone she wasn't; someone she hated. It was turning her into a bitter, miserable version of herself. She was no longer Sky, she was … she was … Rain Cloud. A group of girls drew level with her, giggling and whispering. Were they laughing at her? Sky watched them sashay past. They all looked so immaculate, with their ironed-straight hair and their figure-hugging skirts. Sky looked down at her own skirt. It came to just below the knee, which in this school seemed to be about ten centimetres too long. None of the other girls wore Doc Marten boots like her either. They were all in little ballet-style pumps despite the cold. Sky scanned the grey concrete concourse leading up to the grey, concrete building. Why did her fellow students seem to go to such great lengths to look the same? She got that they all had to wear the same uniform but why didn't people customize their uniform to make it look more uniquely them? Why did they all style their hair and make-up the same?

She felt her phone vibrate in her blazer pocket. It was a text from Amber.

Are you at school yet? Do you want to meet up before registration?

Just seeing the word "registration" made Sky shudder. It was as if they were animals being rounded up to be sent to market. She put her phone back in her pocket. The truth was, she didn't want to meet up with Amber because Amber might want to talk about Maali and her dad, and that was the very last thing Sky wanted to talk about. This made her feel like even more of a horrible person. But Maali's news last night ended up triggering an avalanche of terrible memories about her mum.

Sky marched into the building and made her way along the harshly lit corridor. She'd found out about her mum's death on a bright summer's day, which seemed to have gone against all the laws of nature. Surely world-shatteringly bad news should only be delivered on days that are grey and overcast and echo with thunder. But no, that day had been one of the brightest and sunniest of the year. She'd been playing a game of "Kiss, Marry, Kill" with her best friend, Tara, all the way back from school and had arrived home laughing and breathless. She remembered two things so clearly from that day: there was no music playing when she got home and there was always music playing, and her dad was crying and he never cried. It was as if a needle had ripped across the blissful soundtrack to her childhood and all that was left was ominous silence. Sky's eyes began to smart. Damn. This was the last place she wanted to cry. She swallowed hard and made her way to her form room. The bell to round them up hadn't gone yet so there was only her form tutor, Mrs Bayliss, and Vanessa in the room. Sky went and sat beside Vanessa.

"Hello, Sky," Mrs Bayliss called, peering at her over her large, oval glasses. She had long, greying hair and a permanently serious expression. She reminded Sky of an owl.

"Hi," Sky replied, deliberately not saying the obligatory "Miss". She looked at Vanessa, who was engrossed in the red-raw skin around her fingernails again. "Hey."

"Hi." Vanessa didn't look up.

Sky suddenly felt really tired. She didn't have the energy to try to be friends any more.

Sky flinched as the bell in the corridor screeched and the sound of a student stampede came thundering towards them.

The first period was English. They were studying the

First World War poets, which had given Sky the tiniest flicker of hope. Surely this class would be OK. And if there was one lesson she enjoyed, at least there'd be something to look forward to. Of course, she got lost on the way, so by the time she reached the classroom the door was shut and there was an almighty racket coming from inside. Sky's heart sank. Maybe the teacher was off sick. The thought of being left alone as the new girl in an unsupervised class was about as appealing as being fed to the lions at London Zoo. But as she peered through the pane of glass in the door she saw a teacher standing at the front of the class. He looked very young – and very stressed.

"Quiet, please," he implored as Sky came into the room.

There was a temporary hush but it seemed to have been caused by Sky's arrival rather than the teacher's pleadings. Once again, she felt all eyes burning into her.

"Can I help you?" the teacher asked.

"Yes, I'm here for English. I've just started here."

"Oh." He looked flustered and angry, like he hadn't been told.

Sky felt her hackles rise. It wasn't as if she wanted to be there either.

"Name, please."

"Sky. Sky Cassidy."

"Sky?" said a girl with black hair and a mean, pouty mouth. "What, as in *the* sky?"

Sky nodded.

The girl smirked.

"Sit down. Sit down," the teacher said, gesturing at an empty space on the table across from pouty girl.

The lesson was terrible. Sky had clearly been put in the class for people who had no interest in poetry – or at least the ones who didn't have any interest had complete control of the class; the others just sat there quietly, staring into space. It didn't help that the teacher appeared to be deeply unhappy too.

When the bell finally rang for the end of class, something inside of Sky snapped. If she couldn't even enjoy a poetry lesson at this school there was no hope. She marched out of the classroom and along the corridor, ignoring her map and timetable and heading for the nearest exit.

Maali pushed past the crowd of tourists congregating on Brick Lane and made her way into the gift shop. She didn't normally come out for lunch but this morning she'd been given some divine inspiration. She knew it was divine because there was no way she could have come up with something so inspired on her own. *Why don't you give him a framed copy of the photo you took of him and Mum at Christmas*, her inner voice had said in Chemistry, completely out of the blue. Maali had taken the photo on Christmas morning, when her parents weren't looking. They were standing together peeling vegetables by the kitchen sink, and her dad was looking at her mum with such an expression of pure love it had taken Maali's breath away. If she gave him a framed copy when she visited him after school he could keep it by his hospital bed and hopefully it would cheer him up.

Maali bought a green frame – her dad's favourite colour – and stepped back out on to the street. The sun had finally made an appearance, albeit a pale and diluted one. "Excuse me, please," Maali said as she passed a guy standing in the middle of the pavement looking at his phone.

"Hello, stranger!" the guy called after her. The sound of his voice caused her to freeze in her tracks. It couldn't be… She turned slowly. It was. Ash was standing there, grinning at her, looking even more handsome than she remembered him in his faded jeans and scuffed leather jacket.

"H—hello." Maali felt completely thrown off balance.

"How have you been?" Ash asked, walking towards her. "I've missed seeing you around. And not just because it made me finish *The Lord of the Rings* way quicker than I'd have liked to." He laughed, causing his cuteness to climb several notches.

Maali felt a warm glow as she remembered that day in the City Farm café and how Ash had told her that he wasn't just pleased to see her because talking to her would make the book he was loving last longer. A soft-focus flashback came into her mind. Ash and her at the table in the corner of the café, talking and laughing. Then the flashback went from soft focus to neon glare as she remembered the arrival of Ash's girlfriend, Sage. She cringed as she thought of the way they'd kissed – the way she'd imagined herself being kissed by Ash during the thousands of daydreams she'd had about him. "I have to go," she said crisply. "I have to get back to school."

Ash looked genuinely disappointed. "Oh, that's a shame. How did your story turn out in the end?"

Maali looked at him blankly.

"The one about the pig farmer."

Maali cringed as she remembered the lame excuse she'd come up with to go and see Ash. Telling him she needed help with a story about pigs. It seemed so immature and pathetic now. *She* seemed so immature and pathetic – unlike the ultra-sophisticated, swishy-haired Sage.

"Which way are you going?" Ash asked.

Maali gestured down the road.

"Great. Me too. I'll walk with you."

Maali couldn't believe it. It had been bad enough seeing signs of Ash everywhere lately but making their paths actually cross like this seemed downright cruel. *Lakshmi, why are you doing this to me?* she silently moaned.

"So, how's your New Year been so far?" Ash said.

Maali thought of her dad. "Oh, you know."

Ash grinned at her. "No, I don't know. That's why I'm asking."

Maali felt as if her heart was being crushed. It was like the two causes of her current sorrow were pressing in on her and she could hardly breathe. "I have to go," she muttered and, spotting a gap in the traffic, she raced across the road.

"Are you OK?" Ash called after her. He shouted something else but it was drowned out by a passing lorry.

WHY THE CAGED BIRD CRIES

BY Sky Cassidy

Maya knows why the caged bird sings
but I know why she cries.
She cries because she misses her wings
and the endless open skies.

Why does life have to be so hard?
Why so many rules?
Why the mortgage and the nine-to-five?
Why the soulless schools?

We all have the right to express ourselves,
we all have the right to be free.
We all long for passion and fire and dance,
we all are as wild as the sea.

Maya knows why the caged bird sings
but I know why she cries.
She cries because she misses her wings
and the hope of the bright blue skies.

Chapter Thirteen

Sky placed her notebook on top of her Maya Angelou anthology and took a sip of her peppermint tea. Finally, she was starting to feel like herself again. It had taken a bracing walk around St James's Park, several cups of tea, a read of some of her favourite poems and quickly scribbling out one of her own to shed the hot and bothered, bitchy alter ego school had turned her into. She breathed a sigh of relief. And now she was back in her favourite place in all of London, the Poetry Café. She and the guy serving behind the counter were the only ones in there. Jazz was playing softly in the background and the only other sound came from the occasional ringing of the phone. It was an oasis of quiet and calm in the middle of the Covent Garden craziness. It was coming up to four-thirty – the time when she should be arriving home from school. But Liam was teaching yoga classes in Shepherd's Bush this evening and wouldn't be back till gone ten. She still had all the time in the world and no need to go anywhere or do anything. It was a wonderful feeling.

Sky took her phone from her pocket and clicked on the inbox. She had three more messages from Amber, which she hadn't been able to bring herself to reply to yet.

Hi, I'll meet you at the canteen at lunch. We can go outside if you like? Wherever you'd like to go...

Are you at school today? I'm waiting by the door.

I take it you're not in. Hope all is OK.

Sky felt wracked with guilt. She'd been feeling so crappy earlier she hadn't been thinking straight. It was so rude of her not to reply to Amber. She quickly started typing.

I'm so sorry – had to leave after first period – wasn't feeling well. Will explain all when I see you. S x

She sat back in her chair, wondering what to do next. She was getting pretty hungry. Should she stay here and eat or go and grab a slice of pizza in Leicester Square and listen to the buskers?

The door to the café flew open, bringing in a burst of cold air. A guy stood in the doorway looking around. He was about eighteen, with brown skin and afro hair twisted into mini dreadlocks. He was grinning the kind of goofy grin you'd get if you'd just won the lottery. His gaze fell on Sky and she felt a weird jolt of recognition, as if she knew him from somewhere.

"Hey," he said warmly, like he knew her too. "How's it going?" He spoke with a strong London accent but his voice was soft, which took the edge off it.

"Good," Sky said. "How are you?" OK, this was weird. Why did he seem so familiar?

"Great," he said, shutting the door behind him and coming over. He was carrying a large sports bag, which he put down on the floor by her table. "This is the Poetry Café, right?"

Sky nodded. "Yes." She followed his gaze around the empty tables. "It's a bit quiet at the moment but it should liven up later. They have events downstairs in the evening. Readings and things."

"I know." His eyes were dark brown and they sparkled when he grinned. "I'm meant to be reading here tonight."

"Really?" Sky's heart skipped a beat. A poet!

"Yeah. Can't you tell?" He held out his hands in front of her and made them quiver. "I'm terrified."

Sky laughed. "Don't be. It's a very friendly crowd. At least it was when I read here."

"You've read here?" He pulled out a chair then stopped. "Is it OK … if I join you?"

"Of course. Yeah, I read here a while ago." Sky loved being able to say this – it made her sound so worldly and interesting, so unlike a stupid, grumpy schoolgirl. "It was the first time I'd ever read one of my poems in public. I was really scared too but it was fine. It helps that it's not that big."

He glanced around the narrow café and nodded before looking back at her. "I'm Leon." He held out his hand across the table.

"Oh." Sky quickly took hold of it.

There was a split second of awkward silence before he shook her hand and started to laugh. "See, I told you I was nervous. I've never been anywhere like this before. Do people shake hands here?"

Sky laughed. "I don't think so. At least, no one's ever shaken my hand here before."

Leon groaned. "I'm sorry. It's just – this is very different to the places I'm used to performing." He looked up at the menu on the blackboard. "I mean, what the hell is quin-o-a?"

Sky laughed. "It's actually pronounced *keen-wa* and it's pretty gross so you haven't been missing much. Where do you normally perform, then?"

"Oh, the youth centre on my estate. This community centre in Vauxhall where they do spoken word nights. Nuttin' fancy." Leon took off his jacket. His arms bulged with muscles. Sky spotted a tattoo of a word just beneath his t-shirt sleeve but she wasn't close enough to read what it said.

"You didn't tell me your name." He leaned back in his chair and grinned at her.

Sky felt a stab of anxiety. She'd come to hate telling people her name over the past two days. "Sky," she muttered.

"For real? I mean, that's not your performance name?"

She shook her head.

Leon whistled. "Cool. Great to meet you, Sky."

She grinned back at him. "Great to meet you too."

"I'm really worried about Sky," Amber said, sitting down on her bed.

Rose took off her coat and slung it over the back of Amber's chair. "Why? What's up?"

"She was only in school for one lesson today. She said she wasn't feeling well but I think it's because she's really hating it there."

Rose nodded. "Makes sense. I mean, it must be really tough to start school again at sixteen. I don't get why her dad won't just let her stay home."

"I think they might be having money problems. She said he's having to teach more yoga classes so he's not able to home-school her any more."

Rose sat down on the bed next to Amber. She was wearing a black shift dress over patterned leggings and biker boots. As always, she looked as if she'd stepped straight from the cover of an edgy fashion magazine. "I'll text her later, make sure she's OK. So, how's the existential crisis?"

"Worse than ever." Amber sighed. "The other day I even started wondering if I ought to be taking science A levels."

"Science?" Rose stared at her. "But I thought writing was your thing."

"It is – was. But I keep getting blocked."

"I had been wondering," Rose said. "I was starting to think my notifications for Wilde at Heart had stopped working. You haven't blogged for ages."

"Exactly." Amber looked down into her lap. "I wish I could be more like you."

"You do? Why?"

"Well, you're so sure of what you want to do with your life — so focused on your dream."

Rose laughed. "That's funny because I wish I could be more like you."

Amber stared at her, shocked. "Why?"

"Because you don't care about being different — the way you dress and stuff. I think I'm getting there — by coming out to you guys, I mean. But I still haven't plucked up the courage to come out to my mom or at school yet."

Amber frowned. Did Rose think the same as Chloe and the other bullies at school — that she dressed the way she did because she was gay? "I — I'm not gay, you know."

Rose stared at her. "I know that. I just meant — you don't try to be like everyone else." Her face fell. "Not like me."

Amber felt a surge of panic. Rose was trying to open up to her. What should she do? What should she say?

"What do you mean?" she asked. That was good — put the focus back on to Rose. If she kept asking questions she could delay the awkward moment when she'd have to give advice.

"Messing around with that boy last year. Sending him that photo." Rose suddenly looked really down-hearted.

Amber cleared her throat. "Yes, well, sometimes you need to do the wrong thing to work out what the right thing is." She looked at Rose anxiously. Did what she'd said make sense? To her relief, Rose started nodding.

"Yeah. You're right. I like that. Thank you." She grinned and started playing with the silver rose pendant on her necklace. "I definitely know what the right thing is now, that's for sure." She looked at Amber. "Have you ever been in love?"

Oh God! Having emotional heart-to-hearts with friends was like negotiating your way through a minefield. Just when you think you've dodged one potential disaster, another appears. "Er, no, not really. I don't really..." she tailed off. Better to say nothing.

"You don't really what?"

"I don't really like boys." Amber's face started to burn. "I mean, I'm not gay. I'm just not really anything, I suppose." This was excruciating. She didn't know what she wanted to do with her life and she didn't have a sexuality. It was official – she was a complete non-person!

"What do you mean, you're not really anything?" Rose frowned. "Of course you're something. Maybe not being interested is your thing."

"Maybe." Amber didn't think so, though. The whole world was built around couples.

"You're going to figure all this out, you know."

"Really?"

"Yes. You've just had a knock-back, like I did last year – but without the nudity." Rose gave an embarrassed grin. "I know it must have been really tough to get that email about your mom, but you're going to get through it. Seriously, you don't need to know who she is to figure out who you are. And when you've figured that out you're going to be stronger and more awesome than ever, I promise."

Amber smiled at her. "Thank you."

"No worries. And I'm here any time you need to chat, OK?"

"OK."

"I have some news, by the way," Rose said. "To do with my dream."

"Really? What is it?"

"I'm going to be running a cake stall in Spitalfields Market every Saturday, starting this week!"

"No way!"

"Francesca gave me the job."

Amber studied Rose's face. Why was she blushing bright red? "Your boss at the cake shop?"

"Uh-huh. She's branching out into market stalls and she wants me to run the first one. I'm so psyched. It's going to be such a great experience."

Amber smiled. "Well done. I'm so – you're so – I'm proud of you."

"Really?" Rose looked like she didn't quite believe her.

"Yes. After everything you went through last year – it's

great that you didn't let it make you give up on your dream."

"Are you kidding me? It was my dreams that kept me going … and my fellow Dreamers."

As Rose smiled at her, Amber felt a prickle of hope. This was why she'd set up the Moonlight Dreamers – because she believed so passionately in the power of dreams. And even though she felt lost right now, she knew it would be her dreams that would help her find her way again. Once she worked out what they were.

Chapter Fourteen

All the way to the hospital Maali had felt excited about seeing her dad, but as she followed her mum to the ward, her heart sank. An old man was lying in the first bed they walked past. He was wearing faded pyjamas and his skin was wrinkled and paper-thin. His breath rasped as he struggled to sit upright. Maali quickly looked away. It felt intrusive to see complete strangers displayed in their pyjamas like this. She kept her eyes fixed on the floor until her mum stopped by a bed at the far end of the ward. When Maali looked up she had to stop herself from gasping. Her dad was propped against a bank of pillows. His hair was greasy and his face unshaven. Even though it had only been a day since she last saw him, he looked so much worse – and so weak.

"Dad," Maali said softly. Don't look upset, she told herself sternly as she walked over to him.

"Maali," he replied in a coarse whisper.

She perched on the edge of the bed. A thin tube linked to a drip was attached to his arm.

"It's so I don't get dehydrated," he told her, following

her worried gaze. "It's good to see you."

"You too," Maali replied. Although it wasn't good to see him like this – not at all. No wonder her mum hadn't wanted Namir to come with them. No wonder she'd warned Maali not to expect too much.

"Do you want some water?" her mum asked.

"Yes, please."

Maali watched as her mum took a jug of water from the bedside cabinet and poured some into a plastic cup. Then she carefully lifted it to Maali's dad's lips and he took a sip. It was horrible to see him like this – so vulnerable. He was always the strong one, and so full of life.

"How was school, pet?" he asked. Even his eyes had lost their sparkle, as if the virus had swept through his body and chased away all of his joy.

"It was OK." Maali reached into her school bag. "I brought you a present." She took out the framed photo and handed it to him.

"Oh, Maali, this is lovely." His hands trembled as he held the picture. "Look," he said, showing it to her mum.

"I thought you could keep it by your bed while you're here – to remind you of Mum and home."

"It's beautiful," her mum said, her voice wobbling slightly. "When did you take it?"

"Christmas morning."

"Thank you," Maali's dad said, his eyes shiny with tears.

Maali smiled at them bravely but fear was fluttering like

a trapped bird inside her ribcage. She hated seeing her parents like this.

As Maali climbed the stairs to her attic room later that night, her legs felt heavy as lead. Normally she could find hope in any situation but not today. The hospital visit had left her feeling drained. She knelt before her shrine. "Please, Lakshmi, I need your help. Please, please give me a sign that things will get better. That my dad will get better. Or at least let me know how I can help." She gazed at the figurine. It looked cold and lifeless in the dark. Then Maali had a terrible thought. Why would God do this to her dad? Why would he put anyone through such pain? It felt so cruel. And then another terrible thought struck her. What if there were no gods and goddesses? What if Amber and Rose were right and it was all a sham? Maali prayed every day. She meditated. She tried to live in the most loving way possible and so did her parents and yet this was how they were rewarded. It didn't seem fair and it didn't make sense. Don't be so stupid, of course God exists, Maali told herself as she got undressed and into bed. The sheets felt icy cold against her skin.

"And next on the open mic, we have Rebel Writer."

Sky watched as Leon made his way up to the front of the room. He'd been so nervous before but as soon as he reached the mic he seemed more at ease. She watched wistfully as he took his time to adjust the microphone stand. On the two occasions she'd read her poems in public she'd been so terrified she wouldn't have dared to touch the mic in case it fell over.

"Hello," Leon said softly. His eyes twinkled under the spotlights as he met her gaze. "I'd like to read you all a piece I wrote called 'Be the Change'."

Sky sat back in her chair and closed her eyes as he started to read. She wanted to let the words soak in without any distraction. Leon's poem was all about the discrimination he faced being black. How, right from the age of five, certain teachers treated him differently. How he and his friends would get stopped all the time by the police. How people sometimes looked scared when he got on a bus. How tired he was of constantly feeling he had something to prove – that he wasn't a gangster or a dealer or a thug. It was heartbreaking, but then the whole mood of the poem changed. Leon talked about how he'd been really angry at first but then he'd read a quote from Ghandi about being the change you want to see in the world and this had transformed everything. "Be the change, be the change, change the be, be the change," the refrain went, over and over, melodic and hypnotic. She could see now why it was called performance poetry. His voice lilted up and down. Every line, every word was recited with exactly the right cadence. Softer, then louder, pausing for emphasis. She could tell that he must have put as much thought into the performance as he did into the writing. Sky was in awe. This was how she dreamed of performing someday. Rather than blurting her work out as quickly as possible, she longed to have the confidence to experiment with her voice, to pause for effect, and not forget her lines.

The poem came to an end. Leon stood at the mic, eyes closed. There was a moment's silence, then the audience burst into applause. Leon opened his eyes and looked straight at Sky and grinned. Sky's hands stung from clapping so hard. He came and sat down next to her, giving her arm a quick squeeze. Sky's stomach fluttered in response.

"That was great. You were great," she whispered. She felt so proud, and once again it was as if she'd known him for years.

"Really?"

She loved that he looked genuinely surprised – that he wasn't aware of how talented he was. "Yes, really."

After the open mic was over they walked through Covent Garden together. Even in deepest, darkest, coldest January the streets were full of tourists and revellers and the narrow roads hummed with rickshaws and black cabs.

"How are you getting home?" Leon asked, swinging his sports bag over his shoulder.

"Tube, from Leicester Square. How about you?" Sky asked casually but hoping so badly he'd be going the same way.

"Same. Whereabouts do you live?"

"Currently, Camden."

Leon looked at her questioningly.

"It changes. My dad and I live on a houseboat."

Leon grinned. "Oh man, that must be great."

"It is. How about you? Where do you live?"

"Willesden – in a tower block. And yep, it's as grim as it sounds." He cleared his throat. "I really enjoyed tonight."

Sky felt a strange jolting sensation deep inside her. "Me too." Part of her was praying that he'd ask to see her again but a deeper part of her, the part that had recognized Leon as soon as he walked through the door, felt certain she'd be seeing more of him. It was a very weird feeling, nervous and calm at the same time.

"I was wondering…"

"Yes." She glanced up at him. He was looking straight ahead.

"Would you like to meet up some time? I'd love to hear some of your work."

Sky smiled. "Of course. That would be great." They reached a crossing crowded with people. She felt Leon's arm, solid and strong, lightly touch her shoulders, shielding her from being jostled. It felt so nice. So safe. They crossed over. All of the noise and chaos of London faded into a background haze. It was as if she and Leon were the only two in focus. Like this was a pivotal scene in the story of her life. One that was meant to happen.

Leon rode the Tube with her to Camden, even though he should have got off two stops before.

"You sure you'll be OK getting home from here?" he asked as the train pulled into the station. "You don't want me to walk you?"

"No. I'll be fine. Thanks."

As a crowd of people surged to the door to get off, he once again put his arm lightly around her shoulders, blocking her from everyone, like a solid wall of muscle. She loved the way he was so gentle and strong all at once.

"OK, well I better head back to Euston," he said as they reached the part of the station where the tunnel divided. He rooted around his bag and pulled out a pen. "Give me your hand." He grinned. "Don't worry, I'm not going to shake it again."

"Oh, I wouldn't mind. You have a very nice handshake."

His dark eyes shone. "I do?"

She blushed and looked away. "Yes."

He took her hand in his. It felt warm and strong. "Well, you have a very nice hand."

Somewhere in the distance, the sound of a busker singing *Imagine* by John Lennon came echoing through the tunnel. Sky felt a shiver of joy. Now, every time she heard that song, she'd think back to this magical moment.

Leon started writing something on the back of her hand. "My number," he explained. "If you'd like to meet for more poetry and handshakes – any time."

"Thank you." Again, she felt the weird mixture of sheer joy that she had his number and the certainty that she was always meant to get it.

"Well, I'll be seeing you," Leon said, slinging his sports bag over his shoulder. "I hope."

"You will," she replied and their eyes connected for what seemed like ages. Then another swarm of people surged towards them and carried them their separate ways.

When Sky arrived back at the houseboat she could smell incense from the tow-path. Liam was back already. She felt a moment's apprehension but she was so happy she doubted anything Liam could do or say would spoil her mood. She made her way through the narrow kitchen and into the living room. Liam was sitting on the floor, strumming his guitar.

"Hey, Dad, sorry I'm back so late."

"Where have you been?" Liam put down the guitar and got to his feet. He looked more relieved than angry.

"I went to the Poetry Café after school. A friend of mine was reading there." It wasn't a lie. Leon was a friend now. He just hadn't been before.

"Ah, OK. And how was school?" He studied her face anxiously.

"It was fine." Everything felt fine now. Her entire world – even the worst parts – had been cast in the warm glow of meeting Leon.

"Ah, that's grand." He hugged her. "I knew it would get better. The first day was bound to be the worst. I got a couple more private clients from tonight's class, so hopefully we should be OK for the mooring fees."

"That's great, Dad." Sky breathed a sigh of relief. As long as she could stay in London, she'd be happy.

When she got into her bunk later, she thought of Leon's

poem, trying to remember the lines. She wondered what it must be like to face constant discrimination because of the colour of your skin. She felt ashamed that she'd let a little mild teasing about her name get to her so much. That was nothing compared to what some people had to face day in, day out. But Leon wasn't bitter and sulking about it, he was out there writing and speaking about it, trying to change things for the better. She pulled her duvet up to her chin and gazed into the darkness. That was how she wanted to live her life – not bitching and moaning from the sidelines but actually doing something. Being the change she wanted to see in the world.

WHAT IF YOUR *THING* ISN'T A THING?

As teenagers we're constantly being asked to define ourselves. Through our appearance, through our behaviour, through the bands we like and the clothes we wear and through our sexuality.

There's this constant need to categorize. Like society has to know exactly where we fit in.

But what if you don't fit in?

What if there's no neat little pigeonhole or label for you?

What if your *thing* isn't even a thing?

For example: what if you don't like any kind of music? Or what if you don't have a clue what you want to do when you leave school? Or what if you just aren't interested in boys or sex ... for example.

Does anyone else ever feel like this?

Does anyone else feel the pressure to fake it sometimes just to fit in?

Maybe more of us need to find the courage to speak our truth.

If you don't fit in, say so, instead of pretending to be something you're not.

If how you are doesn't exist as a *thing*, be brave enough to create your own thing.

Who knows, there could be thousands of people out there all hoping and wishing they weren't alone, when the truth is, they're not. It's just that they're all being silent.

I'm going to leave you with a favourite Oscar quote of mine that I know I've used before on this blog but it's perfect for this topic:

"Be yourself; everyone else is already taken."

Be yourself. Be proud of yourself. And dare to speak loud about yourself.

Till next time…

Amber

Chapter Fifteen

It was the last lesson on Friday, which, according to Sky's timetable, meant it was PSHE, which, according to her school planner, stood for Personal, Social and Health Education. All of the groans, Sky thought as she made her way to her form room. As long as Mrs Bayliss didn't expect her to share anything personal, she should be OK. Just one more hour and then she'd be free again – for two days at least. Today had been way more bearable. Nothing had changed – or not on the outside. School was as depressing as ever and she still felt completely out of place, but the difference was that she no longer cared. The glow she'd felt after meeting Leon continued to surround her like an aura. Meeting him had made her realize that there was more to life than school; there was still a whole world of interesting people out there for her to get to know. Sky walked into the classroom and sat down next to Vanessa.

"All right?" she said.

"Hmm," Vanessa replied.

Sky wasn't sure if it was a "hmm"' in agreement. Trying

to read Vanessa was like trying to read a closed book. She looked down at her own hand. Leon's number was still there, slightly faded now. She'd stored it in her phone and written it in her notebook but she couldn't bring herself to remove his trace from her skin.

"So, today we're going to be talking about anxiety," Mrs Bayliss said, writing ANXIETY in big red letters in the centre of the white board.

Not the greatest start, Sky thought. She should have written it in green. Everyone knew green was a more soothing colour.

"So, what does anxiety mean to you?" Mrs Bayliss asked, looking around the class.

Sky stared down at her lap to avoid eye contact.

"It means when you get stressed about something, Miss," Cara called out. "Like when you have a panic attack."

"Good," Mrs Bayliss said, adding the words STRESS and PANIC ATTACK to the board. "What else?"

"Anxiety is when you really worry about something," another girl said.

"Yes." Mrs Bayliss wrote WORRY on the board. "Anything else? How does anxiety make you feel?"

"It makes you feel really scared," a girl sitting at the front of the class said.

"Thank you, Prithi." Mrs Bayliss added the word SCARED.

"It makes you not want to eat anything," another girl said.

Sky watched as Mrs Bayliss wrote LOSS OF APPETITE on the

board. Wow, this class was a laugh a minute.

"It makes you not able to sleep, too," Prithi added.

Mrs Bayliss wrote INSOMNIA on the board. "Anything else?"

"Alone," Vanessa muttered.

"What was that?" Mrs Bayliss strained to listen.

"It makes you feel really alone," Vanessa said, slightly louder.

"Nah, that's just 'cos you've got no friends," a girl called Jessica called out from behind them. Vanessa's face flushed red. Sky turned round and glared at Jessica.

"What's up, *Sky*?" Jessica spat out her name like it was an insult. Sky continued to glare.

Mrs Bayliss finished writing ALONE and turned back to the class. "How many of you have experienced anxiety before?" About two thirds of the class put their hands up. As Mrs Bayliss looked around the room she seemed genuinely concerned. "Sadly, anxiety is affecting more and more people these days, especially young people, but the good news is, there's lots of help available. So today we're going to look at the different ways of treating the symptoms."

"What about the causes?" The question popped out of Sky's mouth before she had time to remember to put her hand in the air. In other lessons this might have got her a telling off from the teacher, but Mrs Bayliss didn't seem to mind. "Good question, Sky. Let's take a moment to look at the causes of anxiety. Anyone got any suggestions?"

"Life?" Vanessa muttered, but so quietly only Sky heard her.

"Homework and exams," Cara said, to a loud murmur of agreement.

Mrs Bayliss wrote HOMEWORK AND EXAMS on the board in blue.

"Too much pressure," another girl called.

"Too much pressure from what?"

"School and parents."

"And the internet," another girl called out.

"How does the internet make you anxious, Philippa?" Mrs Bayliss asked.

Philippa blushed and shrugged. "I don't know. It just does."

"It makes you constantly compare yourself to others," Cara said. "Like, when you see people on your social media having a great time, it can make you feel stressed about your own life – that it's not good enough. That *you're* not good enough."

Sky thought of Rose and what she'd gone through last year when her ex-boyfriend posted the topless photo of her on Instagram. "People are really quick to judge you on the internet too," she said. "On social networks and things."

Philippa and Cara nodded and smiled at Sky.

"Thank you, Sky." Mrs Bayliss wrote SCHOOL, INTERNET and PARENTS on the board. "Anything else?"

"Society," Prithi said.

"How does society make you anxious?" Again, Mrs Bayliss looked really concerned.

Prithi shrugged. "I don't know. The way it always expects so much."

Mrs Bayliss added SOCIETY to the board. "Right, so now we've looked at the causes, let's take a look at all the ways you can get help if you're suffering from anxiety."

As Mrs Bayliss started talking about breathing techniques Sky stared at the board. As she'd already realized, something was wrong here, something felt off. All of the emphasis was on treating the symptoms instead of the cause. It was like the assembly the other day when the Year Head had basically told them to go to their doctors if the exams got to be too much. No one seemed to be asking why so many people were suffering from anxiety. No one seemed to get that there had to be something seriously wrong.

"Don't you think we're missing the point?" Sky said just as Mrs Bayliss was about to show them a deep-breathing technique.

"Sorry?" Mrs Bayliss stared at her.

"Well, shouldn't we be trying to change the things that are making us anxious instead of trying to learn how to cope?" *Be the change. Be the change.* Leon's words echoed in her mind. She looked down at his faded number on her hand and felt a rush of adrenalin.

"Yeah," Philippa said. "Why should all the pressure be on us to change?"

"Well, I don't really see how we're going to get society to change," Mrs Bayliss said.

The atmosphere in the room was different. Sky could feel it. Everyone was really paying attention now. "Why not?" she asked. "People have changed society before. Loads of times. Look at Nelson Mandela – and the suffragettes."

"And Gandhi," Prithi said.

Sky felt a shiver run up her spine. The mention of Gandhi had to be a coincidence. Didn't it?

"I know, but real change takes a long time to achieve and you all have important exams in just a few months – and that isn't going to change." Mrs Bayliss looked at Sky but she didn't seem angry, she seemed more apologetic. "So you need to learn some techniques to help you deal with any stress the exams might make you feel. Does that make sense?" There were a few nods. "OK, everyone, sit up straight and close your eyes. I'm going to count to four as you inhale and then four again as you exhale."

This is bullshit, Sky thought. You could always find an excuse not to make a change. She bet the suffragettes had thousands of reasons not to chain themselves to railings and be force-fed in prison but they still campaigned for the vote and they still brought about massive change. She snuck a glance around the classroom. Most of the class had their eyes closed, but Philippa and Prithi were both smiling at her. Vanessa leaned towards her. "Thank you," she whispered.

"What for?" Sky whispered back.

"Saying the truth."

* * *

Now I know how a ghost must feel, Maali thought as she trudged along Brick Lane on the way home from school. She felt so empty and weightless. Her dad was still in hospital. Her mum had texted at lunchtime to say there'd been no change and he would need to have more tests. Maali had never, ever doubted the existence of God. She knew that the Hindu gods and goddesses had been created to teach people different lessons, but she had never doubted that they were all aspects of the divine. Until now. Now she couldn't shake the uncertainty that had come over her last night. And it felt horrible.

She was passing the old warehouse next to the brewery when a sign caught her eye. Or rather, a word on the sign: PHOTOGRAPHY. She stopped to read it. There was always something going on in this warehouse; normally it was clothes-related – a vintage sale or a fashion show. But today there was a photography exhibition and, even better, it was free. Maali slipped in through the door. Her mum was at the hospital and Namir was at Auntie Sita's – it wasn't as if she had anything to rush home to. She climbed the narrow stone stairs and emerged into a huge open space. The brick walls were painted white and a labyrinth of exposed pipes ran across the ceiling. The room was divided into four sections, each with a theme: Power, Truth, Hope and Love.

Maali made her way to the first section. The theme of Power was obvious in some of the photos and more subtle in others. She preferred the subtle ones. It felt so satisfying to work it out. She stared at a black and white shot of a small child leaning on a lamp post. The lamp post was leaning out of alignment so it looked as if the kid was bending it with a super-human strength.

She made her way into the section on Truth. The photos here had a slightly edgier feel. There were pictures of food-banks and immigrants and drug addicts. The one she liked best was of a homeless man sleeping on a sheet of cardboard in a shop doorway. The photo had been taken from street level and a pair of legs in pinstriped trousers and shiny shoes was walking past. The legs were a blur, while the homeless man was in sharp focus. That was the real truth about London – beneath the sheen of wealth and glamour there was a seam of abject poverty.

Maali began browsing the section marked Hope. Although it was cold in the warehouse she felt herself slowly start to thaw inside. There was one picture in particular that she couldn't peel her eyes from: a legless, shaven-headed man in a wheelchair flinging a basketball into the air. The expression on his face as he watched the ball go was one of pure joy. This was why she loved photography so much – the way a picture was able to convey so much without the need for words. She sighed as she thought of how long it had been since she'd taken a photo. In all of her obsession with Ash and then the stress over her dad, her passion for photography had been shoved to the very back of her mind. But it was still there, pulsing away like a living thing.

She made her way into the final section, Love, feeling

slightly apprehensive. Love used to be her entire reason for being. Now it felt scary, like one of those thick, dark forests from children's fairy tales where witches and monsters lurk at every turn. The first photo was a close-up of a chubby, smiling baby. Maali's heart softened. The next was of a large, jagged heart spray-painted on to the wall of an off-license. Maali's favourite was of an elderly couple sitting on a bench, smiling at each other and holding hands. There was something about their gaze that reminded Maali of her parents and the loving gaze she'd captured in her photo of them. She looked closer. The skin on the man's face was so old it hung down in folds. The woman's face was as lined as a tortoise's. She wondered what the couple had been through in all their years together; what each of the wrinkles represented. There were laughter lines at the sides of the woman's mouth, but she also had a pair of frown lines between her eyes just like Maali's mum. The couple must have been through some tough experiences together and, at their age, they must have been aware that their time together would soon be coming to an end. But they were still smiling. They were still full of love. *And your parents will be too*, her inner voice said. Or was it Lakshmi? Maali sighed. She still wasn't sure what to believe but the exhibition had at least given her a glimmer of hope. To build on that glimmer she decided to set herself a photography project. She was going to start taking photos with the themes of Hope and Love and she was going to keep on taking photos until she'd found enough evidence to believe in them again.

Chapter Sixteen

Hi, Mom — I'm gay.

Mom, I have something to tell you — I'm gay.

Mom, guess who likes girls instead of boys? Me!

Rose shook her head as she made her way along a crowded Camden High Street. She'd had enough of holding it back — tonight was the night she was going to come out to Savannah. But how? She wished she had Sky's way with words. She could have written it all in some deeply moving poem that would blow Savannah's mind and make her see the earth-shattering beauty in her daughter's sexuality.

Roses are red, violets are blue, your daughter's gay and it's high time you knew.

Oh geez. She kept telling herself she shouldn't feel so stressed. Her mom was a model, for chrissakes. The fashion industry was Gay Central. But Rose had read enough websites about coming out to know that even the most enlightened of parents can weird-out when it comes to their own kids.

As Rose approached the cake shop she felt a fluttering in her stomach and a new troop of worries filed into her mind.

What if Francesca wasn't gay? Rose knew she was single but she'd never mentioned any previous partners. What if she was like Amber and not into guys or girls? But Amber was different. She seemed so self-sufficient and self-contained. Francesca was so passionate and full of life. It was impossible to imagine someone like her not falling in love and having desires and making out. OK, get a grip, Rose told herself as she opened the door and went into the café.

"Rose!" Francesca cried from behind the counter. Her hair was swept back from her face with a floral bandana and her frilly apron was covered in flecks of flour. "I have been trying a new recipe – for your stall. I need you to tell me what you think."

Rose followed Francesca into the kitchen at the back of the shop. It was filled with the rich aromas of chocolate and hazelnut and … Rose sniffed the air … a hint of coffee.

"I've created a mocha recipe," Francesca said, pointing to a tray of freshly baked cupcakes. "But I'm not sure what flavour to use for the frosting. What do you think?" Her eyes gleamed with excitement as she looked at Rose. She looked so adorable Rose had to turn away.

"Well, the obvious choice would be chocolate, I guess," Rose said. "Or coffee."

"Yes – but we do not do the obvious," Francesca said.

"Very true." Rose looked at the cakes and frowned. What went with coffee and chocolate? "How about caramel?"

Francesca nodded. "That could work."

"Or caramel and orange?" Rose said.

"Ooh yes! I like it!" Francesca went over to the fruit rack and grabbed a couple of oranges. "Let's try a cream cheese frosting with orange." She handed the fruit to Rose. "Could you zest these for me, please?"

"Sure."

As soon as the frosting was made Francesca piped some onto one of the cakes. Then she cut a bite-sized piece and beckoned to Rose. "You try first," she said, holding the piece of cake up to Rose's mouth. At first, Rose was barely able to chew, let alone swallow. Being this close to Francesca had sent her body into some weird, lust-fuelled lockdown.

"What do you think? Does it work?" Francesca asked excitedly.

Somehow, Rose regained the use of her mouth. She closed her eyes as the cake melted and the rich, deep mocha and caramel flavours mingled with the clean, zesty orange. It tasted awesome. Relief and happiness washed over her. "Yes, I think it does," she said, opening her eyes and grinning at Francesca.

Francesca clapped her hands together. "Now I must try." She popped a piece of cake into her beautiful mouth and closed her eyes. "Oh my!" she sighed. Rose watched, transfixed, as her face became a moving portrait of pleasure. What if she came out to Francesca right now? What if she told her how she felt about her? They were so close it would only take the slightest of movements for their lips to meet. They could melt together in a mocha-orange flavoured heaven and then—

The timer on the oven began to bleep.

"Aha, the other cakes are ready." Francesca ran over to the oven and pulled out a huge tray of cupcakes. "I love this combination of orange, caramel and mocha." She put the tray on the counter and smiled at Rose. "You have such a gift for this – and we will have so much fun tomorrow. It will be just like when I was starting out with my stall in Montmartre. But now, we must get to work." She handed Rose a piping bag.

Rose sighed. Yet again, the moment was gone.

As Rose made her way to the station later she spotted something in a shop window that made her stop in her tracks. It was one of those shops that was all about the tourist, crammed full of I ♥ LONDON t-shirts and tea towels emblazoned with a map of the Underground. But there in the corner of the window display was what looked like a collection of Hindu gods. They were dark gold and speckled with plastic jewels. Rose went inside and started browsing the shelves. She found the statuettes at the back. Most of them were of male gods but there was one goddess. Rose wasn't sure if it was the one Maali was always going on about, but she looked fierce. One of her four arms was holding a sword and another one a severed head. She was wearing a garland of skulls and she looked like she was dancing. Rose took her down from the shelf and over to the counter.

"Is this a Hindu goddess?" she asked the guy behind the counter.

He nodded curtly. No smile. No words. Typical London customer service. It was just like New York and Rose loved it.

"Cool. I'll take her."

As she left the store she fished in her pocket for her phone and sent Maali a quick text.

Hey Maals, hope all ok with your dad. I got you a gift. Can't wait to see you tomorrow! Xoxo

Just as she was about to put her phone back in her pocket it pinged with a new message. It was from Sky.

Hey! Quick question – asking for a friend – if a guy gives a girl his phone number how long should she wait before calling him? S xx ps she really likes him and doesn't want to blow it.

Rose looked at the message and started to grin. Yeah right, asking for a friend! She pressed call.

Sky looked at Leon's number on her phone, her finger hovering over the call button. Ever since she'd got home from school she couldn't stop thinking about him. But if she rang too soon would she look too eager? And if she rang too late would he have forgotten all about her? No guy had ever given her his number before. The sum total of her romantic experience had been holding hands with a boy she'd met at an ashram in India when she was fourteen. But this was different. Why hadn't she given Leon her phone number? Then at least she wouldn't have to go through this mental torture. Her phone started to ring and for a brief moment she actually thought it was him – until she realized that that was totally impossible. It was official – she was going insane. She looked at the caller ID. It was Rose.

"Hello."

"Hey, you dark horse." Wherever Rose was sounded noisy. Sky could hear voices and traffic in the background. "So, who is he, then?"

"Who's who?" Sky grinned.

"The guy whose number you've got."

"It isn't for me. I was asking for a—"

"Yeah, right. Who is he? I need the deets!"

Sky lay back on her bunk. There was no point in trying to lie to Rose. She was like a pit bull when she got wind of a good story – she wouldn't let go until she had answers.

"He's just someone I met at the Poetry Café."

"A poet?"

"Yes."

"OMGenius! That's so perfect. What's his name? How old is he? Where does he live? Oh man, so many questions, so little time." Sky heard the sound of a traffic crossing bleeping.

"Listen, I have to get on the Tube now but will you promise to ring me later to spill all? I'll give you a box of my finest cupcakes tomorrow."

Sky laughed. "OK. I'll call you later."

"But in the meantime, I have a tip for your imaginary friend. Why don't you – I mean, why doesn't she – just text him? Way less stressful and then it's down to him to call you – I mean her. OK, gotta go. Later, alligator!"

Sky stared at her phone. Why hadn't she thought of that? It would be so much easier. She opened a new text message. But what should she write?

Hi, it's me, Sky. It was lovely to meet you yesterday...

She paused. They'd only met yesterday. Was it too soon to text? Arrghh, this was a nightmare!

She looked at the framed photo of her mum on the wall. "I wish you were here," she whispered. "I wish you could tell me what to do." She listened to the water pouring through the lock gates further along the canal. Usually this sound was the most soothing thing in the world. But now she felt waves of sorrow as she thought of all the moments like this when the pain of losing her mum would come back to haunt her. Every new relationship, on her wedding day, if she ever became pregnant. Her dad was great but it wasn't the same. Sometimes you just needed a mum. She put her phone down. It suddenly seemed pointless to text Leon if her mum wasn't there to share any of the joy with her. Sky reached for her notebook and began to write.

Amber looked down at her well-worn London pocket map. If she'd read it right, Rose's road should be the next on the left. She'd tried using the GPS on her phone once before on a trip to the British Museum but it had been a disaster. For some reason it thought she was in a car and had sent her on a circuitous route around the one-way system. Just like everything else, the old way of doing things seemed so much more reliable. She saw the sign for Rose's road and turned on to it. The houses here were huge and the further she walked up the hill, the huger they got. Finally she reached Rose's address. There was a beautiful old tree outside, its branches forming a canopy over the pavement. Amber walked up to the front door and knocked on the brass door-knocker. She wondered if Rose's mum would be home. The world of fashion was alien to her, but even she'd heard of Savannah Ferndale. Her name regularly appeared on the covers of newspapers and magazines – usually next to words like PARTY or FUN-LOVING or, more recently, CELLULITE. She heard footsteps echoing inside and the door opened. A woman wearing a skin-tight, miniscule dress stood in the doorway, looking Amber up and down. She was tiny, with long golden hair and dramatic, Cleopatra-style eye make-up.

"Good evening. I'm Amber." Amber cringed as she realized how formal she must sound. "I'm here to see Rose."

The woman smiled. She was stunningly beautiful, with finely chiselled cheekbones and full lips, just like Rose's. "Come on in, Amber." She spoke in a slow, Southern drawl. "Come on out of the cold."

Amber stepped into the hallway. A huge chandelier, formed from hundreds of glass dewdrops, hung from the ceiling.

"Rose, honey, your friend's here!" Savannah called up the wide staircase. Then she turned back to Amber. "I love that whole masculine vibe you've got going on, it's seriously cool. Where did you get that coat? And the shoes. Are they vintage?"

Amber nodded. She'd never been told she had a "vibe" before. "I got them from Retro-a-go-go – the vintage store I work in on Brick Lane."

Savannah smiled. "Oh, Brick Lane's awesome, isn't it? Here, let me take your coat."

Amber took off her coat and handed it to her, praying Rose would hurry up.

"And that suit is divine." Savannah stared at her. "Have you ever done any modelling? You have such a great look. Such a distinctive jawline."

"Leave her alone, Mother. She came to see me, not get recruited for a catwalk campaign."

Amber felt a rush of relief as Rose came running downstairs, barefooted, in a pair of fleecy pyjamas. She linked her arm through Amber's and led her over to the stairs.

"Have you guys eaten?" Savannah asked. "Would you like me to order you some – pizza?"

Rose stopped and stared down at Savannah, her mouth wide open in shock. "Pizza?"

Savannah nodded. "Yes. I can order you some before I go to Margot's book launch."

"What, like real pizza, with cheese and gluten and everything?"

"Yes! It's good to have a treat every now and again."

"Sure, that would be great." Rose turned to Amber and whispered, "Quick, let's order now before she changes her mind."

They ordered their pizzas and then Rose led Amber along the landing into her bedroom. The room was a riot of recipe books and clothes and CDs strewn everywhere. "'Scuse the mess." Rose cleared a space on her king-sized bed and gestured at Amber to sit down. "So, we are gathered here today because, as I told you in my text, I found one of my mom's psychometric tests in her study." Rose picked up a folder from the top of a heap of books on her desk. "She got obsessed with these things a couple months ago when the press started going on about her cellulite and she was thinking about ditching modelling for another career."

Amber settled back against the pillows. "So, what are they exactly?"

"They're tests that figure out what kind of person you are and what kind of career you should be doing. Companies use them all the time when they're hiring people. But do you still need help with that?" Rose sat down on the bed, next to Amber. "I saw you started blogging again. Great post, by the way."

Amber frowned. "Yes, I do, and no, it wasn't."

"What do you mean?"

"I wasn't honest enough in the blog. I just skated around the issue. The writing didn't flow. It was like – like having creative constipation!"

"Yeah, but at least you made a start."

Amber shook her head. "I still don't know if I should be blogging. I still feel really blocked."

Rose handed her the folder. "OK, looks like you do need this."

Amber opened the folder. She wasn't entirely convinced that a test would give her the answers she was seeking but at this point she was willing to try anything.

"All you have to do is answer the questions as quickly and authentically as possible. So don't try to figure out what they want you to say – just answer from the heart, OK?"

"OK."

"And while you do that I'll just have a little browse for some recipe ideas." Rose opened up her laptop.

As Amber began to read the questions her heart sank. They were all so dreary and unimaginative. Who cared if she strongly agreed, moderately agreed or disagreed with statements like "I enjoy repairing things" or "I adapt well to change"? She thought of Oscar Wilde and what his response would have been if someone suggested he do a test like this. She was certain it would have been something withering and dripping with sarcasm. She began circling answers randomly. She still wasn't sure how she was going to find out who she truly was but she knew for certain that the answer didn't lie in a multiple-choice quiz.

Chapter Seventeen

As soon as Maali's alarm clock went off on Saturday morning her eyes were drawn to her shrine. *Get up and pray,* her inner voice urged, *it's a new day. Start it afresh, as you mean to go on.* But it was as if doubt had pinned her to the bed. *What if you don't exist?* she thought, looking at Lakshmi. *What if it's all an illusion?* From downstairs she heard the sound of a door opening. Her mum was getting ready to go back to the hospital. Soon Auntie Sita and Uncle Dev would be arriving to open up the shop. She used to love it when they came over because it meant laughter and good food and fun. But now it meant illness. Maali's gaze fell upon her bedside cabinet and the piece of paper she'd propped there before she went to bed. She'd written HOPE AND LOVE on it in huge capitals, to remind herself to stay positive. With a heavy sigh she got out of bed and pulled on her dressing gown.

She found her mum downstairs in the kitchen, sitting at the narrow table, resting her head in her hands.

"Morning," Maali said, pretending she hadn't noticed the

way her mum's shoulders were drooping, as if they carried the weight of the world.

"Morning, pet." Normally her mum would spring up and begin to make tea and pop bread into the toaster, but not today. She just sat there, staring into space. Worry started gnawing at Maali's mind. Was there something she wasn't telling her? Did she know why her dad wasn't getting any better? Was he going to get even worse? She went over to the sink and filled up the kettle.

"Do you need me to do anything in the shop before we open?" Sometimes her mum liked her to make a window display of boxes of burfi. It would be good to do something creative – to take her mind off everything else.

But her mum shook her head. "We're going to need you to take care of Namir today while Auntie Sita and Uncle Dev work in the shop."

"Of course." Maali opened the kitchen cupboard and stared blankly at the breakfast cereals. It felt as if the filter on her world had been turned to black and white. Everything that had once brought her joy and filled her life with colour was fading fast.

By the time Rose's alarm went off she had already showered, grabbed a cup of coffee and dried her hair. She'd been way too excited to sleep. Today was the day she got her first taster of running her own cake-making business. OK, so it was only a stall in a market and it wasn't actually hers, but she would be in charge. Or at least she would be if she proved herself to Francesca. She flung open her wardrobe doors and stared at the rails of clothes inside. She didn't just want to prove herself to Francesca, she wanted Francesca to notice her. She wanted Francesca to be attracted to her. Rose shook her head and laughed. She had never, not ever, gotten like this over a guy. When she'd been seeing Matt, she usually dressed down in a bid to stop him pawing at her. Now the opposite was true. As she took in the row of skirts and dresses she imagined Francesca's gorgeous chestnut eyes gazing at her and wondered which outfit she'd like best. Rose held on to the wardrobe door to try and get grounded. She had to get a grip.

She finally decided on a short gingham skater dress with thick woolly tights and her beloved biker boots. She applied a coat of lipstick in exactly the same ruby red as the check in her dress and grinned at her reflection. *"Ooh, Rose, mon chéri,"* she said, mimicking Francesca's French accent. "You are looking so kissable!" She grabbed her phone and bag and headed downstairs.

Although it was only six o'clock, Savannah was up and sitting at the breakfast bar in her bathrobe, poring over her laptop. "Hey, honey, where are you off to so early?" She glanced up. "You look awesome!"

Rose grinned. "Thanks, Mom. I'm off to work on the cake stall in Spitalfields. Remember me telling you? The owner of the cake shop has asked me to run a stall there for her."

"Oh yes, of course. Sorry, I forgot." Savannah looked back

at her laptop and Rose felt a wistful pang. It must be so cool to have parents who actually paid attention to what you were doing, who actually showed an interest, like Liam did with Sky.

"*Entertainment Today* are saying that your dad and Rachel have gotten engaged. Is that true?"

Rose shrugged. "How should I know?"

"Well, did they say anything to you when you were in New York?"

"No."

"Did they seem like they might be about to get engaged?"

"What? Like, was Dad permanently getting down on one knee?"

"No! I don't know. Did they seem more in love? No, scrap that. I don't want to know." Savannah snapped her laptop shut. "I think I'm going to go back to bed. Have a good day, honey. I'll see you later."

Rose watched as Savannah walked out into the hallway. Then she gave a huge sigh, trying to exhale all the confusion, shock and disappointment that were now threatening to engulf her excitement. Were her dad and Rachel engaged? And if so, how come the internet knew about it before she did? She thought about giving Jason a quick Google on her phone but then she remembered her New Year's resolution. Her parents were not going to ruin today. She wasn't going to let them. Today was all about her and achieving her most heartfelt dream.

* * *

The loud honking of geese woke Sky with a start. She burrowed further down in her bunk as they splashed about in the canal right outside the boat. As she gradually came to, she took a moment to see how she felt. Was today going to be a good day or bad? It was weird how you never quite knew what mood you'd be in when you woke up. Last night she'd felt so down, thinking about her mum, but today ... yes, today she was definitely feeling lighter. Instead of texting Leon, she'd ended up writing a letter to her mum. This was something Liam had recommended she do shortly after her mum died. "You can still talk to her," he'd said. "You can still tell her how you're feeling." Sky knew that Liam sometimes did this when he was meditating. He talked to her mum inside his head. But to her, writing had felt a more natural form of communication. So every now and then, when the pain of missing her got too much to bear, she would pour her love out onto the page. She sat up in her bunk and looked out of the porthole. A group of ducks huddled together on the far bank, their beaks tucked under their wings, fast asleep. She loved the view from this side of the boat, away from the tow-path. It was easy to imagine you were in the middle of the countryside instead of the heart of London. As she looked out a thought popped into her mind, perfectly formed, as if someone else had placed it there: there's no need to be afraid of texting a boy. If he's the one for you, he'll be happy to hear from you. A smile spread across Sky's face as the full meaning of the words sunk in. Of course – it made perfect sense. If a boy liked you he'd be happy to hear from you. And if he wasn't happy to hear from you, it meant he wasn't for you after all. She grabbed her phone from the floor and began composing a text.

Amber had been dreaming that she was a shepherd but every time she tried to round up a sheep the ghost of Oscar Wilde started bellowing at her. "You are a Moonlight Dreamer not a sheep-rounder-upper! A dreamer by moonlight, not a rounder-upper by daylight!"

"But this is what the test told me I should do!" Amber cried.

"To hell with the test. Tests are for fools!" Oscar retorted. Then he started singing "Morning Has Broken", his voice growing louder and louder. Halfway through he continued, "Pancakes are cooking, down in the kitchen, coffee is brewing, come and get served."

What the hell? Amber sat up and rubbed her eyes.

"Is anyone alive in there?" Gerald called from the other side of the door.

"Yes! Was that you singing?"

"Of course it was. Who did you think it was? Pavarotti? Although that would be an easy mistake to make, I have been told I sound just like one of the great tenors."

Amber slumped back on the bed.

"Darling?" Gerald called. "Are you getting up? Don't forget you've got work today."

"Yes, I'll be down in a minute." Amber took a deep breath. It was OK. She wasn't a shepherd – despite that stupid test of Rose's telling her that her ideal job would be working on a farm – it was only a nightmare; she still had time to find her true dream.

Chapter Eighteen

Spitalfields Market buzzed with the low hum of chatter as the traders began setting up their stalls for the day. Pale sunlight filtered in through the glass panels in the roof high above them. It was Rose's favourite type of winter's day, cold and crisp with a forget-me-not-blue sky. She took this to be a good omen. As she adjusted the tray of orange, caramel and mocha cupcakes she imagined that this was her own stall. The first day of her brand-new business. Francesca had gone back to her van to get the final tray of cupcakes so Rose was all alone. She took a look around. A girl dressed all in black with an asymmetric curtain of purple hair and a silver nose ring was setting up on the stall to her right, unlocking trays of jewellery. The stall to her left was still empty. It was larger than the rest and had a banner over it saying: THE MAD HATTER. Maybe it was a stall for Alice in Wonderland memorabilia. Rose came out from behind her stall and looked at the cake display. Should the red velvet surprise go next to the banana and butterscotch or would they be better by the lemon meringue? Before she could decide she heard a loud clattering and turned to see a wiry, middle-aged man pulling a trolley towards her loaded with boxes. What was left of his hair was shaven and white and he was wearing a perfectly pressed, pale-grey suit and the shiniest shoes Rose had ever seen.

"All right, mate'?" The man stopped by the Mad Hatter stall and looked Rose up and down.

Rose's middle finger twitched, ready for action. She was so not in the mood for any old-aged perverts today.

"You must be the new girl in town." The man stepped towards her and held out his hand. "I'm Melvin, but you can call me Mel – the Mad Hatter." He gestured at the stall.

"Oh – right." Rose shook his hand. "I'm Rose. Good to meet you."

"Good to meet you too – especially if you do mate's rates on them cakes. They look well nice."

Rose smiled. "Thank you."

"This your business, is it?"

Oh, if only she could say yes. "No. It belongs to a friend of mine. She owns a cake shop in Camden. But I'm looking after the stall for her."

"Nice one." Mel started opening his boxes and placing rows of hats on his table. He had everything from shiny top hats to felt fedoras and fat bowlers and trilbies. Amber would love it. But before Rose could text her about it, Francesca returned. She was wearing a Fifties-style dress in a tulip print and bright red stilettoes. She looked incredible. Something that Mel the Mad Hatter had clearly clocked too, judging by his goggle-eyes as she walked past.

"The last one," Francesca announced, placing the box of cakes behind the stall. She looked at Rose, her eyes wide with concern. "I hope we did not bring too many. It is so hard to tell how it will go."

"It'll go great," Rose said, but she felt nervous. The market would be open soon. People would be arriving. What if nobody bought the cakes? What if the stall was a failure? She clenched her hands into tight fists. There was no way she was going to let that happen. This was her big chance and she wasn't going to blow it. Francesca placed a hand on her arm, setting off a chain-reaction of tingles that travelled all the way to the tips of her toes.

"Thank you so much for doing this," she said.

Rose could barely shift her gaze from Francesca's lips. They were so red and shiny and ... kissable. "I haven't done anything yet," Rose mumbled.

"No, but you agreed to do this and you're going to be wonderful."

Rose looked into Francesca's eyes. They were so brown and—

"'Scuse me, are you the boss lady?" Mel called over, breaking Rose's trance.

Francesca spun around. "What? Oh, yes." As she went over to introduce herself, Rose sighed. There was no doubting how she felt about Francesca but did Francesca feel the same about her? Was there a spark between them or was it just one way? Rose glanced back at the jewellery stall. The purple-haired girl was looking at her. Rose smiled. She guessed she ought to make friends with her other neighbour – it was probably good market etiquette.

"Hey, I'm Rose."

The girl nodded curtly. "Yeah, I heard." She turned away.

Rose stared at the girl's back. What the hell was her problem? But before she could say anything she felt a tap on her shoulder. She turned to see a woman in front of the stall, holding a purse.

"Could I have a couple of the orange mocha cupcakes, please?" she asked, pointing to the display.

Rose started grinning like a fool. She had her very first customer.

Amber let herself into Retro-a-go-go. The store's owner, Gracie, herself an example of prime vintage, was sitting behind the counter on a Seventies barstool, pretend-puffing on her empty cigarette-holder – her bizarre way of beating the habit. Old-time jazz was crackling from the record player in the corner.

"All right, darlin'?" Gracie rasped. Her perfectly set white hair was tinted pink and she was wearing matching baby-pink lipstick. "You're gonna be very pleased with me. I only went and got a new stash of books at the antique fair yesterday. They're out the back. You get first dibs before we put them out for the punters."

"Cool!" Amber slipped behind the counter and smiled at her.

"Do me a favour," Gracie said, before taking an extra-long inhalation. "Give the stockroom a bit of a tidy up while you're out there."

"Of course." Amber was glad for a reason to be tucked away from the customers for a while. She was still feeling slightly unsettled after her bad dream. She went into the cluttered back room and looked around. As usual, it was a treasure trove of vintage clothes, handbags and shoes. And there, in a corner, was a fresh pile of old books. Amber breathed in the musty air. She didn't understand why people flocked to gleaming, soulless shopping centres every Saturday when they could be coming to places like this. Chain stores were so bland and samey. But vintage stores were full of wonder. Every item had a past. Every trinket told a story.

She started looking through the books and a familiar name leapt out at her from one of the spines. Oscar Wilde. It was a copy of his play *The Importance of Being Earnest* – an early edition by the looks of the yellowing pages and fraying spine. Amber began flicking through and a slip of paper fluttered out and landed on the floor. Amber picked it up and caught her breath. Someone had written a quote in pencil. It was really faded but she could still make out the words.

"I never travel without my diary. One should always have something sensational to read on the train."

It was a quote from the play – Amber recognized it immediately. She stared at the paper. It had to be a sign. Normally she was the one who asked Oscar for advice, whenever she played her "What Would Oscar Say" game, but today it was as if Oscar was talking to her of his own accord. First in her dream and now this. But what was he trying to tell her? She studied the quote again. He was telling her that he wanted her life to be "sensational" – for the things she did to make a riveting read.

As if talking to Oscar himself, she whispered, "But how?"

Sky came out of her sun salutation and into child's pose.

"Shall we do a shoulder-stand?" Liam asked.

She nodded and smiled. It was ages since they'd practised yoga together. After all the tension of the past week it felt great. True yoga – the kind that had been practised in India for centuries before it became the latest fitness craze in the West – was all about getting your body and mind in harmony so that you could connect with the universe or the divine. But in their practice this morning Sky had felt it was all about re-connecting with her dad. She pushed herself up into a shoulder-stand, supporting the small of her back with her hands. As the blood rushed down her legs, she felt all of the tension of school seeping out through her shoulders. *Give your tension to the mat*, her dad would say when he was teaching a yoga class. *Feel it soaking into the ground.*

I wonder if he's texted back. Sky tried to push the thought from her mind and lift herself higher into the pose. It didn't matter. If it was meant to be, then he would. If he didn't, then she wouldn't have lost anything. When she felt ready, she came out of the pose and lay on her mat.

"I'm going to have to skip savasana," Liam said, getting to his feet.

"Tut tut, bad yogi," Sky said with a grin. Savasana, or lying still in the corpse pose, was considered the most important part of a yoga routine. Time for your body to integrate all the movements it had been through and for the mind to be still. As Sky lay there she felt a warm glow spread through her, as if her whole body was giving a relieved smile. Outside, on the tow-path, she heard a child giggle and the ducks quack. All felt well with the world.

When she was ready, Sky slowly got to her feet and wrapped her blanket round her. She put the kettle on the stove and popped some bread in the toaster. Then she went to her cabin and looked at her phone. The notification light was blinking. It's probably from one of the Moonlight Dreamers, she told herself as she picked it up. But in that place deep inside her she already knew it was from Leon.

I'd love to! What are you up to today?

Chapter Nineteen

As Maali watched Namir climb the slide for what felt like the four-hundredth time she started to wish she'd been raised a Buddhist rather than a Hindu. If ever a situation called for the Buddhist teaching of patient acceptance, then this was it. They'd been in the freezing-cold park for so long she'd lost all feeling in her hands and feet, and her will to live was draining by the second.

"Are you sure you don't want to do something else?" she called to her brother.

"Like what?" he called back.

Maali stared at him blankly. That was the trouble. There was nothing else to do. They'd been to the cinema and had Happy Meals in McDonald's. What else could they do? Her mum had told her to stay out for as long as possible so that Namir didn't go stir-crazy cooped up in the flat. She looked at her phone. It was only two o'clock and there was still no news from the hospital about her dad.

"Can we go on the swings?" Namir cried as he shot down the slide and landed in a heap at the bottom.

"Sure," Maali replied.

The chains were rusty and the seats were cold and damp, but at least swinging might warm her up. Maali gave Namir a push, then she sat on the swing next to him. It had been years since she'd actually been on a swing and she'd forgotten how much she used to enjoy it. As she pushed herself higher she felt her gloom ease a fraction. The cold wind felt refreshing as it whistled through her hair.

"Let's pretend we're pterodactyls!" Namir shouted, swinging past her. "And we're flying off to kill a deadly T-rex."

He looked so happy and excited. And all just from being on a rusty old swing in the middle of a cold, grey park. Maali felt the sudden urge to capture the moment in a photograph. She fumbled for her phone and switched it to camera mode.

"I can see the T-rex," Namir said, pointing to a huge Alsatian running through the park. He laughed as he swung himself higher. As Maali swooped past him she took a picture. Then she took another and another. She loved the way Namir slipped into the world of his imagination so easily. She loved seeing the joy it brought him. And she realized that while you had your imagination you still had hope. Because in the world of your imagination, anything was possible. You could fly like a bird. You could become a roaring dinosaur. Your dad could get better.

An hour later they made their way back along Brick Lane. As usual for a Saturday, the narrow street was crowded with map-reading tourists and bearded hipsters. The hope Maali had felt on the swing was allowing her to dare to imagine that there might be some good news from her mum when they got home. But as soon as they walked into the shop and she saw the grave look on Uncle Dev's face, her hope faded.

"Have you heard from Mum?" she asked.

He nodded. "Sita will tell you. She's in the kitchen." He turned to Namir. "You stay with me, little man. Help me serve some customers."

Maali slipped behind the counter and into the back of the shop, her heart pounding. Auntie Sita was standing by the cooker, looking at her phone.

"Maali!" she said, coming over to give her a hug.

"What's happened? Uncle Dev said there'd been news from the hospital."

Auntie Sita nodded. "Yes. Your dad needs to have … a brain scan."

Maali leaned against the counter as she tried to absorb this latest development. "What? Why?"

"The doctors think it might be something in his brain that's causing the sickness."

"But how? It has to be his stomach – the vomiting virus – doesn't it?"

Auntie Sita shook her head. "He should have been getting better by now but he isn't responding to any of the treatment. And one of the doctors who saw him today said that sometimes when there is a problem with the brain it can affect the balance and cause nausea."

"But what kind of problem?"

Auntie Sita smiled at her reassuringly. "We don't know yet – that's why they're doing the scan. All we can do is pray it will be OK."

Maali nodded but the last thing she felt like doing was praying. She'd prayed enough already, hadn't she? And look what had happened. "Is it OK if I go up to my room for a while?"

"Of course. We're here if you need us."

"Thank you."

Maali marched up the stairs to her attic bedroom. The pale sun was shining down on her Lakshmi figurine, exposing a thin layer of dust.

"Why is this happening?" she yelled at the statue. "Why are you doing this?" Lakshmi stared back at her blankly through her painted eyes. Maali couldn't believe she'd put so much faith in the goddess before; confiding all her secrets and problems and asking her advice. It seemed so pointless. The goddess seemed nothing more than a toy. Maali looked around her room, tears spilling from her eyes. She grabbed a scarf from the back of her chair and shook it out. Then she went over to her shrine and flung the scarf over it. There was a dull thud as the statue toppled onto its side.

Chapter Twenty

"If you had to pick five words to live your life by, what would they be?"

Sky looked at Leon questioningly. "To live my life by?"

He nodded and stretched his legs out, staring at his snowy-white trainers.

Sky leaned back against the bench and looked up at the sky. Huge pale grey clouds were building on the horizon, like fantastical mountainous worlds. When they'd met earlier at Euston station, neither of them had known where to go. So Leon had placed his hands over her eyes and got her to point randomly at the Underground map. They would go wherever her finger landed — like a travel version of the party game Pin the Tail on the Donkey. They'd ended up in Pinner, a small London suburb near the end of the Metropolitan line. At first Sky had been disappointed: Pinner didn't seem to have much to offer other than the standard high-street shops, but then they'd come across this beautiful park.

"Poetry," she said as she looked at the line of tall fir trees on the far side of the duck pond.

"Yeah." Leon nodded enthusiastically.

"And nature."

Sky watched a small terrier tugging on its lead, eager to chase a squirrel. What else would she like to live her life by? "Love." She immediately blushed, but Leon was looking at her intently as if he wanted her to go on.

Sky thought of the Moonlight Dreamers. "Friendship." She had one more word to choose. What else did she want to live her life by? She thought of school. "And courage." She looked at Leon, eager to shift the spotlight. "How about you?"

"Why courage?" he asked.

She swallowed hard and looked away. Should she tell him? "Because you can never create the life you want if you don't have courage. If you don't have courage you end up living everyone else's dreams."

Leon nodded in agreement but he suddenly looked sad.

The whole time they'd been together, Sky had swung between moments of feeling really close to Leon and remembering that they really didn't know each other at all. This was starting to feel like one of those moments.

"Whose dreams are you living right now?" he asked.

"What, right in this moment?"

He nodded.

"My own." She felt the tips of her cheeks start to burn.

"Me too." He grinned at her and suddenly she was back in the security of feeling like she'd known him her whole life. "But when you're not here in – what's this place called again?"

"Pinner."

"When you're not here in Pinner, picking words on a park bench, whose dreams are you living?"

It was like he knew what she was going through.

"My dad's. The school's. The government's."

"And that's a bad thing?"

She nodded. "My dad recently made me start secondary school for the first time in my life."

"What? You'd never been to secondary school before?" His gape-mouthed look of surprise was almost comical.

"No, he'd always home-schooled me, but now he needs to work more and he's worried about me getting good grades in my GCSEs and A levels so I've had to go to school."

Leon whistled. "That must be … interesting."

"Yeah – it is. But the weirdest part is that I wasn't prepared for how angry it would make me feel."

"Because you were made to go there against your will?"

"No. Well, that made me angry too, but it's more school itself. I wasn't prepared for school to make me angry. I thought it would make me bored or fed up or lonely but it just seems so … so …" Sky searched for the right word … "so harsh. And backward."

"Backward? You mean the people?"

"No! The system. It's like it's built to destroy people – well, to wear them down."

"It is."

Sky looked at him questioningly.

Leon sat forwards and pulled his hoodie up against the cold. "Think about it. Society doesn't need a bunch of free spirits who know their own minds and follow their own paths. Society needs a bunch of sheep to blindly do whatever it tells them. School's where it all begins. It's where we get trained to be good little sheep."

"But why don't people do something about it? Why do they just accept it?"

Leon shrugged. "They're too afraid? Too dumb? Too busy playing Xbox or watching TV?"

Sky sighed. "It's so depressing."

"Maybe. Maybe not."

"What do you mean?"

"It depends where you stand. If you're one of the sheep it's depressing. If you're one of the free spirits –" he looked up at the sky and grinned – "if you're one of the free spirits you can be the change."

Sky grinned. Being with Leon was like putting her heart on recharge. She could feel herself filling with courage and determination.

"What year are you in?" he asked.

"Eleven. How about you?"

"Thirteen."

"Oh wow, so you're doing your A levels?"

"Yep, so I can get the golden ticket and go to university – and end up thirty grand in debt." He laughed. "So, you live with your dad?"

Sky nodded.

"What about your mum? Do you ever see her?"

Sky shook her head. Normally she hated it when this question came up but Leon seemed to have a knack of putting her at ease. "No, she died."

Leon turned to face her, his expression full of concern. "I'm sorry. That must be tough."

She nodded. Usually people got really awkward at this point and would cough and fidget and try to change the subject, but Leon was looking at her, his gaze calm and focused.

"What was she like? Do you – do you mind me asking?"

"No – not at all. She was..." Sky looked at the clouds. Their edges were tinted pink in the afternoon sun. "She was like sunlight. She was so joyful and bright and she never said a mean thing about anyone. And she had this amazing laugh, like a bell tinkling. She never got bitter – not even when she was really ill. Not even when she lost all her hair." Sky felt a lump forming in the back of her throat.

Leon shuffled closer to her on the bench. So close his leg was touching hers. She could feel the warmth coming through his jeans.

"She sounds like a beautiful person."

"She was – inside and out. I know that sounds like such a cliché but it was true. She was so funny and kind. She was ... she was too good to die."

"The good people never die."

"What do you mean?" Sky glanced at Leon. He was staring straight ahead and he looked really sad. She wondered if he'd lost someone too.

"They live on in the things they said and did – they live on inside us."

"Did you … lose someone?"

He nodded. "My best friend, Tyrone. He was stabbed. Three years ago."

"Oh, I'm so sorry."

"It's OK." Leon cleared his throat. "Do you want to write a poem together?"

"What, now?"

"Yeah. Why not?"

"OK. What about?"

"How about courage?"

"All right. But how are we going to do it?"

"Throw some words at me. What comes to your mind when you think of courage?" He got to his feet and held out his hand. "Come on, let's walk. I always think better when I walk."

She grabbed his hand and he helped her up. He didn't let go as they started to walk around the pond. "Strong, brave, fierce…" she began.

"Fierce. I love that word. What else?"

Sky thought back to the PSHE class and how she'd felt when she found the courage to speak up. "Free."

"Yeah. And who do you think of when you think of courage?"

182

"Oh – I don't know … the suffragettes. Refugees. Malala. She's so courageous."

"Too right." Leon led her down a winding path into the trees. "These trees remind me of courage too. The way they're so tall and strong."

Sky gazed up into the branches. This close they were even more majestic. She closed her eyes and breathed in the scent of pine. "When fear tears through the forest…" she began.

"Stay rooted like the tallest pine," Leon continued.

Sky gazed at the tree trunk. "Inside you are rings of truth and wisdom and…"

"Love," Leon said softly.

"And love, no amount of pain can touch." She felt him moving closer and gripping her hand tighter. High above them, a breeze rippled through the leaves.

"Your branches may bend," Leon said softly, "but your courage…"

"Your courage stays firm and strong." He was right in front of her now; if she tilted her head forwards just a fraction it would be resting on his chest. She wanted to add something more, something about how the important thing was remembering you had that reserve of inner strength, but he was so close and her heart was beating so hard that it seemed to be drowning out her thoughts.

"Can I…?" he whispered, pulling her to him.

Yes! she wanted to cry. Instead she nodded and leaned into him. She felt his strong arms wrap around her and his head come to rest on the top of hers. She took a deep breath, and with it came an important realization. Sometimes you don't know what you've been missing ... until you find it.

Chapter Twenty-one

Rose had never realized that the human body had smile muscles. But now, as she served what felt like the millionth customer at the cake stall, her jaw was aching from its customer service work-out.

"Thank you. Have a nice day," she said as she handed a box of cupcakes to the customer. She turned to Francesca, who was rearranging the ever-diminishing display. "That's it, we're all out of red velvet."

Francesca grinned and shook her head in disbelief. "It is incredible. You are incredible!" She grasped Rose's hand. "You are such a natural at this."

Rose beamed with a mixture of pride – and desire. Working in such close proximity to Francesca all day had done nothing to dampen her feelings for her. In fact, they were even stronger. Dealing with the frantic rush at lunch-time had definitely been bonding – as had their chats during the rare moments of quiet. And now Francesca was calling her incredible. Or, in her French accent, "incredeeeble".

"Thank you." Rose could feel herself starting to blush so

she quickly looked away. The girl at the jewellery stall, who Rose had found out was called Jet but Rose had nicknamed Eeyore, was sitting on her chair, sullenly tapping into her phone. As if aware of Rose's gaze, she suddenly looked over – and glared. Rose shook her head and turned away. What an idiot.

"Well, you ladies certainly got off to a rocking start," Mel said, striding over. He was wearing a pale grey top hat now, to match his suit. He looked like one of those old time East End gangsters, like the Kray twins, en route to a wedding. Rose had grown quite fond of him as the day had gone on. He was constantly singing and joking with the customers and it was good to have one friendly neighbour, at least. Rose checked the time on her phone and felt a buzz of excitement. She'd be meeting the other Moonlight Dreamers soon.

"Is it OK if I buy some cakes for my friends?" she asked Francesca. "I'm seeing them right after we finish here."

Francesca frowned and shook her head. "I will not hear of such a thing!"

"I'm sorry?" Rose panicked. Had she said something wrong?

Francesca grabbed a large cake box from under the stall. "You do not have to buy them! Take whatever you want."

"Seriously?"

"Of course! It is your bonus for doing so well. And while I think of it…" Francesca opened the till and took out some notes. "Here are your wages."

Rose had been enjoying the experience of working on the stall so much she'd forgotten she was actually getting paid for it. As she stuffed the money into her jacket pocket she felt awash with happiness and pride. For the first time in her life the money she was holding wasn't a handout from her mom or guilt induced compensation for never seeing her from her dad. It was all hers, earned fair and square.

"Make sure you spend it on something fun," Francesca said with grin.

Rose nodded but she already knew what she was going to do with the money. She was going to invest it in her own business account.

Maali rolled onto her back and gazed at her bedroom ceiling. Her face was slick with tears. What was she going to do? How was she going to get through this fear about her dad? On the pillow next to her, her phone bleeped. It was a text from Rose. Oh crap! She was meant to be meeting her and the other Moonlight Dreamers in – Maali checked the time – thirty minutes. In all of her sorrow over her dad she'd completely forgotten. She read the text.

Yo Maals! I got let off work early – don't worry, I haven't been sacked! So me and Amber have gone straight to Café 1001. Meet us in there whenever you're ready and then we'll go get something to eat. Love ya xoxo

Maali felt the faintest glimmer of hope. Maybe all was not lost. She might not have Lakshmi any more but she still had the Moonlight Dreamers. She got out of bed and looked at herself in her wardrobe mirror. Her eyes were puffy and red from crying and her hair was messy. She quickly pulled a brush through it and rubbed some soothing coconut oil into the skin around her eyes. Then she made her way downstairs.

In the shop, Uncle Dev was cashing up and Auntie Sita was sweeping the floor while Namir played with his toy dinosaurs behind the counter.

"Is there any news from the hospital?" she asked.

Uncle Dev shook his head.

"Only that your dad is still waiting to have his scan," Auntie Sita replied.

"Would it be OK if I popped out to see my friends?" Maali asked. "Just to the café round the corner. I can be home in two minutes if you need me."

"Of course," Auntie Sita replied.

"And you promise you'll text if you hear anything?"

"Absolutely." Auntie Sita nodded. "You go and see your friends. We'll let you know if anything happens."

Amber took a sip of her cappuccino and glanced across the table at Rose. She looked so beautiful – and so happy. Clearly her first day on the stall had been a huge success. "I found something in the shop today and I think it might be a sign," Amber said, taking a scrap of paper from her pocket.

"You do?" Rose leaned in towards her. "What is it?"

"It's a—"

"Hi, guys." Maali appeared at the table and slumped down into one of the armchairs. "I am *so* glad to see you."

"Are you OK?" Rose leaned towards her. "Hey! Have you been crying?"

Amber stared at Maali. Her eyes did look bloodshot.

Maali nodded. She hugged her bag tightly. "I'm sorry. It's just been such a terrible day and I don't know what to do."

Rose grabbed her hand. "OK. Deep breaths. Is it to do with your dad?"

"Yes, the doctors don't think he has the vomiting virus any more. He has to have a brain scan."

"What?" Rose stared at her.

Amber felt a pang of guilt at ever feeling bad about not getting to know her surrogate mum. At least she had two parents and they were both healthy. "Why does he have to have a brain scan?" she asked.

"I'm not sure. Apparently the symptoms he's been having might not be caused by a virus after all – it could be there's a problem with his brain." Maali looked terrified.

"Shit." Rose took hold of Maali's hand. "OK, first of all, we don't know for sure that there's something wrong with his brain, the docs only think there might be, right?"

Maali nodded.

"And second of all, even if there is something up with his brain – at least you guys will finally know what's been making him sick and then hopefully the docs will be able to do something to make him better."

"Hopefully," Maali said.

"And third of all," Rose continued, "you've got us, so you're not going through this alone, OK?"

"Thank you." Maali's eyes started to well with tears.

Rose got up and gave her a hug. "Can I get you a hot chocolate? You look like you could use a little sugar."

Maali nodded.

"Oh, and I got you this." Rose reached under the table and handed her a brown paper bag.

Maali wiped her tears away. "What is it?"

Amber watched as Maali opened the present. Inside was a gold statue of a woman with four arms. One was holding a sword and the other a severed head. Amber guessed it was some kind of Hindu goddess but she wasn't sure if it made the ideal gift in the circumstances. She looked slightly menacing to say the least.

"She is one of your goddesses, isn't she?" Rose said. "The guy in the shop said she was but he wasn't exactly forthcoming."

Maali nodded. "Yes. It's Kali."

"Do you like her?" Rose looked concerned. "I saw her in the shop and I thought of you. There was something about her. I don't know – I'm not into all that God business but she looked kind of fierce and I figured you could use some strength right now."

Maali gave a weak smile. "Thank you. She's great."

"OK. I'll get you your drink and we'll talk some more. Then we need to decide where to eat." Rose checked her phone. "Has anyone heard from Sky? She hasn't replied to my text."

Amber and Maali checked their phones and shook their heads.

Rose frowned. "Weird. It's not like her to be late. Ah well, she knows where we are."

As soon as Rose left, an awkward silence fell upon the table. Amber could feel it gathering around her like an oppressive fog. *Don't offer her a mint. Don't tap her on the back*, her inner voice urged. *Say something helpful, something loving.* She began to flick through the database of Oscar Wilde quotes stored in her mind until she found the perfect one. Or at least she hoped it was...

"Can I – can I share an Oscar Wilde quote with you?"

Maali smiled at her gratefully. "Of course."

Amber cleared her throat. "'Keep love in your heart. A life without it is like a sunless garden when the flowers are dead.'"

To Amber's dismay, Maali's eyes filled with fresh tears.

"Oh dear. I'm sorry – I – I didn't mean to upset you – I—"

"You haven't. It's lovely. And it's true. It's just so hard..." Maali held her head in her hands.

Amber coughed. She looked nervously around the café. She adjusted her waistcoat. Then she got up and she went and crouched beside Maali's chair. "You are – er – the most loving person I've ever met. So, er, don't stop. OK?"

Maali looked at her and started to grin. "Really?"

Amber nodded.

Maali flung her arms around her. "Thank you!"

"You're – welcome. Anyway, better get back to my seat." Amber extricated herself from the younger girl's embrace and sat back down. She did feel slightly awkward from the exchange but most of all she felt a warm glow.

COURAGE
BY Sky and Leon

When fear tears through the forest,
stay rooted like the tallest pine.
Inside you are rings of wisdom and truth
no amount of pain can touch.
Your branches may bend,
but courage turns your trunk to steel.

When fear rips through the valley,
ride the current like an eagle.
Inside you, a heart beats new life and love
no amount of tears can drown.
Your feathers may ruffle,
but courage turns your wings to steel.

Chapter Twenty-two

As the train pulled into Harrow-on-the-Hill, Sky looked at the station clock and her heart sank. She was supposed to have met the other Moonlight Dreamers ten minutes ago and she was still almost an hour away. Being with Leon had been like being in a cocoon away from the rest of the world, a cocoon of words that made her lose all track of time. After their hug they'd carried on walking for a bit, finishing their poem. Then they'd gone to a tearoom overlooking the duck pond and feasted on muffins and flapjacks and peppermint tea, and Googled their favourite poems to read to each other.

She pulled her phone from her bag. She had two new messages – both from Rose. The first said that Rose had finished work early and told Sky to meet her in Café 1001. The second said that they'd decided to eat at Cinnamon curry house on Brick Lane at six. Across from her, Leon tapped away on his phone. She wondered who he was texting. It occurred to her that he knew way more about her than she did about him. Back in the park it had felt lovely to have him show so much interest but now it made her feel a little unsettled. They'd be going their separate ways soon. She needed to know more about him. To make him less dream-like and more real.

"So, what are you doing tonight?" she asked, in what she hoped was a tone of casual interest rather than blatant nosiness.

"I'm going to see one of my brothers in Hammersmith. How about you?" Leon put his phone in his jacket pocket and smiled at her.

"I'm having dinner with some friends." Sky felt a sudden burst of gratitude. How lucky was she to get to spend the afternoon with Leon and then have an evening with the Moonlight Dreamers! She couldn't wait to tell them what had happened.

"Nice." He leaned towards her. "So, when are we going to meet again?"

Relief unknotted the tension in her shoulders. "I don't know. When do you want to?"

He grinned. "Soon."

She laughed. "Me too."

"OK, I'll call you tomorrow." He leaned even closer and whispered, "I really like you, Sky-Blue."

"I really like you too," she whispered back.

"Good."

When the train drew into Finchley Road he took hold of both her hands. "I'll be seeing you then," he said softly. His face brushed hers and for a second, she thought he was going to kiss her, right there on the crowded train. But instead he looked at her and smiled. "Later, Sky-Blue."

"See you later."

As the train pulled out of the station and Leon disappeared into the crowd on the platform, Sky sat back in her seat and gazed out of the window. The sun had set and the clouds were turning dark, charcoal grey. She felt so different, so alive … and she never wanted this feeling to end.

Sky raced down Brick Lane. She loved it best at night, when the darkness chased all of the grey away and the lights sparkled like jewels. The narrow cobbled pavements were crowded and outside every Indian restaurant, staff were trying to entice diners in.

"Free bottle of wine if you eat here," a young Indian guy said to her with a grin.

Sky smiled and shook her head. Normally she found these guys annoying, but tonight she didn't think she could find anything annoying. She was too high on words and poetry and Leon.

Finally — after being offered everything from wine to free vegetable samosas to a wilted rose in a plastic tube — Sky spotted Cinnamon. She slipped inside and breathed in the delicious aroma of curry, cumin, cardamom…

"There she is!" Rose cried, and Sky saw the Moonlight Dreamers at a table at the back.

"Hey! I'm so sorry I'm late!" she exclaimed.

"No problem," Amber said, shifting up to make more room.

"It's so good to see you," said Maali, touching her gently on the arm.

"Where have you been?" asked Rose.

Sky grinned. "I've been to Pinner."

"Where the hell is Pinner?"

"At the end of the Metropolitan line." Sky shivered as she remembered Leon's hands over her eyes as she pointed blindly to the map.

"And why would you want to go to the end of the Metropolitan line?" Rose asked.

"Why not?" Sky laughed. "Actually, I chose it at random."

"What, you just thought to yourself, where shall I go today, and Pinner popped into your mind?" Rose passed her the plate of poppadums. "Don't worry, we haven't ordered yet. We waited for you."

"Thank you." Sky took a poppadum and opened the leather-bound menu. But it was hard to concentrate. She was way too excited. "I went out with the poet guy. The one I met the other night."

Maali looked up from her phone. "You've been on a date?" she said wistfully.

"Well, I'm not sure I'd call it that but—"

"Er, hello, what would you call it then?" Rose said with a grin. "Girl meets guy. Girl likes guy. Guy gives girl phone number. Girl texts guy. Guy texts back – or did he ring?"

Sky shook her head. "No, he texted."

"OK, guy texts back and says, how'd you fancy going to the end of the Metropolitan line with me. Little bit weird, yes, but definitely a date."

"He didn't ask me to go to Pinner, he made me choose it — randomly."

"What, like in a lucky dip of Tube stations?"

"Kind of. He made me choose a station from the Tube map without looking. He put his hands over my eyes and I had to point somewhere on the map and wherever I pointed to was where we would go."

"That's so romantic." Maali sighed.

"So what happened?" Rose said. "What did you do in Pinner?"

"We went to the park and we wrote a poem." Sky ducked behind the menu to hide her blushes.

"Oh my God, that's like your perfect date!" Rose exclaimed.

Sky peeped over her menu and nodded. "Anyway, enough about me. How did your first day on the stall go?"

"It was awesome with a capital AWE," Rose said. "Seriously, I had the best time."

"That's great." Sky looked at Amber and Maali. "And how about you guys?"

Maali instantly looked away. "My dad's had to have a brain scan," she said quietly.

The joy started to drain from Sky's body. "A brain scan? Why?"

"They think there might be something wrong with his brain that's making him ill."

"Oh." Sky couldn't think of what else to say. All she could think of was the time her mum had to have a scan, when they discovered her cancer had spread to her lymph glands.

"It's OK," Maali said, smiling at the others gratefully. "These guys have really cheered me up."

"That's good," Sky said ... but inside she felt a horrible sense of foreboding.

Chapter Twenty-three

Maali let herself into the flat. What news would be waiting for her this time? She'd last heard from Auntie Sita half an hour ago, telling her that there was nothing to report, but recent events had taught her that things could change in an instant. Everything was deathly quiet in the flat. Maali went into the living room and saw her mum kneeling on the floor in front of their family shrine. Wisps of patchouli-scented incense coiled around their statue of the elephant-headed god, Ganesha.

"Mum!" Maali rushed over and threw her arms around her.

"Hello, pet." Her mum looked and sounded exhausted.

"How's Dad?"

"He's OK. He was sleeping when I left."

"And what about the scan?" Maali looked at her anxiously.

"We should find out the results from the consultant tomorrow. Did you have a nice time with your friends?"

"It was OK. They were really nice – about Dad."

Her mum nodded. "That's good."

"Mum?"

"Yes?"

"Dad is going to be OK, isn't he?"

"I hope so, pet. We have to wait and see … and pray." She looked at Ganesha.

Maali's mouth went dry. Her mum *hoped* her dad would be OK but she didn't *know*. Not wanting to get upset in front of her, she stood up.

"I think I'll go to bed."

Her mum nodded, her gaze still fixed on the golden statue. "OK, love. See you in the morning."

As soon as Maali got to her room and saw her covered shrine she remembered the present Rose had given her. She took the statue from her bag. Kali was the goddess of time, responsible for destruction and creation, and therefore considered one of the most powerful. Maali had never been that drawn to her before. When she was little she'd been terrified of Kali and the sword and severed head she was often depicted as carrying. She'd much preferred Lakshmi for her beauty and serenity, but now…

Rather than smiling sweetly like Lakshmi, Kali stared at Maali determinedly. There was a fierceness about her expression that tugged at something deep in the pit of Maali's stomach. She went and fetched her book of Hindu gods and goddesses from the shelf and turned to the page about Kali. *"Kali shows us how our worst fears can become love and how the death of the old can herald the birth of the new,"* she read. *"She is the beauty at the centre of destruction and the calm at the eye of the storm."*

Maali sat back and gazed at the goddess. She certainly felt as if she were in the eye of a storm right now. And she wished she could turn her worst fears about her dad into love. The Oscar Wilde quote Amber had shared with her earlier had hit her hard.

"Keep love in your heart. A life without it is like a sunless garden when the flowers are dead."

She didn't want her life to be like a sunless garden of dead flowers. She didn't want to be fearful. She still wanted to believe in love. Could it be that her prayers had been answered? Maali got into her pyjamas, turned off her lamp and slipped beneath her duvet. She placed the Kali statue on the pillow next to her. "Will you help me become strong?" she whispered. "Will you help me find love in my heart again? And will you help me help my parents, too?"

The statue stared back at her bravely, as if to say "of course". Maali snuggled down and closed her eyes. Maybe what she'd been feeling wasn't that there wasn't a god, it was that the aspect of the divine she needed to call upon had changed. Before, when life had been relatively easy, it was fun to focus on beauty and prosperity, but now she needed something tougher and grittier to cling to. She needed to believe in a goddess who feared nothing and no one – not even death.

* * *

Rose typed "Jason Levine" into Google and started to scroll through the search results. She wondered if any other kids had to do this to find out whether their dad had gotten engaged. She'd returned home from her meal with the Moonlight Dreamers to find that Savannah was out. Rose had been so busy all day that she hadn't had time to call her dad but the question had kept niggling at the back of her mind. If it was true, then why hadn't he told her? She'd tried calling him on the walk home from the station but his phone had gone straight to voicemail. So now she had to resort to Google. The trouble was, her dad was notoriously private. He refused to have any social media accounts and didn't even have a private Instagram, so she was relying on the kind of tittle-tattle sites that had made her life a misery last year. There was a story on *Entertainment Today* but it was dubious, to say the least. There was a grainy shot of her dad and Rachel inside a jewellery store in LA and a quote "from a source close to the star" who said that Rachel, and Jason were "more in love than ever" and it was only a matter of time before they tied the knot. The article went on to quote the same source as saying Jason was "way happier" with Rachel, as she was "much more understanding of his career and the needs of an actor". Although it didn't outright say it, the "much more" was clearly a dig at Savannah. Rose felt a rush of anger on behalf of her mom. No wonder she'd been so pissed this morning. Who the hell was this source close to her dad? If she ever found out they'd be in big trouble.

She pulled her phone from her pocket and started writing a text to her dad.

So, wassup? Are you guys engaged?! Or is the celebrity rumour mill full of crap as usual?

Rose sighed and put her phone down. It was happening again. Her parents and their non-stop dramas were totally killing her buzz. She went over to her cupboard and took out a packet of cacao and some coconut sugar. Savannah had finally allowed her to have baking ingredients in the house but the deal was she had to keep them separate from her mom's stuff, which consisted mainly of a couple packs of couscous and some rice cakes. Savannah got most of her meals delivered by a company called *Calorie Control Patrol – We Deliver, You Get Thinner*. It was exactly as grim as it sounded.

Rose put a couple of cups of almond milk in a pan and added the cacao and sugar. She needed to draw her mind away from her parents and back to her own life. She leaned against the kitchen counter. Today had been so awesome. Sure, it had been hard work, but it was so satisfying to see the customers so happy. Watching the cakes fly from the stall. Bantering with Mel. She thought about what she'd do if the stall was actually hers and she had a great idea – she'd create a signature cupcake for Spitalfields, something inspired by the area. She started pacing up and down, trying to think of what flavours she'd use. She thought of the curry houses lining Brick Lane. She needed something with a dash of spice, something with a kick. Chilli or cayenne pepper – with chocolate. That would work. Her mouth started watering at the prospect.

The notification on her phone went off, wrenching her from her daydream. It was a text from her dad.

Hey honey, yes, I did pop the question to Rachel yesterday and she said yes! I'm so sorry you had to find out the way you did. I was going to Skype you tomorrow to tell you face to face but the bloody internet beat me to it. So sorry about telling your mum too. But you know how she presses my buttons! Much love, Dad xxx

Rose frowned at the text. Only in her dad's world could Skype count as "face to face". And he must have meant to put "not telling your mum", otherwise it didn't make any sense. She was about to call him when she heard the door slam.

"Hey, Mom! I'm in the kitchen." She heard the clip-clop of her mom's heels on the tiled floor as she got up to stir the pan. "Do you fancy a hot chocolate? I just made some."

"How could you?" Savannah stood in the doorway glaring at her.

Rose's in-built alcohol sensor twitched into action. From the way Savannah was leaning on the door frame and the slightly smudged eye make-up – not to mention her completely OTT reaction to the hot chocolate – she estimated at least half a bottle of bubbly had been consumed.

"Calm down, Mother, I've made it with almond milk and cacao and coconut sugar. It's actually good for you."

"I'm not talking about the hot chocolate. I'm talking about you."

Savannah marched into the kitchen and stared at Rose.

"Me?" Rose's heart began to sink. What the hell was going on?

"Yes. You. How could you tell him before you told me?"

"Tell who what?"

"Your father."

"Dad? Oh, are you talking about the engagement?"

"No! I am not talking about the freakin' engagement." Savannah sat down at the breakfast bar. Up close she looked really tired rather than drunk. "I'm talking about your sexuality. How could you have told him – and that – that – brain-dead surf monster – something so personal before telling your own mother? And why haven't you told me?" Her expression shifted and she looked at Rose hopefully. "Or was that arsehole lying to me to hurt me? Did he make it up? Is it all just a way to get to me?"

"OK, let's rewind a second." Rose took the pan from the heat and came to sit by Savannah. "What happened? What did Dad tell you?"

"He did make it up. I knew it! I knew you'd never do that to me. That bastard. I—"

"Whoa, wait a minute. Can you please tell me what he said?"

"I called him this afternoon to ask if the story about his engagement was true and he told me that you'd told him you were gay."

"And this came into the conversation about his engagement how?"

Savannah looked sheepish. "I might have got a little angry about the fact that he hadn't even told his own daughter before the internet got hold of it. I might have also called him a selfish son of a bitch for getting engaged to a woman you barely know."

"But how did my sexuality come into the conversation?"

"He said that I was a fine one to talk; that I didn't even know my own daughter's sexuality – and that you were very close to Rachel, that you'd told her you were – you were gay – before you even told me. But was he making it up? Was he just trying to hurt me?"

Rose felt awful. She shook her head.

"What? You are?"

Rose nodded.

"And you told that – that surf monster – before you told me?"

"She's not a surf monster, Mom, she's actually—"

"Yes, she is! Have you seen her Instagram?"

"No, I – wait, how have you seen her Instagram?"

"It's full of pictures of her in her bikini and bullshit

quotes about riding a wave of love. Anyway, that's not the point. The point is, how could you tell her before you told me?" Savannah pulled her cigarettes from her bag. "I'm your mom," she said in a little voice before lighting one.

Well, try acting like it for once, Rose's inner voice snapped. She took a deep breath to try to stay calm. "I hadn't planned it. I hadn't wanted to tell them first. It just kind of slipped out."

Savannah angrily exhaled a cloud of smoke. "It slipped out. The fact that you are gay just slipped out."

"Yes." Rose felt tears welling. Shit, this was not how she had wanted this conversation to go. Not at all. She decided to see if honesty was actually the best policy. "If you must know, I was trying to get Dad's attention. I'd been there over a week and all he wanted to do was talk about his movie – when he wasn't actually away rehearsing for his movie. I wanted to tell him something that would make him pay attention for once."

Savannah frowned. "But why didn't you tell me first?"

Oh, for God's sake! Rose was feeling really mad now. No matter what happened to her, her parents always seemed to twist it back on to them. Even something as important as her sexuality had to end up being about them. It was pathetic. It was beyond pathetic. It was … oh, where was walking dictionary Amber when she needed her?

Rose stood up. "I wanted to tell you. Ever since I got back, I've been trying to find the right time. But there's never the right time because you're always in the middle of some kind of drama." Rage had taken her over now and she couldn't stop the torrent of words. "You're either moping about getting old or putting on an ounce of weight or what Dad's doing. Who gives a crap what the rest of the world think? Why can't you just be happy being yourself? And being a mom. A proper mom. All the modelling and the fame, it's all phoney bullshit. Quit feeling sorry for yourself and start counting your blessings, 'cos from where I'm standing, you've got loads." She walked to the door, then turned back to face her mom. "Yes, I'm gay. Yes, I told Dad and Rachel before I told you. So you can turn it into another episode of the Savannah Ferndale soap opera or you can actually be a real mom for once and suck it up and support me."

All the way up the stairs and across the landing, Rose managed to keep herself from crying, but as soon as she got into her room and threw herself down on her bed the tears started pouring down her cheeks. She cried for all the times she'd felt like this, all the times she'd felt so shut-out and ignored by her parents. All the times she'd felt second-place to their fame and careers. All the times when she was younger and had been left with nannies or au pairs who would spend most of their time quizzing her about her parents or snooping through their things. And she cried with disappointment that — even after everything that had happened last year with the internet storm over her photo — Savannah still hadn't changed. She still put herself first. Rose stopped crying and listened. Maybe this time would be different. Maybe Savannah would realize what an idiot she'd been and come up to console her. But all she could hear was the wind in the trees and the whine of a distant police siren. All of the joy from the day had gone. She rolled onto her side and hugged her pillow.

Chapter Twenty-four

Amber sat down at the table nearest the canteen door so Sky would see her when she came in.

"Hey, freak."

Amber internally groaned as she looked up to see Chloe and the rest of the OMGs standing at her table, their pouting mouths all freshly painted.

"These seats taken?" Chloe gestured at the empty chairs.

Amber nodded.

"What, by all of your imaginary friends?" Chloe's friend Sarah sneered.

"Yes, actually," Amber snapped. "And they're way better company than you."

"You're such a weirdo," Chloe hissed.

"And?" Amber stared at her. She didn't care what Chloe thought of her. She had way more important things to think about — like how Maali's dad was. And how she was going to follow Oscar's advice and make her life sensational.

"And what?" Chloe said.

"Wow, conversation with you is riveting," Amber

muttered just as Sky appeared at the table.

She looked from Chloe to Amber and raised her eyebrows. "Everything OK?"

"Yes, everything's great. They were just going." Amber looked pointedly at Chloe.

A scowl flickered on to Chloe's face and she leaned down to speak in Amber's ear. "You think you're so great, don't you, now you've actually got a friend. But I know what you're really like – and I bet the readers of your stupid blog would love to know too." Chloe turned back to the other OMGs. "Come on, let's get out of here."

Amber stared after Chloe, her heart pounding.

"What the hell was that about?" Sky said.

Amber shrugged. "She's just being her usual charming self." But inside she didn't feel so self-assured. She knew that Chloe had read her interview with Rose and therefore knew about her blog, but she'd assumed she hadn't looked at it since.

"Do you want to get out of here for a bit?" Sky asked.

Amber nodded.

Outside was cold and grey and the air was filled with a fine drizzle.

"How's your day been so far?" Amber asked.

Sky sighed. "Not great. Why do teachers get so uptight about homework? Seriously, it's bad enough having to be here for seven hours a day. I can't believe they expect us to work most of the weekend, too."

"Oh dear," Amber said. But she was only half concentrating. Her mind was too full of thoughts of Chloe and the OMGs killing themselves laughing over her blog. And just when she'd started posting again. Why did this have to happen now?

"And if they're not going on about homework, they're obsessing over revision. It's not as if our mock exams count for anything." Sky looked at Amber. "They don't count towards our final grades, do they?"

"No. They're more of a trial run."

"So they're pointless." Sky sighed and looked back at the grey brick building. "Just like school."

Rose added another pinch of cayenne pepper to the frosting and gave it a stir. Ever since her blow-up with Savannah at the weekend, the atmosphere at home had been thick with tension. Savannah was acting as if nothing had happened, being falsely bright and cheery but with just enough iciness to let Rose know that she was still pissed off at her. Rose's coping strategy had been to throw herself into devising a signature cupcake for the stall and daydreaming about Francesca. She tasted the frosting. Now it was perfect. She filled up an icing bag and started piping swirls on top of the batch of chocolate and chilli cupcakes she'd made earlier. The first time she'd ever piped icing it had come out uneven but now she knew exactly how much pressure to exert on the bag and exactly how to move her wrist. Once she'd iced the cakes, she stepped back to admire them and all of her tension disappeared. They looked great. Now for the finishing touches. She'd found some mini chilli peppers at Camden Market and figured they'd make the perfect decoration. She gently placed one in the centre of each cake. Perfect. Now she needed to show them to Francesca. If she liked them, Rose could make a fresh batch for Saturday. As she thought of seeing Francesca again, and watching that beautiful mouth biting into one of her cakes, her skin tingled with excitement.

Sky trudged through the crowded concourse at Camden Tube station, her heart as heavy as her backpack of school books. She'd gone up to Covent Garden after school. She couldn't face going home, because going home would mean there'd be no excuse not to make a start on her homework. The problem was, she now had so much homework she didn't know *where* to start. Sky had refused on principle to do any over the weekend but today she'd had three more assignments heaped on top of the two essays that were due. She tapped her Oyster card on the reader and slipped through the barrier. The air outside was crisp and fresh – a welcome change to the muggy air of the Underground. She quickly checked her phone – still no call or message from Leon. She'd hoped she might find him in the Poetry Café but there'd been no sign of him. And why should there have been? As she started to make her way up the High Road she felt sad and desperate and consumed with disappointment.

He'd said he'd call her on Sunday and now it was Monday night. What if he didn't call at all? What if the dream was over? And it *was* a dream. The longer that went by without her hearing from Leon, the less real the whole thing seemed. The less real *he* seemed. Like some fantasy guy she'd conjured up in her imagination to distract her from the harsh realities of school. This was no good. She hated feeling this way. There was only one person who could snap her out of this mood. She stopped by a lamppost and typed a text to Rose.

> Hey! How are you? Where are you? Don't suppose you want to meet? Don't worry if it's too late but I could really do with your advice. S xx

All through dinner, Maali could tell something was wrong. It wasn't anything that Auntie Sita or Uncle Dev had said, it was more what they hadn't said. When Maali had asked if there'd been any news on the scan results, they'd said they "weren't sure". How could they not be sure? Either they knew or they didn't. Her mum hadn't been any clearer either, sending her a text in the afternoon saying that she'd tell her what had happened when she got home. Surely if it was good news she'd have told her by text? Surely only bad news needed to be told face to face? Maali stirred her curry listlessly with her fork. She wasn't able to eat even a mouthful. Fear gripped her throat like a vice. Downstairs the front door slammed shut and all of them apart from Namir jumped. Uncle Dev and Auntie Sita were clearly as nervous as she was. They all watched silently as Maali's mum walked into the room. She took one look at them and burst into tears.

Uncle Dev leapt to his feet. "Sis! Come here." He wrapped his arms around her.

Maali sat still as stone. What had happened? Why was she crying?

"What's wrong, Mum?" Namir asked in a little voice.

"Oh, nothing, pet, Mummy's just tired." Their mum broke away from Uncle Dev's embrace and wiped her eyes.

"Why don't you and I go and watch your dinosaur movie?" Auntie Sita said to Namir. "Let Mum have some dinner."

"OK," Namir said, but he was still looking at his mum anxiously.

Once Sita and Namir had left, Maali's mum came over and took hold of Maali's hands. "We got the results of the scan," she said, her eyes glassy with tears. "Dad – he … he has a brain tumour."

Maali sat motionless at the table while beneath her it felt as if the entire world had fallen away.

Cake Ingredients

200g butter (room temperature – or your blender won't
be happy!)
200g light brown sugar
3 eggs
200g self-raising flour
100g unsweetened cocoa
½ teaspoon ground cinnamon
1 teaspoon mild chilli powder
¼ teaspoon cayenne pepper
A few drops of milk if needed

- Beat the butter and sugar.
- Stir in the eggs, one at a time. (Don't be put off by the gross appearance.)
- Combine all the dry ingredients in another bowl.
- Slowly (and I mean SLOWLY!) sift the dry mix into the butter, sugar and eggs mix, then fold in.
- Stir in a few drops of milk if needed.
- Spoon the mixture into cupcake cases (you'll need about 12) and place on a baking tray.
- Bake in a pre-heated oven at 160°C / gas mark 2 for 20–25 minutes.
- Test them with a skewer to make sure they're cooked.

(The skewer needs to come out clean – if it's covered in weird gloopy stuff, it's not ready.)

- Leave to cool on a wire rack before icing.

Frosting Ingredients

450g icing sugar, sieved

85g unsalted butter

40ml milk

25g unsweetened cocoa

I teaspoon vanilla extract

¼ teaspoon cayenne pepper

- Cream the butter, cocoa and cayenne pepper.
- Slowly add half the icing sugar.
- Add the milk and vanilla.
- Slowly stir in the remaining sugar.
- Pipe the frosting onto the cakes.
- Decorate with mini chillis – or, if you're really brave, chilli flakes.

Chapter Twenty-five

Rose let herself into the patisserie and looked around. One of Francesca's assistants, a red-haired Scottish woman named Claire, was behind the counter and there were a couple of customers sitting at the tables.

"Hey," Rose said, coming up to the counter.

Claire smiled. "Hello, Rose. You're a bit late for work experience. We'll be closing soon."

"I know. I just came by to see Francesca. I have something to show her."

"Ah, OK. She just popped out." Claire gestured to an empty table nearby. "Why don't you take a seat? Would you like a drink?"

Rose shook her head. She was too nervous. She'd decided that tonight was the night she was going to tell Francesca she was gay. She wasn't exactly sure how she was going to do this. On the way over on the train she'd dreamed up a scenario in which she'd stayed behind after the shop had shut and Francesca had conveniently said to her in passing that she was gay. "So am I!" Rose had exclaimed in response.

At which point Francesca had turned to her and smiled. "You and I are so alike, my darling Rose." And then, finally, they'd kissed. The kiss had tasted of lipstick and chocolate and chilli and it had gone on for ever.

Rose sat down at the table and took a deep breath. She had to get a grip. She didn't have to tell Francesca tonight, she reminded herself. She could always tell her another time. But at least if she told her now, she'd get it out there. Then, if Francesca *was* gay, she'd probably tell Rose and at least that would leave the way clear for something to happen.

But *would* something happen? Rose thought back to when Francesca had given her the necklace. There had definitely been a spark between them then, especially when Francesca put the necklace on her. Rose hadn't imagined it. She was certain. And again on Saturday, when Francesca had told her how "incredeeeble" she was. The way she'd looked at her, the way her huge dark eyes had widened and sparkled...

The door burst open and Francesca stepped in. She was wearing tightly fitting black trousers, with sky-high red stilettos and a matching halter-neck top. Her hair was piled up on top of her head, with a few loose tendrils spilling down around her face. She looked stunning. Rose could hardly move, let alone speak.

"Rose!" Francesca exclaimed. "What are you doing here?"

"I – uh – I made some cakes for the stall. A new recipe. If you – if you like them, I thought it might be good to..."

Rose fell silent as a dark-haired, heavy-set man walked

into the shop behind Francesca and placed his hand on her shoulder.

Francesca spun round and smiled at him. "Rose, Claire, this is Pierre. Pierre, these are my wonderful staff."

Rose tried with every muscle in her face not to frown. Who the hell was Pierre?

"*Bon soir*," Pierre called over to her.

He was French. Rose relaxed a little. Maybe he was her brother.

Pierre put one of his hairy, chunky hands on Francesca's waist and pulled her to him. OK, so maybe French siblings liked being super-affectionate. He planted a kiss slap-bang on her beautiful lips. The lips Rose had dreamed of kissing for months. Francesca giggled.

"Excuse us," she said, grinning at Claire and Rose. "We haven't seen each other since Christmas."

Pierre said something in French and started nuzzling her neck. Rose felt like she was going to puke. Every kiss he planted on Francesca, every giggle and coy look she gave him in return, felt like pins bursting Rose's heart-shaped balloon. How could she have been so wrong? How could she have been so stupid? Rose hated feeling like this. She needed to get out of there. She took her phone from her bag, ready to fake an excuse. But there was a text from Sky. It sounded urgent too. Perfect.

"Oh, I'm so sorry. I've got to go."

"But I only just got here!" Francesca cried. "What are

these cakes you were talking about? Stay for a drink."

"I can't. I'm sorry. My friend's having an emergency." Rose waved her phone as if producing evidence. "I only popped in because I was passing. Lovely to meet you," she said through gritted teeth to Pierre. "I'll see you at the stall on Saturday," she said to Francesca as she walked past her to the door.

"Of course. See you then. I hope your friend she is OK."

"Me too." Rose practically ran from the shop. Shit. Shit. Shit. She felt as if her heart were being crushed by one of those machines you get at salvage yards. The kind that can squash an entire car into the size of a shoe box. The worst thing was, she couldn't be angry with Francesca. It wasn't as if she'd cheated on her, or even told her that she was gay. This disappointment Rose was feeling, that was eating her up from the inside, was all her own doing. She needed a drink. She saw an off-licence up ahead and stormed inside. She grabbed a bottle of wine from the shelf.

"Are you over eighteen?" the Asian guy behind the counter asked.

"Are you kidding me?" This was all she needed. She hardly ever got ID-ed. "I'm twenty-three and I've got three kids," she snapped at him. "Why do you think I need the wine?"

"OK. OK. Just checking," the guy said, scanning the wine and putting it in a bag.

Rose pulled a ten-pound note from her jacket pocket. It was from her wages from Saturday. The money she was supposed to be putting into a savings account for her business. She was too angry and upset to care. She came out of the shop and called Sky. Sky answered on the first ring.

"Rose! Where are you?"

"Camden. How about you?"

"Same. Just came out of the Tube."

Rose looked down the High Road and in the distance she could just make out Sky's fluffy blonde hair.

"I'm up ahead of you. Outside the off-licence. I'm the one waving the wine bottle, which kind of sums up my night."

"Oh dear."

"Yeah." Rose watched as Sky started running towards her.

"Have you got enough for two?" she said breathlessly.

Rose saw a flicker of light in the dark tunnel of her disappointment. "Sure have."

Amber logged into her email account. She had twenty-seven new messages. Normally, this sight would make her happy but, following her earlier altercation with Chloe, she felt a twinge of unease. She quickly scanned her inbox. One was her word of the day from Dictionary.com but the rest were all comment notifications from her blog. Amber's heart sank as she saw that most of them came from a new poster: someone called @ChloGlo. She clicked the first one open. It had been posted on her latest blog.

Well, you defiantly don't fit in!!! What a freak!

Chloe – it had to be. And how typical that she should make Amber's most irritating predictive text error of all time. She hated it when people put defiantly instead of definitely. Amber opened the next notification.

Why don't you tell ur readers why ur not interested in boys and sex. Cos ur a lesbian!

Amber's face flushed. But, despite knowing that what she'd see was bound to hurt her, she clicked open another.

Why don't you do a blog about what happened to you in PE last year?

Right – that was enough! Amber walked over to her bedroom window and opened it wide. Outside, a crowd of people on a Jack the Ripper tour followed their guide down the cobbled street. Over to the right she could hear the gentle thud of a bassline coming from one of the bars in the Truman Brewery. She breathed in deep lungfuls of cold night air, trying to get rid of the nausea building inside her. Her blog had been her sanctuary. The one place she felt free to be herself – or at least write about herself – in an honest and open way. And even though she'd been blocked recently, she'd hoped that once she got over her current identity crisis she'd be able to start writing freely again. Now Chloe had ruined it. With her snooping around and commenting,

Wilde at Heart would be just as bad as school.

Amber felt tears burning her eyes as she deleted the comments one by one and changed the blog setting to offline. It was so unfair. Why did the bullies always win? There was a knock on her door.

"Amber, darling!" Gerald called. "Daniel's popping to Rosa's for some Thai food. What would you like?"

"Nothing," Amber replied, choking back her tears.

Gerald poked his head round the door. "What's wrong?"

Amber frowned. Since when did Gerald become observant? "Nothing's wrong." She turned back to look out of the window so he wouldn't see her face.

"Is it – is it about your mother?"

"No. I'm just not hungry." But instead of leaving like he normally would, she heard Gerald come into the room and close the door.

"When I was your age I was prone to gazing mournfully out of windows whenever something was wrong."

"I'm not gazing mournfully out of the window," Amber said, turning to gaze mournfully into the room.

"Hmm," Gerald said, staring at her critically, the way he did at his unfinished paintings.

"I'm just a bit fed up with someone at school, that's all," Amber said.

"And what did this someone do?" Gerald asked. Despite being nearly sixty, he still had a powerful presence about him, especially when he looked angry or concerned, like now. And seeing his concern made Amber's resolve waiver. She wiped her tears away.

"She likes to make my life hell," Amber muttered. "But it was OK when it was just at school. I'm used to it at school, but now – now she's read my blog and she's making my life hell there too."

"How?"

"By posting nasty comments about me." Amber sat on her bed, feeling a horrible mixture of sadness and shame. "It's OK, I've taken the blog offline."

Gerald frowned. "What does that mean?"

"She won't be able to see it. No one will be able to see it."

Gerald went over to the window and looked outside. "When I was your age I spent a lot of time gazing mournfully out of the window because of the horrible things people said about me."

"What kind of things?"

"Poofter. Nancy-boy. Queer. Queer was an insult back then. Simply being gay was. Gay men routinely got attacked. Beaten black and blue just for loving another man. But do you know what I realized during all those hours of staring mournfully into space?" He turned to face her.

Amber shook her head.

"I realized that I had a choice. I could either let the bullies win – or I could make sure that I won. I could be proud of who I was and what I did and who I loved. And I could say, to hell with the imbeciles who would rather stew in their own hate like ... like sour dumplings!"

Amber bit on her lip, unsure whether she was about to laugh or cry.

Gerald sat down on the bed next to her. "Don't let the haters hurt you, darling. Don't give them that power. Now, you know that my knowledge of the worldwide interweb thingy is about as detailed as a news report in the *Sun*, but surely there must be some way to stop people posting hateful things on your blogger."

"Blog," Amber corrected. "I can block her. But she'll probably keep creating new accounts – or getting her friends to post for her."

"Then keep blocking. But most of all, keep creating. Keep writing and reaching for better, darling. As our good friend Oscar would say: 'We are all in the gutter, but some of us are looking at the stars.' Keep looking at the stars. Don't look at the gutter, and whatever you do, don't listen to the guttersnipes." Gerald placed his arm around her shoulders and Amber leaned into him.

"Thank you," she whispered.

Daniel appeared in the doorway. "Hurry up, guys. I'm about to die of starvation here. Oh, is everything OK?"

Daniel sat down on the other side of Amber and both he and Gerald looked at her questioningly. She nodded. Because if it wasn't OK right now, she felt certain it would be, with dads like these, supporting her like a pair of beloved book-ends.

* * *

"I can't believe how dumb I've been," Rose said, taking a swig from the bottle of wine.

"Me too." Sky bit into a hot, salty chip. They'd come down to the canal to get away from the noise of the High Road and were sitting on a bench staring glumly into the dark water.

"Gee, thanks."

"No, I don't mean you. I mean me. I can't believe how stupid I've been."

"Yeah, but at least you had reason to believe the poet guy liked you. At least he actually asked you out. I've been crushing on someone who isn't even attracted to my entire gender!" Rose passed the wine to Sky.

Sky leaned back on the bench and took a swig. She didn't really drink alcohol and she didn't normally like wine, but tonight it actually tasted quite good, warm and fruity. The perfect thing to wash down the chips and wash away her stress over Leon. You haven't been stupid. You've been unlucky."

"Yeah, story of my life."

Sky sighed. She hated seeing Rose so defeated. It reminded her of the time she'd had to smuggle her to the safety of the houseboat to escape the internet storm over her photo. "Don't worry. You'll find someone." Sky cringed. That sounded so pathetic.

"I don't want someone, I want *Francesca*." Rose stood up and looked at the sky. "Where the hell's the moon when you need her?"

Sky followed her gaze. The sky was orangey-black from the light pollution, with not a single star visible. "It's too cloudy."

Rose sighed. "Great."

"It's still there, though." Sky took another large swig of wine. And another. It seemed to get better with every mouthful. She was feeling quite light-headed now, her thoughts becoming hazy. "I know, why don't we tell it to the moon? Why don't we get how we're feeling off our chests?"

Rose nodded. "OK, but it's not going to be pretty."

"It doesn't have to be. It just has to be honest."

"OK." Rose took the bottle from her and had a drink. Then she stood in the middle of the darkened tow-path and looked up at the sky. "I'm really pissed off," she said. "Like, so pissed off I could explode. How come whenever I try to do the right thing it always ends up being the wrong thing?" She took another swig of wine. "Why's life so full of wrong turnings? Why..." She put the bottle on the bench and looked down at the ground. "Why couldn't she have liked me the way I like her?"

Sky watched Rose. She looked so beautiful. Even in the darkness you could see the arc of her cheekbones and the bud-like outline of her full lips. There was no way she'd be on her own for long. If only she could see that too. Rose's hair started to gleam silver. The moon was emerging from behind a cloud. "Look," said Sky, pointing to it.

Rose looked up. "Wow." She gazed at the moon for a

moment. Then she sat back down on the bench and turned to Sky. "Your turn."

Sky stood up and gazed at the moon too. Wispy black clouds were scudding across it. "I'm so disappointed he hasn't called," she said quietly, feeling really self-conscious.

"Hey, sister, how about a little more rage?" Rose said.

Sky laughed. "All right. I'm really, really pissed off that he didn't get in touch when he said he would." She felt anger building inside her. It felt good, better than the pathetic moping feeling she had been experiencing. "I mean, why tell a person you want to see them and that you'll call them tomorrow if you don't really mean it? What kind of loser does something like that?"

"Yes!" Rose cried.

Sky was on a roll now. The warmth from the wine was blending with her anger and making everything feel slightly blurred at the edges. "I can't believe I fell for it. I can't believe I was so stupid. I mean, he probably does this kind of thing all the time. He probably takes random girls to random Tube stations every day of the week. That's probably his – his – thing! He's probably been to every place on the goddam map." Sky paused. Why had she said "goddam"? She never said "goddam"! She felt the sudden urge to giggle. But she mustn't. She was telling it to the moon, godammit! "He's probably written poems with random girls all over London. I should—"

A phone started ringing. Sky ignored it.

"And another thing…" She took a step towards the canal. The ground seemed to lurch slightly, as if she were on a boat. She started to laugh and turned to Rose. "It's like the canal path's a boat!"

"Hmm, I think maybe you need to sit down."

"And drink more wine?"

"No! No more wine. You could answer your phone, though."

"Is that my phone?"

"Uh-huh."

Sky burst out laughing and went over to her bag. She pulled her phone out. "Oh no!"

"What?"

"It's him!"

Chapter Twenty-six

"But why can't I come with you?" Maali begged her mum.

"Because we don't know what time they'll be moving him. It might not be until this afternoon." Her mum took a sip of her tea. A plate of toast lay cold and untouched on the table beside her.

Maali sighed. After yesterday's news she desperately wanted to see her dad, but he was being moved to a specialist brain hospital and her mum didn't want her getting in the way. She hadn't quite said it like that but that was what she meant. Maali could tell.

"Maybe you can come and see him after school," her mum said. "Hopefully he'll be moved by then."

"School?" Maali stared at her. How could she expect her to go into school? "Mum, I don't think I—"

"What?" Her mum got up from the table and tipped her uneaten toast into the bin. Her face was thin and pinched with worry.

"Nothing."

Her mum came over and placed her hand on Maali's

shoulder. "I promise I'll text you as soon as we know when he's being moved."

"OK."

Maali set off for school like a zombie. The only way she could cope with the enormity of what was happening was to pretend that it wasn't happening. To pretend that her dad wasn't in hospital at all — that he was back home, getting ready to open up the shop, laughing and joking as usual with her mum. She came to a standstill outside the mosque. She couldn't do this. It was too hard. It was too much to take. She closed her eyes and took a deep breath. *Just keep taking one more step*, a voice said firmly inside her head. *Just one more step*. Maali opened her eyes and took a step. And another. And another. And slowly but surely, one step at a time, she made her way to school.

Sky sat down at the form-room table, her mouth dry and her head pounding. For once, Vanessa wasn't there first. Sky rummaged in her bag for a pack of mints. She was paranoid that when Vanessa did arrive she'd be able to smell the stale wine on her breath. She took her phone out along with her mints and placed it on the table. She'd let Leon's call ring out last night. Rose had praised her for playing it cool and not picking up but the truth was, she'd felt anything but cool when she saw his name on the caller ID. She'd felt ecstatic. She'd also realized she was drunk and she hadn't wanted him to hear her like that. She'd shoved her phone in her bag and pretended to Rose that she didn't care, but as soon as she'd got back to the houseboat and seen the voicemail icon at the top of the screen, she'd been overjoyed. She'd played his message so many times that she knew it by heart.

"Hey, Sky-Blue, I was just wondering what you were up to Wednesday night. I've been invited to be a guest on a radio show about poetry and I wondered if you'd like to come along. Give me a call." Then there was a couple of seconds' silence before … "It's Leon. Bye."

Sky glanced around the room. Mrs Bayliss was busy helping someone with their homework. She should have time to play his message once more. She put her phone to her ear and tilted her head forwards so that her hair fell over it.

"Hey, Sky-Blue, I was just wondering what you were—"

"Is there some kind of emergency, Miss Cassidy?"

Sky jumped at the sound of Mrs Bayliss's voice right behind her. She turned to face her, dropping the phone into her lap. "What? I – no…"

Mrs Bayliss held out her hand. "Give it to me."

"What?"

"The phone."

The class fell silent.

Vanessa came bursting through the door and crashed into the seat next to Sky.

"Give me the phone," Mrs Bayliss said, looking straight at Sky.

Sky's face flushed. "I can't…"

"School rules, I'm afraid. If you use your phone in class it gets confiscated until the end of the day."

"The end of the day?" Sky looked at her, horrified.

"Yes."

"But I need to call someone," Sky said, desperately trawling her hungover brain for some kind of excuse.

"I'm sure it can wait. Now give it to me, please."

Sky gave Mrs Bayliss the phone. This sucked. How could they take away her personal property like that? It wasn't as if Mrs Bayliss was teaching at the time. She hadn't even taken the register yet. This was so unfair.

Sky scowled as Mrs Bayliss walked back to the front of the class.

"Bad luck," Philippa whispered across the aisle to Sky with a sympathetic smile. A few of the other students were smiling sympathetically too.

"It's best to go to the toilets if you need to use your phone," Vanessa whispered. "That way they can't see you."

"Do you have something you want to share with us, Vanessa?" Mrs Bayliss snapped.

Vanessa shook her head. "No."

"No, what?"

"No, Miss."

Mrs Bayliss slung Sky's phone into her desk drawer and locked it. Sky pictured Leon's message locked in there too and she felt as if her head might explode from the injustice of it all.

* * *

Amber stood outside the school library looking for Sky. She'd texted her to come and meet here instead of their usual place but morning break had started almost ten minutes ago and there was still no sign of her. Maybe she wasn't in today. Maybe she was taking another day off. Amber looked around inside the library but there was still no sign of Sky. Why did she have to be off today of all days? Amber could really do with her advice on how to deal with Chloe and the blog and, well, everything.

Sky paced up and down the corridor outside the canteen. There was no sign of Amber and she had no way of knowing if she was even in today, thanks to Mrs Bayliss confiscating her phone. She decided to go outside to get some fresh air. Hopefully if Amber was in she'd think to find her there. The sky was a slab of grey, like a concrete ceiling to match the concrete school below. Sky went around the side of the building to the path leading to the tennis courts. It was usually a lot quieter here and she needed to think. She wouldn't be able to call Leon back until after school now. What if he took her silence as a no and invited someone else to go with him tomorrow? Going to a radio interview sounded so interesting. Why should Mrs Bayliss be allowed to take her phone and ruin her life like this? What if she had a genuine emergency? What if her dad needed to get hold of her? She marched further down the path, feeling angrier with every step. This place sucked so much and the worst thing was, she didn't have a clue how to make it better.

Rose rolled onto her stomach and started scrolling through Netflix. Since waking up she'd binge-watched the last four episodes of *Making a Murderer*, and now she needed to find something else suitably grim.

She'd woken with a pounding headache from last night's wine, which had done nothing to help lift the general malaise she was feeling about Francesca. Though she'd tried to drown her sorrows in the bottom of a bottle, that was Savannah's party trick. Rose didn't want to turn out like her; that would be her very worst nightmare.

Rose heard Savannah coming out of her bedroom across the landing and she coughed loudly, just so she'd know she was skipping school. Within seconds there was a knock on her door.

"Rose? Are you in there?"

Rose closed her laptop and sat up. She hoped it would be a quick telling-off this time. She didn't have the energy for another of their fights. "Yeah."

"Can I come in?"

Well, that was a first. She couldn't remember Savannah ever having asked permission to enter her room, especially when she was mad at her.

"Yeah."

Savannah came in. She was wearing leggings and a

vest-top so tight you could see her ribcage jutting out. "Did you leave these in the kitchen?" She held out the container of cupcakes Rose had made for the stall. When she'd got home last night she'd dumped them on the kitchen counter before coming to bed. So no doubt Savannah was about to yell at her for leaving cakes lying around the place. She got out of bed and grabbed the box.

"Don't worry, I'll get rid of them."

"What do you mean?"

Rose pulled a hoodie over her pyjamas and put on her slippers. "I'll throw them in the outside bin. It'll be like they never existed," she said as she marched downstairs. This was so typical of Savannah. There was no mention of the fact that she hadn't gone into school, but leave a goddam cake lying around and there was all hell to pay.

"Why are you throwing them out?" Savannah called down from the landing.

Rose stopped by the front door.

"Because that's what you want, isn't it? I forgot, OK? I got home late and I forgot the no-cake-in-the-kitchen policy." She opened the door and nearly jumped out of her skin. Savannah's *Vagina Vows* buddy, Margot, was standing there draped in a floor-length, purple faux-fur coat. She was beaming so widely Rose could see all of her fillings.

"Good morning!" Margot boomed. "Is your lovely mother there?"

"No," Rose muttered, "but my selfish mother is."

"I beg your pardon?"

"Nothing. Go on in." Rose left the door open and stalked over to the bins. What had she been thinking, making the Spitalfields Surprise cupcakes? It wasn't her cake stall. It wasn't her place to create a new cake. That was up to Francesca. Beautiful, passionate Francesca. Rose shuddered at the image of Pierre pawing at Francesca with his chunky, hairy hands. Eew. Gross. She lifted the lid of the bin and threw the whole box in.

"Rose!" Savannah cried from the front door.

"What?" Rose stared at her. Surely she didn't want to have a fight out here and in front of Margot.

"I didn't want you to throw them out."

"What were they?" Margot said, staring at the bin.

"Nothing," Rose said, pushing past them into the house and running upstairs to her room. "They were nothing."

When the school bell finally rang for the end of the day it was like the starting pistol in a race. Sky leapt from her desk and rushed to her form room. What if Mrs Bayliss wasn't there? What if she'd gone home already and her phone was still locked away? But she was there, hunched over her desk, marking a huge pile of books that teetered next to her.

"I've come to get my phone," Sky said, standing in front of her desk.

Mrs Bayliss looked up. The make-up she'd been wearing at the start of the day had smudged away and wisps of her grey hair had worked their way loose from her bun. She looked really, really tired. "Ah, yes," she said with a sigh. She took a key from her jacket pocket and opened her desk drawer. "I hope you understand why I had to confiscate it."

"Not really, no," Sky said. Then, realizing Mrs Bayliss was holding the phone and could lock it away again at any moment, she added, "But I guess it's the rules."

"Yes, it is." Mrs Bayliss peered over her glasses at her. "It may surprise you to learn this, Sky, but it's hard enough to capture the attention of thirty teenagers at the best of times. If you all started phoning and texting during class we'd have no hope of teaching you a thing."

"But you weren't..." Sky stopped herself. "I'm sorry. It won't happen again."

"Good." Mrs Bayliss handed her the phone.

Sky shoved it into her blazer pocket.

"It must be hard to come into a secondary school so late in the day." Mrs Bayliss leaned back in her chair. "How are you coping?"

"Yeah, it's – I'm OK."

"Good. Well, if you need anything – any help with anything – do come and see me." She looked genuinely concerned.

"Thanks." Sky wasn't sure what to make of this latest development. Maybe Mrs Bayliss was feeling guilty for taking her phone.

Once she was safely outside and off school property,

she checked the phone for any new messages. There were a couple from Amber about meeting her in the library at first break. Nothing from Leon. But why would there be? He was waiting for her to contact him. She went to his number and pressed call.

Amber let herself into the house and began trudging up the stairs.

"Honey, you're home!" Daniel burst through the kitchen door and greeted her with a massive hug. "Come here, we've got something to tell you."

Amber came into the kitchen. Gerald was standing by the counter, holding an envelope in his hand.

"We thought you could do with a little cheering up," he said, holding the envelope out to her.

"So we got tickets to see *The Picture of Dorian Gray* at the Donmar tonight – starring Ralph Fiennes!" Daniel said, barely able to contain his excitement.

"But I thought you said tickets were harder to find than a tax inspector's heart." Amber stared at Gerald. The play was only on for a limited run before it went to Broadway. Tickets had sold out within minutes.

"They were," Gerald said.

"So how did you…?"

"Your father used his powers of persuasion," Daniel said with a grin.

"My not too inconsiderable powers of persuasion," Gerald

said with a boastful grin. "Ralph and I go way back. I knew him when he still pronounced the *L*."

"This is – this is amazing!

"And we're having drinks at the Oscar Wilde Bar in the Hotel Café Royal beforehand," Gerald said. "It's where he fell in love with Lord Alfred Douglas." He gave Amber a hefty slap on the back. "Did it work?" He looked at her anxiously. "Has it made you feel better?"

Amber grinned. "Yes! It's made me feel loads better! Thank you!"

Maali sat cross-legged in the darkness in front of her shrine. The statues of Lakshmi and Kali stood side by side, illuminated by the flickering light of a candle she'd placed between them.

"I need your help," she whispered to the goddesses. "I need it more than ever before."

Rain pattered gently on the skylight above her and trickled down the glass like tears. Maybe even the gods were crying at this latest news. Maali was beyond crying, though. It was as if fear had frozen her tears in their ducts. Tomorrow afternoon, surgeons would be operating on her dad, attempting to remove the tumour from his brain. Her mum had tried to tell her that this was good news, that they would be removing the thing that was making him so sick. But there seemed to be so many "what ifs" attached to this promise. *What if they aren't able to remove it? What if they remove it but it comes back?*

And worst of all, the question Maali hardly dared ask: *What if it's cancerous?*

Maali continued staring at the goddesses. "Please," she pleaded. "Please make it OK."

The rain pounded relentlessly on the skylight.

Amber walked into her bedroom and switched on her desk lamp. Something had happened to her in the theatre tonight. Something profound. As she'd sat there in the darkness, watching Oscar's words so powerfully brought to life by the cast, she'd felt inspired. And – although she'd been struggling with writer's block for the past few weeks – she now knew without a shadow of a doubt that she was born to be a writer. That she was born to create magical new worlds with words. She didn't need to know who her mum was to know that. Oscar's gift with words had sparked a feeling of recognition and desire deep inside her. They always had. She'd just lost sight of that fact. She picked up her book of Oscar Wilde quotes.

"How can I reignite my writing dream?" she whispered as she flicked to a random page and began to read. The quote she landed on was short but sweet.

"When good Americans die they go to Paris."

Amber read it again. The words *"go to Paris"* echoed in her mind. Oscar Wilde had gone to Paris after his release from jail. He had died there. Amber thought back to her trip to Paris last year with her dads and the Moonlight Dreamers. Seeing Oscar's grave had been a dream come true, but what if she visited some of the places he went to when he was alive? Would that inspire her to write again? It would certainly give her something interesting to write about. But how was she going to go to Paris? Who would she go with? Gerald had an exhibition in New York coming up. He and Daniel would be away this weekend. *He and Daniel would be away this weekend!* An idea began to form in Amber's mind that filled her with nervous excitement. What if she went to Paris on her own? That's what Oscar would do. It's what he *had* done. And what better way for her to clear her head and get over the recent disappointments ... *and* have something sensational to write about in her diary.

Amber walked over to the window and looked outside. The rain was lashing down in sheets now, running in streams down the side of the road and pouring down the guttering. It seemed symbolic somehow, washing all of the grime away.

Chapter Twenty-seven

"Do you remember the time when you were little and you wouldn't go to bed because you thought there was a monster outside your bedroom?" Maali's dad asked her.

Maali nodded. Any minute now the doctors would be coming to take her dad away, to operate on him. *Don't cry. Don't cry. Don't cry*, she told herself, biting down on her bottom lip.

"And you demanded I come up and kill it," her dad continued. His cheeks looked even more sunken and his chin was now covered with a full beard, flecked with grey. He looked so old and frail, like he'd aged twenty years in a week.

The operation will make him better again, Maali told herself.

"But it turned out the monster was just the shadow from the coat-stand." Her dad laughed feebly and took hold of her hand. His grip was weak and his fingers trembled against hers. "Do you remember what I said to you when I put you to bed that night?"

Maali shook her head. Right now she couldn't think of

anything other than the fact that her dad was about to go for surgery.

"I told you that so many of our fears are just shadows."

Maali gulped. Was he telling her not to be afraid? But his illness wasn't a shadow. It was life-threatening and all too real.

"I love you, pet," he whispered.

"I love you too." Maali somehow managed to say the words without crying.

"They're coming," her mum said. She jumped up from her seat and kissed Maali's dad on the forehead.

Maali turned to see a team of orderlies approaching.

Fear swelled inside her. She wanted to jump in front of the bed and yell at them not to take him. Instead she sat numbly in her chair.

One of the orderlies greeted them cheerily as if they were about to take her dad on a fun day out rather than for life-saving surgery.

But what if it doesn't save his life? Maali's inner voice whispered. *What if you never see him again?* Maali clenched her fists so tightly her nails dug into her palms. *Shut up!* she told herself. *Shut up.*

"See you soon," her dad said, smiling at Maali and her mum. But there was fear in his eyes. Maali could see it.

"I love you," her mum said, stroking the side of his face.

The orderlies unlocked the wheels on the bottom of the bed and began pushing it down the ward. Taking her dad away from them.

"Come on," her mum said, beckoning Maali to follow.

They walked along behind the bed, out of the ward and over to the lift.

"Don't forget ... just shadows," Maali's dad said, smiling.

"I won't," Maali said, somehow summoning the strength to smile back.

The bright strip-lights, the cheery orderly's voice, the *ping* of the lift arriving, all blended into a haze. She heard her dad saying "see you later". Then the lift doors closed and he was gone.

Maali leaned against the wall, suddenly feeling faint. Her mum's arms went around her, hugging her tight.

"It'll be OK, pet. He'll be OK."

They slowly made their way to the drinks machine and sat down. Maali felt hollowed out by terror. What if her dad didn't make it through the operation? What if she never saw him again?

Sky put her phone face-down on her bed but the message Maali had sent earlier that afternoon remained etched behind her eyes.

My dad is being operated on right now. I know you guys don't believe in praying, but please could you keep him in your thoughts? I'm waiting at the hospital and I'm so scared. xxxxx

Sky hadn't set foot in a hospital since her mum died. Just the thought of it filled her with dread. In her experience, people went into hospital and they never came out. What if that happened to Maali? What if her dad's tumour was cancerous? Sky looked around her cabin at the pile of school books on the floor, the pile of homework assignments that were threatening to swallow her whole, and she felt a tightening in her chest. Her phone vibrated and she looked at it, terrified. What if it was bad news from Maali? But it was Leon. She breathed a sigh of relief.

Still on for this evening?

She quickly began to type a reply. Going out with Leon was exactly what she needed – a distraction from all the stress.

Yes absolutely!

Great. I'll meet you outside Borough station at 6. I'll bring my firmest handshake. ☺

Sky put her phone down but almost immediately it pinged again. She smiled, thinking it would be Leon, but it was a WhatsApp message from Rose to her and Amber.

Hey, Moonlight Dreamers, I take it you guys got

Maali's text? I was thinking we should maybe go up to the hospital to see her. Apparently her dad's going to be in surgery for hours. What do you reckon? Xoxo

Sky stared blankly at the message. Going to see Maali would mean going to a hospital. The notification on her phone went off again. This time it was a message from Amber.

Great idea. I was just about to suggest the same. I can get there in an hour. Amber

Sky felt horrible. She couldn't set foot in a hospital, especially not in these circumstances. It would totally freak her out and that was the last thing Maali needed. Maali needed people like Amber and Rose, who would be strong for her and not dissolve into a quivering heap. But how could she get out of going? Sky stuffed her phone into her bag. She could pretend she hadn't seen the message until it was too late to come. That way she wouldn't have to go into the stuff about her mum. But she couldn't pretend she hadn't seen it – it was on WhatsApp – Rose would have seen that she'd already read it. Damn. Sky took her phone back out of her bag and sent a quick reply.

I'm so sorry. Leon invited me to a radio interview he's doing. I can't get out of it. Send Maali my love and tell her I'll call her later. xxx

* * *

Maali walked along the sterile hospital corridors, following the signs for the hospital chapel. Her mum was in the canteen getting a cup of coffee with Uncle Dev. Auntie Sita was at home with Namir. It had been almost two hours since the start of her dad's surgery and Maali was beginning to go out of her mind with worry.

The chapel was a small, plain room with a few rows of pine-wood pews. Maali liked the fact that it was simple and unadorned. There was a stillness about it, a softness to the lighting that made it a welcome refuge from the hustle and bustle of the hospital. She sat down at the end of one of the pews and closed her eyes. It didn't matter that she wasn't by her shrine or that she didn't have her goddess statues to pray to – it had gone beyond that.

"I don't know if you can hear me," she whispered to the simple wooden cross hanging on the far wall. "Or even if you actually exist. But I really hope you do because – well, right now, you're all the hope I've got." She took a deep breath and began saying a prayer over and over again. A prayer made up of just one word: "Please."

Maali wasn't sure how long she sat there whispering "please" – it could have been minutes, it could have been an hour – but almost as soon as she began, she felt a stillness come over her. There was something calming about repeating one word over and over again; it helped bring her breathing back to normal. She felt her phone vibrate in her pocket and her heart skipped a beat. Surely it was too soon for news about her dad. Had something gone wrong? But the text was from Rose.

Maals, I know you're probably with your family right now but just wanted to let you know that if you need us, we're right outside and we're sending you so much love and support. xoxo

Maali stared at the text in disbelief. The Moonlight Dreamers had come to the hospital. Just knowing they were there instantly filled her with strength. She closed her eyes and said another one-word prayer. This time it was "thank you".

Borough station was packed with grim-faced rush-hour commuters making their way home from work. Sky leaned against the wall next to the entrance, trying not to get trampled on. The anxiety that had threatened to engulf her in her cabin started bubbling again in her stomach. It was so noisy and everyone looked so angry. Sky clenched her fists. A police car zoomed past, lights blazing, siren shrieking, setting her teeth on edge. She shouldn't be here. She should have stayed at the boat, tackling her homework mountain, especially when— She felt someone tap on her shoulder.

"All right, Sky-Blue?" She turned and saw Leon smiling at her, his dark eyes warm and twinkly. Instantly her anxiety abated. He was wearing a beanie hat, thick fleece hoodie and baggy low-slung jeans. "Sorry I'm late." He took hold of her hand and instantly she felt more grounded. "Come on, the radio station's just down the road."

Rose looked up at the hospital, at the bright white light of the windows glowing in the dark. She wondered if Maali was behind one of those windows, waiting anxiously to hear about her dad. She turned to Amber.

"Do you think Maals got my message?"

Amber pulled up the collar on her man's winter coat. "I don't know. She might have had to switch her phone off."

Rose nodded. "Do you think it was a dumb idea coming here?"

"No! Of course not. It feels good to be here – to be close to her – even if she doesn't know we are." Amber looked up at the hospital. "I can't imagine what she must be going through."

Rose nodded. "I know. It really puts things into perspective." She took her phone from her pocket and frowned. "I still haven't heard back from Sky." When Sky had messaged to say she was with Leon, Rose had tried calling her to get her to change her mind. Maali's dad being so sick was the biggest crisis to have faced one of the Moonlight Dreamers; surely they should all be together at a time like this. But Rose's call had gone straight to voicemail, as had her three attempts to call since. Sky must have switched off her phone.

"I'm sure she'll be here," Amber said. "She'll probably come straight from the radio thing." She turned and looked around them. The hospital was situated on a large square lined on the other sides by huge Georgian townhouses. In the centre of the square was a communal garden. "Shall we go and wait over there? If we sit on the bench by the gate we'll be able to see Maali if she comes out."

"Good plan." Rose followed Amber. She wanted to believe that Sky was on her way but she couldn't help feeling that something was up; that she was deliberately ignoring her calls. Rose shook off the thought. There was no way Sky would choose to be with a guy over Maali – not at a time like this.

Sky watched from the other side of the desk as Leon adjusted his headphones and leaned closer to the mic. His interview was about to start. The radio station was above a charity shop on Borough High Street. The entrance was a non-descript door on the side of the building. The only hint that there was a radio station there was a tiny printed card on the intercom that said *Riverside FM*. Apparently there were loads of independent radio stations like this hidden away throughout the city. Riverside specialized in broadcasting programmes about the arts and Leon had been invited to guest on a show called *Spoken Word Heard*. The interviewer was a West Indian guy called Nelson Prince who was wearing a faded Black Uhuru t-shirt and a string of large wooden beads.

"Coming up next we have Leon Jackson, aka Rebel Writer," Nelson boomed into his mic. "This young man has been causing quite a stir recently on the spoken word scene. And you're in for a treat tonight, my friends, as he's going to be telling us all about his work *and* performing a couple of pieces for us."

Leon looked at Sky and gave her a nervous smile. Sky smiled back but something felt off. Leon had brought her right to the beating heart of London's underground arts scene. She should be feeling elated. But uncomfortable thoughts kept buzzing round her mind: Maali at the hospital. Maali waiting to find out how her dad's operation had gone. The other Moonlight Dreamers there to support her. It felt wrong that Sky should be here, enjoying herself. *But you wouldn't have been any help*, she reminded herself. *You would have freaked out. Maali's way better off without you there.*

"OK, Rebel Writer," Nelson boomed. "Tell us all about yourself. How did you get started on your writing journey?"

"Why don't we try telling the moon about Maali?" Amber said, leaning back on the bench and tilting her face up to the sky.

"Good idea," Rose said, also looking up.

A half-moon was glowing softly above them, misty-edged from cloud cover. All around them London hummed with noise – car horns, sirens, distant laughter and shouting – but in the darkened garden it felt peaceful.

"Do you want to start?" Rose asked.

"OK." Amber focused her gaze on the moon. Then she pictured what she was about to say being beamed back down to Maali inside the hospital, as if the moon were a giant glowing satellite dish. "I'd just like to say that I hope Maali can feel your presence – and our presence." She pictured the moon's strength pulling tides in and out the world over and she pictured some of that same strength flowing into Maali. "I hope it's making her feel stronger, in what must be a terrible time." Amber looked at Rose. "Do you want to say something?"

"Sure." Rose stood up and stared at the moon. "We really need your help. I know you can't change what's happening to her dad but you can make our girl Maals feel strong. I know you can. And if you have some way of letting her know that we're here for her, that would be awesome too."

"I know," came a soft voice from the darkness.

Rose turned to see Maali standing behind the bench, smiling weakly.

"So, what did you think?" Leon asked as they made their way out of the radio station.

"It was great," Sky replied with a smile. "You were great. I still can't believe you asked me to read."

During one of the show's music breaks Leon had asked if he and Sky could read their "Courage" poem together. Nelson had readily agreed and to her surprise, Sky hadn't felt any of the nerves she experienced performing at spoken-word events. There was something so intimate about radio – just her and the mic and Leon – it was easy to pretend there was no one else listening.

As they stepped out on to Borough High Street, Sky felt much happier. "Thank you so much for this evening," she said.

"It isn't over yet," Leon replied. "Is it?" He looked at her so hopefully it filled her heart with joy. She shook her head. "Good." He took her hand and pulled her into a shop doorway. "There's something I've been meaning to do."

"What?"

Leon took her face in his hands and kissed her gently on the mouth.

Maali looked from Rose to Amber and back again. "Thank you for coming. It made me so happy when I saw your text."

Rose put her arm round her. "Are you kidding? Where else would we be? How's your dad?"

"Still in surgery." Maali checked her phone. Before she'd popped out to see the Moonlight Dreamers she'd given her mum strict instructions to text or call as soon she heard anything. "Where's Sky?"

"She had to go to a radio interview," Amber replied.

"Wow, really?"

"It wasn't her interview," Rose muttered.

Maali looked at her questioningly.

"It doesn't matter," Rose said quickly. "I'm sure she'll get here if she can."

"I'm so grateful you came," Maali said. "It's been so scary."

"Let's sit down." Rose gestured to the bench. Maali sat down and Amber and Rose sat either side of her. For the first time all day she didn't feel alone.

"Do you want to talk about it?" Rose asked.

Maali sighed. "It's been horrible."

"I bet."

"I almost stopped believing in God."

"What?" Rose stared at her. "You can't stop believing in God. You not believing in God would be like – like Taylor Swift not believing in break-up songs."

"I know. But I didn't get why God would do something like this to my dad. It seemed so unfair."

"Life is unfair," Amber muttered. "That's just the way it is."

"But you mustn't let it stop you from being you," Rose added.

"She's right," Amber said. "You can't let bad things beat you."

Maali stared at them. "But you guys don't even believe in God. I thought you'd be happy if I stopped."

Rose shook her head. "All that stuff you say about the gods and goddesses – I might not believe in it, but I do kind of like it, and anyway, it's part of what makes you you."

Maali gave her a relieved smile. "Thank you." She looked up at the moon. "And thank you, Chandra, for bringing my fellow Dreamers to me."

They sat in silence for a moment. Then Maali's phone began to ring. "Oh my God, it's my mum," she stammered.

"It's OK. We're here," Rose said, moving closer.

"Yes," Amber said, placing her hand on Maali's arm.

Hands trembling, Maali answered the call.

"Maali," her mum said, her voice quivering like she was crying. *Why was she crying? What had happened?* Maali's heart plummeted. "He's out of surgery. The operation's done."

Maali gulped. "And was it – is he OK?"

"Yes. They've taken him to the recovery unit."

"I'll be straight up." Maali ended the call and looked at Amber and Rose. "My dad's out of surgery. He's OK!"

Chapter Twenty-eight

As soon as Sky got to school the following morning she went into a cubicle in the girls' toilets to check her phone – there was no way she was going to risk getting it confiscated again. When she'd got home last night she'd texted Maali straight away, apologizing for not coming to see her and asking how her dad was. Maali had replied almost immediately to let her know that the operation was over and her dad was OK. She hadn't seemed upset at all that Sky hadn't come. Then Sky had texted Rose, apologizing for not getting back to her and explaining that she'd had to switch her phone off at the radio station and by the time the interview was over it was too late to join them at the hospital. It was only a white lie. Rose didn't know that the interview had been over by seven-thirty. But Rose hadn't replied. She had no reason to be mad at her. Did she? Sky closed the toilet lid and sat down. Then she took her phone from her pocket. She gave a sigh of relief as she saw she'd got a text from Rose. But her heart sank as she read it.

*Hey, real shame you couldn't be there. We're going
up there again straight after school. Amber will let you
know the details. xo*

It seemed so curt. And Sky couldn't help noticing that
there was only one kiss. Rose always signed off with at least
two. *You're being pathetic*, Sky told herself. *She was probably
just in a hurry when she wrote it.* She leaned over and pressed
the side of her face against the cool wall. Coming in from
the icy cold to the stuffy school had caused her face to burn.
She re-read the text. Amber and Rose were going to the
hospital again. Her stomach began to churn. There was no
way she'd be able to get out of going two days running. She
was going to have to face her fear. She was going to have to
be strong for Maali, no matter how many horrible memories
it unleashed. Sky thought of the day stretching out before
her. All of the teachers she owed homework to; all of the
trouble she was about to get into. Last night, walking along
the South Bank with Leon had been such a welcome escape
from it all. She'd felt so happy as they'd walked and talked
– and, every so often, kissed. But now she was back in the
nightmare that was school, with no escape for hours. And
then she had to go to a hospital and talk about Maali's dad,
who possibly had cancer. Sky closed her eyes and took a
deep breath of the stale air. She had no idea how she was
going to do this.

* * *

"Dad, do you want to hear me roar like a dinosaur?" Namir asked as he plonked himself on the end of the hospital bed.

Maali's dad grinned. "I would love to hear you roar like a dinosaur but I'm not sure the rest of the ward do. Could you roar like a dinosaur who has a sore throat?"

Maali laughed. Even though her dad still looked as frail as he did before the operation, there was a new lightness about him. Her mum had said it was because he was high on painkillers but Maali could tell that it was more than that. He was just as relieved as they were to have the operation out of the way.

"Why don't you and I take a trip to the vending machine?" their mum said to Namir. "That's if you're a dinosaur who likes chocolate?"

Namir was off the bed like a shot. "All dinosaurs like chocolate, silly!"

Maali and her dad watched as her mum and Namir made their way out of the ward.

"How are you doing, pet?" he asked once they'd gone.

"OK. How are you?" Maali studied her dad's face.

"I'm great." He smiled. "Such a relief to get the op out of the way. And to not feel sick any more!"

Maali smiled. But he must have had the same questions hanging over his head that she did, casting clouds over his relief: *Had the tumour been cancerous? Would it come back?*

* * *

Amber came out of the fire exit and looked around. Sky was pacing up and down at the foot of the steps looking really stressed.

"Oh good!" she said when she spotted Amber. "I thought you might not come."

"Why wouldn't I come? We always meet here."

"I thought maybe … never mind. How are you? How was Maali last night? I'm so sorry I wasn't able to join you."

Amber came down the steps. "It's fine. She was OK. Well, as OK as can be expected. And the surgery went well."

"Yes, but…" Sky broke off. "Do they know what it was? The tumour, I mean."

Amber shook her head. "They have to wait a few days for the results of the biopsy."

Sky looked away. She seemed so flustered and on edge.

"We're going back to the hospital to see Maali straight after school. Did Rose tell you?"

"I – uh – I won't be able to make it," Sky said glumly. "I have a detention."

"What for?"

"Not doing my maths homework."

"Oh no! Well, maybe you could join us after your detention? We'll be there for a while, I'm sure."

"No! I can't. I have so much other homework to do. I need to get on top of it or I'll be in detention every day."

Amber stepped closer to Sky. "Are you OK?"

"Yes, yes, I'm fine." Sky looked like she might be about to

burst into tears. "I think maybe I should go to the library. Try and get a start on the homework mountain."

"Oh, OK." Amber stared after Sky as she hurried up the steps.

"Have a nice time with Maali tonight. Send her my love," Sky muttered, before disappearing back into the school.

As Rose made her way along the canal path she felt her anger grow with every step. It had been bad enough when Sky didn't show at the hospital because she was out with Leon, but to blow them out tonight because she had homework was the lamest excuse in the book. Part of her had wondered if the homework excuse was even true. That's why she'd decided to call in on Sky on her way home from the hospital to check for herself that she wasn't out with lover-boy.

She stepped onto the deck at the front of the boat and knocked on the door.

"Rose!" Liam opened the door and grinned at her. "How are ye?"

"Great, thanks."

"And how's your mam?"

"She's OK, I guess. Is Sky home?"

"She is." Liam stepped aside and gestured down the narrow passageway. "Go ahead."

Rose felt a slight wave of relief as she made her way along the boat. At least Sky was at home. At least she hadn't been lying. Then she heard the low murmur of Sky's voice from inside the cabin, followed by a giggle. She must be talking to Leon. Rose rapped loudly on the door.

"Rose?" Sky looked really shocked as she opened the door. Or was it guilt? "What are you doing here?"

"I came to see what's up," Rose said bluntly.

"What do you mean? Wait a second." Sky ran over to her bunk and picked up her phone. "Can I call you back?" She giggled again. "Yes, you too." She put the phone down and turned back to Rose. "Sorry about that, come in."

"Who were you talking to?" Rose said.

"Oh, just Leon."

There was something about the casual way she said it that really pissed Rose off. Bully for Sky that she could be so blasé about having a guy.

"Why didn't you come to the hospital last night?"

"You know why." Sky looked defensive.

"You were out with poet guy."

"Leon. Yes. He'd invited me to go to a radio interview with him." Sky sat down on her bunk.

Rose remained standing. "*His* radio interview?"

"Yes."

"So you didn't have to be there?"

"No, well, yes. I mean, he'd invited me."

"And what, he wouldn't have understood if you told him you had to go see your friend whose dad was having life-saving surgery?"

Sky stared at her. Even in the dim light of the candles

dotted around the cabin Rose could see her face was flushing. "Yes, of course he would," she eventually replied. "But by the time I got your message it was too late. I was already there."

"But I messaged you at five. How long did this interview take? All night?" Rose was really mad now. She could tell Sky was lying. It was written all over her face. And she'd lied again tonight. She hadn't been doing homework after her detention, she'd been on the phone to Leon. "I thought the Moonlight Dreamers was important to you."

"It is."

Rose shook her head. "No, it's not. Not since you met this guy."

Sky stared at her. "What? How?"

"It's like your friends come last now. Everything revolves around him."

"That's not true."

"Yes, it is. You were late for our meeting because you were so busy writing poems in the park or whatever. And twice now you've let Maali down at a time when she really needs us."

"I haven't let her down. I've been texting her."

"Oh, whoop-de-doo!"

Sky got to her feet. "You don't understand."

"Oh, I understand. You're one of those lame girls who dumps her friends the minute a guy comes on the scene."

"I'm not!" Sky looked really angry now.

"Yes, you are, and it's pathetic."

"You're jealous," Sky said, staring at Rose.

"What?"

"Of me and Leon. That's what this is about. You're jealous because I've met someone who likes me back."

There was a horrible silence. Sky's words lodged deep inside of Rose like a knife. "Thanks," she muttered.

"I didn't mean—"

"No, I know exactly what you meant." Rose turned and walked to the door. "Go to hell, Sky."

Chapter Twenty-nine

Clutching her e-ticket and her passport, Amber made her way to the Eurostar terminal at St Pancras. This was it, the day she would finally have something sensational to write about ... hopefully. She pressed her ticket to the scanner and walked through the gate to join the queue of people waiting to go through customs. Her recent trip to Paris with Gerald and Daniel and the Moonlight Dreamers was fresh in her memory so she remembered exactly what to do. She still felt nervous, though. This was the first time she'd ever travelled abroad on her own. But she felt excited, too.

Once she'd put her bag and coat through the X-ray machine she joined the queue for passport control. This was the bit she'd been dreading. What if they were suspicious of a sixteen year old travelling alone? She'd looked it up online and knew that it was allowed, and she'd prepared a cover story just in case – she was off to see her great-aunt Celine from the fictional French side of her family – but it was fine. The grumpy security guard scowled at her and scowled at her passport, then let her through with a grunt. As Amber made her way over to the crowded waiting area she felt awash with happiness. This was it – her adventure had begun.

Maali stepped out on to Brick Lane and took a deep breath of the crisp, cool air. She loved it at this time on a Saturday, before the place was invaded by shoppers and tourists. When the only people around were the road-sweepers and the store-owners getting ready for the new day. She'd wanted to come out with her camera to see if she could find any photos of hope and love. She also craved a little time on her own. The past couple of days since her dad's operation had been a weird confusion of mixed emotions. The surgeon had been very pleased with the results – she'd been able to remove all of the tumour. With every day Maali's dad looked a bit healthier and stronger. He was able to walk and eat. But every day brought them closer to finding out the biopsy results. The happiness they were feeling was as fragile as an eggshell. It could be shattered in an instant.

As Maali walked past the Brick Lane mosque she instinctively thought of God. It had been such a confusing time for her spiritually but the conclusion she'd come to was that as long as she kept it as simple as possible – thinking of God as a source of love and strength and wisdom within everyone – she felt at peace and protected. She took a photo of the mirrored minaret, then carried on walking, looking for other signs of hope and love. She turned down the side street that led to the City Farm. It was far too early for Ash to be there. As she walked across the stubbly patch of grass in front of the council flats she thought of how love-struck she'd felt when she'd seen Ash before. It seemed so silly now. She hadn't loved Ash. She hadn't even really known him. What had happened to her dad had rebooted her somehow. It had made her realize what real love was and that it didn't come in an instant. Like a rare orchid, real love took tender care and time to grow. She went over to the low fence and looked into the farm. Most of the animals were still in their stalls but a white horse was grazing in the far corner of the field. The same horse that had been there the night she'd first met Ash – the one that had been made to look like a unicorn for a drink commercial. It felt fitting somehow that she should see it today – that the thing that had brought her to Ash in the first place should appear just as her crush on him ended. "Thank you," Maali whispered to the horse before taking its picture.

Rose had turned up at the cake stall all fired up to feel differently about Francesca. When not watching depressing documentaries on Netflix and replaying what Sky had said to her on a loop, she'd spent most of Friday coming up with reasons to no longer like Francesca. Most of these involved imagining her with Pierre in various scenarios that made her want to puke her guts up. But as soon as she arrived and saw Francesca putting the cakes out on the stall, as soon as she saw her shiny dark hair cascading in curls around her shoulders, as soon as she saw her hour-glass figure squeezed into yet another beautiful dress, as soon as she saw the way Francesca's face lit up when she saw Rose, all the old feelings came flooding back. And if anything, they felt even more powerful now they were tinged with the tragic air of unrequitedness. Rose wasn't even sure if unrequitedness was a word, but if it was, she was currently it personified.

"Rose! How is your friend? Is she OK?" Francesca cried.

It took Rose a couple of seconds to remember her excuse for leaving the shop on Monday night.

"Yes, she's fine now, thanks," she replied. She couldn't help feeling a bitter pang as she thought back to Thursday night on the canal and how Leon had rung Sky. How he "liked her back", as Sky had put it. Much as Rose hated to admit it, it had made her own pain feel less intense when she'd thought that Sky might be a walking, talking, crying-to-the-moon case of unrequited love too. But no, it wasn't to be. Sky was all loved up and Rose was alone in her pathetic-ness.

"Oh, thank goodness," Francesca said. "You looked so worried about her."

"Yes. Yes, I was." Rose couldn't help giving a bitter laugh. How times had changed. She might have felt a pang of envy about Leon liking Sky but that didn't alter the fact that Sky had been bang out of line letting Maali down.

"I need to ask you a favour and if it is not OK then that's fine, I will totally understand," Francesca said.

"Of course. What is it?" Rose felt a tingle of excitement at the prospect of helping Francesca in some way. It was as if the rest of her body hadn't got the memo from her brain that this was now an entirely futile cause.

"Catherine has rung in sick, which means I'm one short in the shop today. I know I said I'd work here with you for the whole of today but do you think you would be OK on your own for a while? You did so well last week, I'm sure you can do it. And I would pay you extra too."

Rose felt a dull thud of disappointment. "Sure. I'll be fine," she said.

"Oh, thank you!" Francesca hugged her. Her perfume smelled as delicious as ever but this time it was a little too sweet, like something an evil fairy-tale princess would wear to ensnare her victims.

"No problem." Rose pulled away. Jet was staring at them from the jewellery stall. The slogan on her t-shirt read DIE ANGRY! A message Rose felt certain Jet would live up to.

"Melvin!" Francesca called over to Mel. "I will need to leave Rose on her own for a while. Will it be OK for you to keep an eye on the stall if she needs to take a break? In case you need a toilet break," she whispered to Rose.

"Of course, darlin'," Mel called back. "Anything for you girls, especially if there's a cake in it for me."

"But of course!" Francesca cried. She turned back to Rose. "So I will go to the shop now and make sure they're OK. Then I will be back with you in time for the lunchtime rush."

"Sure." Rose wondered if it was actually possible to wilt from disappointment. She felt dangerously close to finding out.

"Cheer up, love, it might never happen," Mel said, appearing at the stall with his trademark cheeky grin.

"It already has," Rose replied glumly. She looked past Mel into the market. A small woman wearing an orange hippy-style poncho, baseball cap and huge pair of sunglasses was approaching the stall. Rose put on her best customer service smile. "Hey, can I help you? Oh my God! Mom! Is that you?"

Savannah nodded and glanced around nervously. "Shh."

"What are you doing here?" Rose's pulse quickened. The only reason Savannah would come here on her own was if there'd been some kind of emergency. "Is everything OK?"

Mel had gone back to his stall but she could see him looking over at them curiously.

Savannah nodded.

"Then why are you here?"

"I wanted to see where you worked."

"You did? Why?"

Savannah glared at her over the top of her shades. "You're my daughter. I care about where you work, OK?"

"OK." Rose looked her up and down. "Where'd you get the poncho from, Mom? Crusty Hippy dot com?"

"Liam lent it to me. I didn't want to be recognized."

"Liam?" This was getting weirder by the minute. "When did you see Liam?"

"Just now. I had something I needed to discuss with him."

Savannah looked at the cakes on the stall. "Did you make these?"

"Some of them."

Savannah nodded. Her huge glasses made it impossible to read her expression.

"So what's the deal? Why are you really here?"

"I'd like to buy some cakes."

Rose could barely keep herself from gaping. "For real?"

Savannah nodded.

"You do realize that they contain sugar and flour and all kinds of fat?"

Savannah pursed her lips. "There's no need to be sarcastic, Rose. I am aware of what goes into a cake."

"All righty then, just checking." Rose picked up the cake tongs. "Which one would you like?"

"I'll take two dozen. Give me an assortment."

"Two dozen? But that's, like, twenty-four!"

"Yes, I am able to count, too."

Rose put the tongs down on top of the glass cabinet. "Mom, what are you going to do with twenty-four cakes?"

"Do you want my custom or not?"

"Yes, of course – but – OK then." Rose took two of the biggest boxes from beneath the stall and started filling them with cupcakes. Her mom might have officially lost the plot but at least Francesca would be pleased. They might sell out again by the end of the day. *Arrrgh!* Rose felt a burst of anger at herself. Why was she still so bothered about making

Francesca happy? She put the cake boxes into a bag and handed them to Savannah. "How did you even get here?" Savannah never went out in public unaccompanied any more.

"Margot drove. She's waiting in a parking bay just outside the market. We're on our way to a *Vagina Vows* workshop."

"Eew, Mom!"

"What? I thought it would be nice to get some cakes for the participants – to have during our break. How much do I owe you?" Savannah got out her platinum credit card and handed it to Rose. "Are you coming home after work?"

"I guess."

"Good. I have something I need to talk to you about." Savannah tapped her pin number into the card reader. "You shouldn't have thrown those cakes out, by the way. They were delicious."

"You ate one?" Rose stared at her, open-mouthed.

"I ate two. I loved the combination of the chocolate and the chilli." Savannah stepped back and looked at the stall. "So, this is what all the fuss is about, huh?"

Rose instantly felt defensive. Was she about to make a dig? "Yes."

Savannah nodded. "OK. Good. I'll see you at home."

"Yes, see ya." Rose watched as Savannah hurried out of the market. The way she walked in public places – head down, shoulders hunched, not wanting to be seen – was the total opposite to her catwalk strut. Rose sat down on the stool behind the stall and tried to take in everything that had just happened. But all she got were unanswered questions. Why had her mom been to see Liam? Why had she come to check out the stall? And what the hell went on at a *Vagina Vows* workshop?

Chapter Thirty

Amber took a sip of her bitter coffee and gazed along the bustling street. As soon as she'd arrived in Paris she'd come straight to Montmartre, one of Oscar Wilde's favourite haunts. As she looked up the hill to the stunning white-domed church at the top she could see why. Montmartre was beautiful. Paris was beautiful. The minute Amber had set foot in the Metro system she'd fallen in love. With its art deco station signs and dramatic station names – names like *Saint-Augustine* and *Château Rouge* and *Notre-Dame-de-Lorette* – it was so different from London. She felt like a character in an arty French movie – mysterious and adventurous and so alive. Here, dressed in her plum-coloured suit and black fedora, she didn't feel like she stood out – she felt like she fitted right in. She loved the way all the cafés had their pavement seats facing outwards so that everyone could people-watch. She loved the lilting voices of the French people sitting around her outside the café. She loved how beautiful and dramatic their conversations sounded. Already she was seeing why writers such as Oscar Wilde had been drawn to Paris – there was so much here to stimulate the imagination. She took out her notepad and began to write.

Sky looked at the pile of books on her cabin floor and sighed. She was supposed to be spending the weekend getting on top of her homework but it was so hard to concentrate. Every time she looked around the cabin she'd get a flashback to Thursday night – Rose had looked so angry and hurt. At the time it had seemed obvious to Sky that Rose was jealous; but now she wasn't so sure. The more time that passed, the more doubtful she became. What if Rose had genuinely been angry out of her loyalty to Maali? Why couldn't Sky have told her the truth about her fear of hospitals instead of letting things get so out of hand? What if Rose never wanted to see her again? What would happen to the Moonlight Dreamers then? Sky looked back at her text books. How could she concentrate on homework when everything had gone so wrong? The alert went off on her phone and she grabbed it, hoping it was Rose. But it was a text from Leon.

Really looking forward to seeing you later Sky-Blue. xx

Sky felt a burst of warmth. Leon had invited her to a spoken word event in Vauxhall that night. **Really looking forward to seeing you too xx**, she typed back. And she was. Right now, being with Leon was the only place she felt free from stress. He didn't know the Moonlight Dreamers. He didn't know about Sky's fear of hospitals. He didn't know what she was going through at school. He didn't know any of it. When she was with him she could pretend she was happy and strong. When she was with him she could escape into a dream-like world of poetry and kisses. Sky looked at her battered notebook next to her bunk. She could escape into that world right now, through her pen. She shoved her homework books into the corner and began to write.

Amber climbed the last of the steps up Montmartre hill. All the way up she'd stopped herself from turning round. She'd wanted to save the view for when she got to the top. It was well worth the wait. As Amber slowly turned around she couldn't help gasping. The whole of Paris lay spread out beneath her, its white buildings glowing pale gold in the winter sun. A crowd had gathered around a busker on the plateau below. He had long dark hair and olive skin and was holding a battered guitar covered in stickers.

"Welcome to Paris!" he cried in a heavy French accent. "The city that can change your life for ever."

As she drank in the stunning landscape, Amber could definitely believe him. When she'd come to Paris last year her sole focus had been to see Oscar Wilde's grave. She'd felt like a tourist, like an outsider looking in. But coming here on her own was a completely different experience. This time she felt the heady Parisian atmosphere – the dramatic place names, the passionate people, the smells of freshly baked bread and cigarette smoke and coffee and wine – soaking into her. This time she felt part of it – an insider, looking out.

"This is a song I think you all will know," the busker said.

A ripple of applause broke out, Amber looked back at Sacré-Coeur. Even though she didn't believe in God and had never once gone to church, she couldn't help feeling awestruck. With its white turrets and domes it looked like the palace from a fairy tale. She turned to look back down the hill and pictured Oscar Wilde standing in this exact same spot all those years before. She hoped he had moments of happiness just like the one she was experiencing before he died. She hoped his final years weren't all sorrow-filled.

The busker started to sing "Let It Be", and a shiver ran up Amber's spine as the crowd joined in.

As Amber hummed along, she pictured all the things she'd been worrying about drifting away like notes on the breeze.

Rose trudged up the hill towards home feeling laden down with gloom. Her day at work had ended spectacularly badly when Francesca had returned to the stall with Pierre in tow to help her pack away. They didn't need his help. They'd done just fine the previous week. It was so cringey seeing them giggling and flirting together. It was the kind of behaviour that would normally make Rose tell them to "get a room". But she didn't want Francesca to get a room with Pierre. She didn't want her doing anything in private with him. The mere thought made her skin crawl. It was weird how everything she'd loved about Francesca – her smile, her accent, her laugh – seemed repellent now it was being directed towards Pierre. All Rose wanted was to get home, take a long bath with one of her mom's smelliest bath bombs and soak all of the stress away.

She opened the door and stepped into the hallway. The first unexpected thing she noticed was her mom's suitcase by the foot of the stairs. The second was the smell. Instead of the usual aroma of Savannah's favourite bergamot and lime-scented candles, Rose was sure she could smell something baking. She sniffed the air. It smelled fruity and spicy and sweet. Maybe Savannah was burning one of the American candles they always had at Thanksgiving. *Pumpkin Pie* or *Cinnamon Spice* or whatever. But as Rose crossed the hall she realized the smell was definitely coming from the kitchen.

"Mom! What's going on?"

Savannah was standing in the middle of the kitchen. In what appeared to be some kind of flour-induced apocalypse. The counter, the floor and Savannah herself were all covered in a white, powdery dust. "I'm baking," she said with a grin.

Rose activated her alcohol sensor. But Savannah didn't appear to be swaying and her speech didn't seem to be slurred. "OK. And what are you baking?"

"A pie." Savannah looked and sounded totally sober. Maybe she'd OD-ed on green juice. Maybe she was experiencing some kind of weird kale-induced high.

"What kind of pie?"

"Apple. I think I might have put in a little too much cinnamon, though." Savannah frowned at the oven. "I was trying to remember my grandma's recipe. Does half a cup sound about right to you?"

"Half a cup of cinnamon? In one pie?!"

"Uh-huh."

Rose sat down at the breakfast bar. "That might be a little on the spicy side."

Savannah sighed. "It's been so long since I baked anything. I used to love it when I was a kid."

"You did?"

"I used to help my grandma all the time. She was such a great baker – must be where you get it from." Savannah sat down opposite Rose and lit a cigarette. "Do you want a coffee?"

"Please."

Savannah rested her cigarette in the ashtray and fetched the jug of coffee and two mugs. "I've been doing a lot of thinking since our – since we spoke about…"

"Me coming out?" Rose offered.

"Yes." Savannah poured a cup of coffee and handed it to her. "I feel like I've really let you down. Again."

Rose instinctively wanted to lie and tell her that she hadn't, but she bit her tongue. It was so rare that her mom apologized, she wanted to hear what else she had to say.

Savannah poured herself a cup. "I was so hurt when your

dad told me you'd told him first — I just did what I always do and I lashed out. I'm really sorry. And I want to make some changes, some serious changes."

"Like what?" Rose took a sip of coffee and braced herself.

"I want to be a real mom. I want to do real mom things, like be there for you and bake you pies." Savannah leapt to her feet. "Shit! The pie!" She grabbed the hand towel and opened the oven. "Oh no! It's burnt." She plonked the pie on the counter. The crust was black and there was steam coming from a crack in the lid. Savannah looked like she might be about to cry.

"It's OK," Rose said quickly. "We can eat around the black bits."

The smoke alarm began to beep and they burst out laughing.

When they finally got the alarm to stop, they sat down at the breakfast bar and Savannah took a drag on her cigarette.

"So, you're gay."

"Yes." Rose looked at her anxiously. She got that her mom was pissed at her for telling Jason first but was she OK about the actual sexuality bit?

"I love you. You know that, right?"

Rose nodded, even though there'd been times lately when she hadn't been so sure.

"And I'm so proud of you." She place her hand over Rose's. "Seeing you today on that stall, looking so grown-up, I felt as if my heart was going to burst with pride."

"For real?"

"For real. So I want you to know that your sexuality makes no difference to me. If anything it just makes me love you more."

Rose felt a lump growing in her throat. "How?"

"Because it's another example of how fearless you are. I love that about you."

"I'm not fearless, Mom. I get frightened a lot."

Savannah squeezed her hand. "Well, then I love how you overcome your fear and don't let it dictate what you do. Not like me." She looked so sad it made Rose's heart ache.

"What are you afraid of, Mom?"

Savannah sighed. "So many things. Growing old, getting fat, losing my career. But I don't want to be like that any more. I want to be more like you."

"Wow." Rose felt stunned. Her whole life Savannah had seemed like the brightest star in the sky. A trailblazer. An icon. Now here she was saying she wanted to be more like Rose.

"When I was with Liam I had a glimpse of how life could be if I stopped being scared, but I blew it. I don't want to blow it with you."

"You really liked him, didn't you?"

Savannah nodded.

"Oh, Mom." Rose went around the breakfast bar and put her arm round her.

But Savannah shook it off. "No. I should be the one

being strong for you. I'm the parent here. So I've made some decisions."

"What decisions?" Rose waited anxiously.

"I've started going to meetings again."

"AA?"

"Uh-huh. I don't like what drink does to me. I don't like how it clouds my judgement and makes me so … so…"

"Irrational?"

"Well, I was going to say impetuous, but OK, irrational. And I'm going to go on a retreat Margot's running."

"Margot? The Vagina lady?"

"Right. She's such a great woman, Rose. She's really helping me to see how I've given away my power."

"OK." Rose wasn't sure what to make of this. Her mom had a tendency to pick up new fads the same way she picked up new outfits. She cast them off just as quickly too. But her giving up the booze had to be a good thing.

"It's only for a few days and Liam's said he'll take care of you while I'm away."

Rose's heart sank. "What, on the houseboat?"

"Yes. So you'll be able to hang out with Sky loads." Savannah looked at her hopefully. "Is that OK?"

How could she tell Savannah she'd fallen out with Sky when she was making so much effort to change? It took everything Rose had to fake a smile. "Of course."

"I really want to be a better mom for you, Rose."

"I know." Rose looked down at the pie. "Shall we try some?"

"If you're feeling brave enough."

"Of course I'm feeling brave enough. I'm the poster child for feeling the fear and eating it anyway." Rose got a couple of forks and they dug through the burnt crust. The apple mixture inside was as brown as mud. They both took a mouthful. The taste of cinnamon was overpowering but Rose somehow managed to swallow it. Savannah, on the other hand, looked as if she was chewing on a wasp.

"Eeeew!" she spluttered, spitting her pie into the ashtray. "Can we please just accept that you are the baker in the family?" She grabbed her coffee and downed half of it. "I'll just focus on the other parts of being a mom. Like – like talking to you about feelings and tucking you in at night. "

"Mom, I'm sixteen! OK, it's a deal … apart from the tucking-in bit." Rose high-fived her over the counter. As she watched Savannah light another cigarette she felt something dangerously close to happy. Savannah might not be the most conventional mom in the world, but she was *her* dysfunctional mom and, right now, she wouldn't trade her for anyone.

Chapter Thirty-one

Sky followed Leon under one of the huge archways next to Vauxhall station. A homeless man sat hunched against the wall, holding out an old coffee cup. His face and hands were streaked with dirt.

"Spare change," he muttered without even looking up as Leon and Sky approached.

Leon fumbled in his pocket and put some money in the cup. "Stay safe, man."

The man nodded. "Thanks. God bless."

Sky felt a pang in her chest as she searched in her pocket for some change. There was so much suffering going on in the world. Why didn't people do more to try to change it? Why did most people choose to look the other way?

"Did you bring something to read?" Leon asked as they reached the end of the archway.

"I brought something but I'm not sure I'll read it. I only wrote it this afternoon — it might be too raw."

"No such thing as too raw when it comes to poetry." Leon smiled. "In my opinion, anyway."

"Maybe." Sky's stomach churned as she thought of what had happened the last time she'd read in front of a room full of strangers.

"Don't be scared," he said, as if reading her mind. "It's a really friendly crowd at this gig. You're gonna be great."

"Thank you."

They crossed a busy intersection and Leon led her into some communal gardens. She felt the back of his hand brush against hers. Then, suddenly, as if of their own accord, their fingers linked, causing Sky's skin to tingle.

"You OK, Sky-Blue?" he said with a grin.

Sky nodded. Right now, she felt OK to infinity.

Amber took a bite of her warm baguette and stared up at Notre-Dame. If Sacré-Coeur was like a palace from a fairy tale, then Notre-Dame was more like something from a gothic horror story, especially now darkness had fallen. Amber loved it, though. She loved imagining the grim-faced gargoyles carved into the stone turrets coming to life at the stroke of midnight, cackling loudly as they scampered about the Parisian streets. She felt certain that Oscar Wilde would have loved Notre-Dame too. Once again, she imagined him standing in exactly the same spot as her, gazing up at the huge cathedral for inspiration. She looked at the time on her pocket-watch. There was just under an hour before she'd need to get back to the station. Time for one more wander.

"Where to next, Oscar?" she whispered as she stuffed her

baguette into her bag. She wandered over to some stone steps leading away from the cathedral. The steps took her down to a quaint little side street. Amber stared in amazement. There in front of her was the most magical-looking bookshop she had ever seen. A yellow and black sign saying SHAKESPEARE AND COMPANY hung over the sea-green shop-front. Golden light shone out into the darkness, illuminating the walls crammed with books inside. There were shelves full of books on the pavement outside, too, as if the shop was literally bursting at the seams. Amber seriously began to wonder if she might be dreaming. As she stepped inside she thought she might actually pass out from excitement. The walls were lined from floor to ceiling with wooden shelves bursting with books and the floor was filled with tables stacked with books. An old-fashioned chandelier hung from the ceiling and the handwritten signs for the different sections were stuck skew-whiff on the shelves. The signs were in English too, Amber realized.

As she wandered further into the shop she fell deeper and deeper in love. She loved the wooden ladders leaning against the walls, reaching up to the highest shelves. She loved the quotes painted on what little space was left on the walls. Especially the one that read: *"Be not inhospitable to strangers, lest they be angels in disguise."* She loved the antique armchairs tucked away in darkened corners. She loved the fact that even the stairs leading to the second floor had bookshelves built into them. And as for the books... As Amber began scanning the shelves she felt like crying for joy. She was standing inside a treasure trove of antique books and first editions. *And* they were all in English!

The next half an hour passed in a blur of words. Then, when it was time to leave, she took a first edition of Oscar Wilde's *De Profundis* over to pay.

"*Bonsoir,*" she said to the pale, thin young man behind the counter.

"Good evening," he replied in a crisp British accent.

"Oh, you're English," she said.

"I certainly am." He took the book from her. "And you are too. I could tell from your French accent. Or lack of. Excellent choice, by the way." He gestured to the book.

Amber smiled. "Thank you." She looked around the shop and sighed. "You're so lucky to be working here."

"I don't just work here. I live here, too," the young man replied, putting the book into a brown paper bag.

"What do you mean?"

"While I write my first novel."

"But…" Amber broke off, speechless, certain she had to be dreaming again.

"They let young aspiring writers stay here for free in exchange for helping in the shop," the man explained. "There are beds tucked away behind the shelves and upstairs."

"But – but that sounds perfect!" Amber exclaimed.

The guy grinned. "I know, right?"

Amber pictured herself one day standing behind the

counter serving people in this magical shop. Sleeping in a little bed tucked away in a corner, surrounded by books. Breathing in inspiration from all the writers who'd gone before her as she slept and wrote. She wanted to cry with joy. She paid for her book and took one last look around the shop. Instead of feeling sad that she was leaving, she felt joyful in the certainty that one day she'd return – to work and write and stay here too. She had a new dream and it was one she was determined to make come true.

"Thank you, Oscar," she whispered as she walked out into the cool night air.

Sky had always liked the name Eloise. She'd liked the way it rolled off the tongue in fat, round syllables. She'd liked the way it sounded like melody and all the harmonious connotations that conjured. But not any more. As she watched a performance poet called Eloise Ebony giggling flirtatiously with Leon she didn't care if she never heard the name again.

The event was halfway through and most of the audience were milling around a table of refreshments at the back of the hall. But not Eloise. She'd come over to Leon as soon as the first half was over and started gushing about how much she "loved his work" and how he was "like, so inspirational". To be fair, Leon had read a stunning piece right before the break, all about what it had been like growing up without a dad. Even though his story was very different from hers because Leon's dad had chosen to leave him and his family, parts of the poem struck Sky to the core: they were so reminiscent of how she'd felt after her mum died. But she hadn't been able to tell Leon any of this because Eloise had got there first, gushing all over him. Tired of feeling like a spare part, Sky had made her excuses and gone to get a drink. As she stood in line for the refreshments table she checked her phone, hoping there might be a text from Rose. But there was nothing. Sky wondered if Rose and Amber had gone to see Maali again and not bothered to invite her this time. She pictured them talking about her the way Rose had done the other night; about how much she'd changed since meeting Leon. She looked over at him. Eloise was now sitting in Sky's chair, leaning close, whispering in Leon's ear. Sky prickled with anger. She hated girls like this, who saw guys as being there for the taking, regardless of who they might already be with. She picked up a plastic cup of lukewarm apple juice and marched back to her seat.

"It would be so awesome to write something together," she heard Eloise saying.

What the hell? Had Leon asked Eloise to write a poem with him, just like he'd done with her? Maybe she'd been right after all when she was drunk the other night. Maybe he did do this kind of thing with all the girls. *It's not as if he's your boyfriend, though,* her inner voice chided. Yes, but we have kissed, she thought. And we did hold hands. *Tonight*, we held hands *tonight*.

"Sky!" Leon said, finally noticing she was back. "Oh, you got a drink."

"Yes," Sky replied bluntly.

"I can get you one," Eloise said, jumping to her feet. She was wearing a leopard-print top, tight jeans and high-heeled boots. Her skin was slightly darker than Leon's and her well-toned arms glistened in the spotlights. She towered over Sky like an Amazonian goddess.

"Thank you. I'll just have water, please," Leon replied.

Sky sat back down. Anger knotted inside her.

"So, what do you think?" Leon asked. "Are you enjoying it?"

"Yeah, it's good," Sky said flatly. But all of her excitement had gone. She didn't want to be here, having to deal with self-obsessed girls like Eloise. She wanted to be with her real friends. She wanted to be with the Moonlight Dreamers.

"Here you go!" Eloise said in a sing-song voice, returning with a bottle of water for Leon.

"Thanks." Leon took the water and looked at Sky. "Did you guys meet? Eloise, this is Sky. Sky, Eloise."

Sky looked at Eloise and forced herself to smile. Eloise's smile seemed equally forced as she sat down in a seat directly across the aisle from them.

As soon as the MC came back on stage Sky's anger started transforming into determination. She was sick of feeling like a victim; sick of not speaking her truth – about school; about Maali's dad and how frightened his illness had made her feel;

how terrified she was that Maali would lose him the same way she'd lost her mum; and now about Eloise. When the MC asked who'd like to read next, her arm shot up, arrow-straight.

FREE TO BE

BY Sky Cassidy

When your day is divided by lessons and bells,
when your head wants to burst from the sounds and
the smells,
when you long to be heard but you're not even seen,
when you know you're unique but you're labelled "*a*
teen",
when your bag is weighed down with homework and
books,
when you're sick of the digs and the jibes and the
looks,
when you start skipping meals 'cos you're told to be
thin,
when the anger you feel forms scars on your skin,
when you pray someone hears your desperate plea:
When will I ever be free to be me?

When your fears lie in wait at the foot of your bed,
when the things that they say won't get out of your
head,
when you can't give them voice so you silently scream,
when you're too scared to act and you can't even
dream,
when you're told that you're anxious and given a pill,
but no one considers that society's ill,

when they dumb you and numb you and give you no
   voice,
so that apathy seems like your only choice,
and nobody hears your desperate plea:
When will I ever be free to be me?

Then you finally decide that enough is enough,
that you just haven't got what it takes to be "tough".
But that doesn't matter because "tough" is for fools,
"tough" makes you sheep, makes you obey the rules.
And you want to question and challenge and thrive,
you want to feel grateful for being alive,
so you open your eyes to a new way to see,
A way that will help you to be free to be.

You look to the others who've blazed this same trail,
you search for examples inside of their tales,
you learn that they all had their own doubts and fears,
you read how pain caused them to cry bitter tears.
But you also find hope in their stories of strife,
and you see how they grabbed this gift of a life,
and they took it and shook it and made it their own,
and they found deep inside them a place to call home.
You cry as you see how they turned fear to gain
but this time the tears that you cry aren't of pain.
This time the tears are of sweet clarity,
Because this time they help you to be free to be.

DEFIANTLY DIFFERENT

My whole teenage life, I've been made to feel wrong for being me.

Wrong for having two dads.

Wrong for dressing the way I do … in vintage men's clothes.

Wrong for not being attracted to boys … and not being attracted to girls either.

Wrong for simply existing half the time.

A lot of you have been emailing me asking why I haven't blogged much lately.

The truth is, I've been feeling really blocked.

And I've been feeling really blocked because I've been feeling really bad about myself for being so different and unsure of who I'm supposed to be.

Then, last week, someone started posting hateful comments on this blog.

My first reaction was to run away and hide. To stop blogging for good.

But that would mean the hater had won. And I'm not going to let her win.

Because now I see that being different is something

to be proud of and something that can lead to a sensational life.

I'm writing this blog post in Paris. And I'm in Paris because I realized that I had a choice. I could either let the haters win or I could choose to wear my difference with pride.

So I'm wearing it with pride outside a café in Montmartre, along with a plum-coloured pinstripe suit and fedora, and thinking of my hero, Oscar Wilde.

Oscar Wilde came to Paris because he felt shunned by his home country, England. The tragedy was, he ended up being shunned here, too. But times are changing. If Oscar was living in the UK now, he'd be totally free to be his true self; to write whatever he liked and to love whoever he liked.

Oscar died in Paris, unloved and alone, because it was so difficult to be different back then.

But it isn't so difficult to be different any more – at least, not where I live. So I feel like I owe it to Oscar to look on the bright side. To see how lucky I am. And to be defiantly different in honour of all the people in the past – and all the people in other parts of the world today – who don't have that luxury. Who get locked up or even killed for being different.

Yes, I might be different, but I'm DEFIANTLY DIFFERENT – and I'm not going to hide away. I'm going to write what I like and dress how I like and

love, or not love, who I like. And I'm going to dream sensational dreams. And let them lead me to live sensational adventures.

I'm going to leave you with this quote from my beloved Oscar, who, even when he was dying alone in a dingy hotel in Paris, had the humour to write:

> *"This wallpaper and I are fighting a duel to the death.*
> *Either it goes or I do."*

I'm really sorry you lost that duel, Oscar, but I'm going to make sure you didn't die in vain, by making my life as sensational as possible and embracing my differences.

Amber

Chapter Thirty-two

As Sky put the finishing touches to her History essay, a flock of geese landed with a splash on the canal outside. It was as if they were giving her an ironic fanfare for finally completing a piece of homework. Sky sat back and sighed. One assignment down, five to go. Even though it was Sunday she'd set her alarm for super early, determined to tackle her homework once and for all. Something had shifted in her last night as she read her poem on the open mic. As she'd spoken her deepest feelings out loud a force had built within her, bigger and bigger, until it felt as if she wasn't just reading the poem – it felt as if she *was* the poem. And as the anger and sorrow and determination and hope of the words all swirled around inside her, as she rode the waves of passion and emotion she had an epiphany. She'd been giving school way too much power, letting it get to her so much. Poetry was her passion – writing it and performing it – and nobody could take that away from her. Yes, school was stressful, but she wasn't going to be there for ever. School wasn't a final destination: it was a stepping stone. And if she viewed it like that – as a stepping stone to much better, brighter things – it lost its ability to overwhelm her. Then, on her way home last night, she'd got a notification from *Wilde at Heart* and read a blog post from Amber that had blown her mind. Amber had gone to Paris! And reading her defiant declaration of being proud to be different made Sky want to jump for joy. Amber had included a photo with her blog – a selfie of her sitting outside a Parisian café – looking so happy and free. Even though she'd been bullied at school and apparently on her blog, she hadn't sat around feeling sorry for herself, she'd done something about it. And that's how Sky wanted to live too. She'd sent Amber a text when she got home apologizing for being a rubbish friend and telling her how inspiring she found her words. Sky smiled as she re-read Amber's reply.

You haven't been a rubbish friend at all. You've been going through a really tough time and we all under-stand. And thank you so much! I've been getting some lovely messages about the blog. Paris was amazing! Amber x

Sky felt a wistful pang. She wanted to believe that her friends understood what she'd been going through recently – but she knew this wasn't true of Rose. She still hadn't heard from her. She scrolled down to Leon's last text.

Thanks for a great night Sky-Blue. And for the great poem. Raw is real! Xx

Sky smiled. When the event finished last night Eloise had come sidling up to Leon, asking if they, but looking only at him, wanted to come to a party in Brixton. To Sky's relief Leon shook his head. "We have an urgent date with a bag of chips," he'd said, putting his arm round Sky. As they'd walked back to the station, sharing a bag of hot, salty chips, he asked her what had inspired her poem and it had all come tumbling out. How she'd been feeling about school, her fear about Maali's dad ending up like her mum, even her argument with Rose. Leon hugged her. Then he'd told her about how, after his friend Tyrone was stabbed, he'd felt so angry at the world he'd shut everyone out – even the people closest to him. "Good friends are hard to find," he said. "You need to keep them close – even when they say things that hurt you."

Sky scrolled through her contacts till she got to Rose, but before she could send her a text she heard Liam making his way down the passageway.

"Sky, are ye awake? I've got a surprise."

"What kind of surprise?" Sky said, opening the door. "Oh!"

Rose was standing there holding a backpack. Her expression was deadly serious, while Liam was grinning like a Cheshire cat.

"She's come to stay with us," he said. "Isn't it grand?"

* * *

Rose sat on the end of Sky's bunk.

"What are you doing here?" Sky said, looking from Rose to her backpack.

Rose frowned. Sky didn't exactly seem thrilled at her arrival, which was pretty darn rude of her. Surely Rose should be the one who was pissed.

"OK, I'm going to head off to the High Road to get us all some breakfast," Liam said from the cabin door. "How does croissants and coffee sound?"

"Sounds awesome," Rose said. It felt good to be back around Liam at least. There was something instantly calming about him. It must be all the meditation he did.

"Great," Liam said. "See you in a bit."

Rose turned back to Sky. She was standing by the porthole on the other side of the cabin, holding her phone. Rose bristled. She'd probably been about to call Leon. "Do you want me to go?" she asked, picking up her bag. The last thing she wanted was to play gooseberry all week; she'd rather be on her own, back in Hampstead.

"What? No! Of course not!" Sky's frown faded. "I'm really glad you're here. You have no idea how glad."

Rose frowned. "Seriously?"

"Yes." Sky started fiddling with the drawstring on her pyjamas. "I was just about to call you."

Rose felt a rush of relief. "Why?"

"To say sorry. And to explain."

Rose put her bag down. "Explain what?"

"Why I've been so weird – about visiting Maali." Sky sat down on the bunk opposite. "It didn't have anything to do with Leon. This is going to sound really pathetic but I have a phobia of hospitals."

"How come?" Rose studied her face for any sign that she was lying.

"Because…" Sky looked down into her lap. "Because that's where my mum died – in a hospital. And ever since Maali's dad was diagnosed with a brain tumour I've been terrified that the same thing's going to happen to him. And when I've thought about having to go to a hospital to see her, I've freaked out. I'm really sorry."

"Why didn't you tell me?" Rose said softly.

"I was embarrassed. I was already feeling bad enough about being such a wuss about school."

Rose came and sat down next to her. "You aren't a wuss."

"Really?"

Rose shook her head. "I'm sorry too."

"What for?"

"Saying what I did about Leon. You were right. I was jealous. I was so gutted about Francesca and when things worked out for you guys I——" She broke off. This fessing up business was hard. "And I was scared I was going to lose you. That you'd lose interest in the Moonlight Dreamers."

Sky looked visibly shocked. "I'd never lose interest in you guys. You're the best thing that ever happened to me."

"Better than poet guy?" Rose couldn't help asking.

"Yes!"

Rose gave a relieved grin.

"I'm really sorry about Francesca," Sky said. "And for saying what I did."

"It's OK." Rose sighed. "I think I've figured out a meaning to it all. Maybe we are meant to meet certain people but it's not always for the reason we think."

"How do you mean?"

"I've been cursing the day I ever laid eyes on Francesca but that's just because I'm gutted that she isn't into me. The fact is, she made me realize what I want to do with my life and she's given me my first break on that path. Maybe that's why I was meant to meet her, to help me achieve my patissier dream, not my, like, gay dream."

They looked at each other and laughed.

"I've really missed you," Sky said, moving closer to Rose.

Rose took hold of her hand. "I've missed you too."

Chapter Thirty-three

"How about a game of I Spy?" Maali's dad said, looking at her and her mum with a grin. A terrified grin. Today was the day they were getting the biopsy results and an icy fear hung over all of them. They'd tried to distract themselves by playing countless games of charades but it didn't work. At any moment now the consultant could come striding into the ward and hand her dad a possible death sentence. Maali looked at the Kali figurine on the bedside cupboard. She'd brought it to the hospital with them this morning to help bring them strength. *Please, Kali. Please let it be good news*, Maali silently prayed. Kali glared back at her fiercely.

Sky got into school half an hour early – a record for her – and made her way to her form room. School wasn't so bad at this time of day, with no other students about. The corridors felt wider and the only sound she could hear was the distant hum of the traffic outside. She opened her form-room door and breathed a sigh of relief: Mrs Bayliss was already there, once again hunched over a pile of marking.

"Excuse me, Mrs Bayliss, I was wondering if I could talk to you about something."

Mrs Bayliss looked up, surprised. "Sky. This is very bright and early for you."

"Yes, I know. I was just wondering…" When Sky had practised this with Rose last night it had gone really smoothly, but now that she was here, standing in front of the real Mrs Bayliss, she felt tongue-tied.

Mrs Bayliss took off her glasses and leaned back in her chair. "Yes?"

"Well, it's just that…" Sky took a step closer. "As you know, I'd never been to a secondary school before I came here."

"Yes."

"And so it's given me a unique perspective … on how things are done here."

Mrs Bayliss stared at her. "Would you care to elaborate?"

For a second, Sky's mind went totally blank, until the chorus from Leon's poem started echoing through it. *Be the change. Be the change.* How could she be the change she wanted to see in the school system if she didn't say anything?

"I just think that the way things are done can be so pressurized." Sky had wanted to say "are" so pressurized but Rose had made her change it to "can be" to be more tactful.

"Well, it's bound to be stressful to come into the school system at such a late stage," Mrs Bayliss said, nodding sympathetically. "As I said to you the other day, if there's anything I can—"

"I'm not talking about for me," Sky interrupted. "I'm talking about for everyone. I mean, you guys don't even hide the fact that it's so — it *can be* so stressful. We have to have classes on anxiety in PSHE. And when Mr Jenkins gave us a talk about our exams, he told us if it all got too much we should see our GPs."

"I'm sure he was only talking about extreme cases, Sky," Mrs Bayliss said. "And GPs can help students if they're struggling to cope."

"By medicating them," Sky snapped, her face flushing red. She took a deep breath to try to regain her composure. She wanted Mrs Bayliss to take her seriously, not think of her as a tantrum-throwing child.

"In some cases, yes. But really, Sky, we're talking about a tiny minority here. Often a GP will refer a student for counselling, or some CBT sessions."

"It's not a tiny minority, though," Sky said, searching through her bag and pulling out a piece of paper. "I've got some figures here and they're really shocking. The number of young people being given antidepressants has gone up by more than fifty per cent in the last seven years. And there've been massive rises in the number of people with anxiety and eating disorders and self-harming, too. And I think the way schools are run has played a big part in that."

Mrs Bayliss was silent for a moment. Sky's heart was pounding so loudly she wondered if she could hear it. "So, what would you, with your unique perspective, as you put it, suggest that we do?" she eventually asked.

Sky came over and stood by her desk. "I think students should be allowed to have more of a say in how things are done."

Mrs Bayliss gave a dry laugh and Sky instinctively prickled, thinking she was being patronizing. "That would be lovely, Sky, and I wish teachers could be given more of a say in how things are done too, but unfortunately, that's not the world we're living in."

"So why don't we change it, then?" Sky looked at her hopefully. It sounded as if Mrs Bayliss was pretty disillusioned with the system too.

Mrs Bayliss sighed. "Ah, to be young and idealistic again." She leaned forward in her chair. "You're really serious about this, aren't you?"

Sky nodded. "I want to do something. I don't want to be one of those people who just mopes around and moans."

"And that's very commendable." Mrs Bayliss looked in her drawer and pulled out a leaflet. "Have you heard of the student council?"

Sky shook her head.

"Well, I think you should make that your first port of call. If you have suggestions for how our students' needs could be better met, the council can campaign for them on your behalf. You could always join them if you like; I know they're always looking for new members. You might also want to look into the Youth Parliament."

Sky looked at her questioningly.

"It's the government who decides how schools are run, Sky, not the teachers – sadly. So, if you want to bring about change you need to put pressure on the decision-makers – the *real* decision-makers."

Sky nodded.

Mrs Bayliss put her glasses back on and picked up her pen. Sky turned to leave.

"I admire your spirit, Sky," Mrs Bayliss said, just as she reached the door. "Try to hold on to it. Don't let the world make you cynical."

Sky turned back and smiled. "Thank you, miss. I won't."

The first person Amber saw when she arrived at school and made her way to her locker was Chloe. Typical. Talk about coming back down to earth with a bump. Amber took a deep breath and braced herself for the onslaught.

"You think you're so good, don't you?" Chloe said, walking over to her. "Swanning off to Paris. Writing all about how great you are on your stupid blog."

A hush fell over the crowd of students at the lockers.

Amber looked at Chloe – at her beige face and bitter stare – and all she could see was unhappiness oozing from every foundation-clogged pore. Why would she need to keep endlessly picking away at Amber if she was happy with her life?

"Why are you so obsessed with me?" Amber said loudly.

"What?" Chloe's glossy, pouty mouth fell open in shock. "I'm not obsessed with you."

"Yes, you are. You must be. All you ever do is hang around me like a bad smell." Amber heard a snigger from the crowd. For once it wasn't directed at her.

Chloe's face flushed. "I'm not obsessed with you. You're the gay one."

"But I'm not the gay one. You know that. You read my blog – obsessively."

The school corridor was completely silent now. Everyone was watching and waiting to see how Chloe would respond.

"You are gay. Your dads are gay. You dress like you're gay," Chloe spluttered.

"No, I don't. I dress like I have flair and imagination – because I do. Unlike you, you pathetic sheep."

"What did you call me?" Chloe stepped right up to Amber, so close that Amber could smell the stale cigarette smoke on her breath.

"I called you a pathetic sheep," Amber replied loudly, not moving a muscle and not breaking her gaze.

"Are you asking for a slap?" Chloe hissed.

"No, but why don't you give me one and see what happens." Amber felt a fury building deep within her. All of the years of fear and frustration, all of the pain caused by Chloe, morphing into a fierce rage. Amber clenched her fists. She'd never hit anyone before but she felt ready. She could practically hear Oscar Wilde in her head, egging her on. She moved even closer to Chloe. They were so close now that they were practically nose to nose, like two boxers psyching each other out before a fight. Then the weirdest thing happened. Amber saw a flicker of fear in Chloe's eyes – and Chloe stepped back.

"Yeah, well, I wouldn't waste my energy on you, anyway," she muttered.

A murmur of surprise rippled along the corridor. Amber remained standing tall as she watched Chloe and the rest of the OMGs skulk off.

"Well done!"

A group of girls made their way over to Amber, smiling.

"You were great," one of them said.

"Yeah, you really put her in her place." Another of them laughed.

Amber's face flushed and she started to grin. All these years she'd felt scared of Chloe but now she couldn't for the life of her understand why. Going to Paris had expanded her world far beyond this school and all that happened here, making Chloe mouse-like in her insignificance.

"Oh my God!" Amber heard Sky exclaim. She turned and saw her beaming at her. "What just happened? You were amazing!" She grabbed Amber in a hug and for once, Amber's instinct wasn't to stiffen but to hug her right back.

"I'm not exactly sure," Amber said. "But it felt really good."

"I bet!" Sky grinned at her. "I'm so proud of you!"

Amber smiled. There was something different about Sky

too. Considering they were at school, she looked remarkably happy. She felt her phone vibrate in her blazer pocket and took it out.

"It's from Maali," she said.

"Any news?" Sky asked, instantly looking anxious.

"No," Amber said, reading the text. "They've got to wait for the consultant to do the rounds – should be some time this morning."

Sky nodded. "OK."

"Do you want to see my Paris photos?" Amber asked.

"Absolutely." Sky linked arms with her. "I can't believe you went to Paris on your own *and* faced down Queen OMG all in one week. You're my hero."

Amber laughed. "I can't quite believe it either! But it's Oscar's fault. He made me do it!"

Chapter Thirty-four

As Rose made her way out of school she checked her phone for about the millionth time. Her heart skipped a beat as she saw that she finally had a text from Maali.

No news. Consultant still hasn't been.

The text was so blunt and so unlike Maali that Rose could practically feel the tension that had gone into typing it. She didn't know how Maali and her parents were coping. She'd found it bad enough to wait all day to hear something; she hated to think what it was doing to them.

Thanks for letting me know. Love you Maals. Stay strong xoxoxoxo ps do you want us to come to the hospital?

Maali replied almost instantly:

No it's ok. Thanks.

Rose looked up and down Hampstead High Street. Unsure of what else to do, she started texting the other Moonlight Dreamers.

Still no news from the hospital. I say we go up there. Sky no worries if you can't come. Amber and I will let you know what happens. xoxo

Sky's heart dropped like a stone as the bus turned off Euston Road. They were almost at the hospital. Next to her, Amber was checking her phone, completely oblivious to the panic welling inside of Sky. She looked down from the top deck. Outside, commuters and tourists were scurrying along the pavements like worker ants, all completely oblivious too.

"Still no news from Maali," Amber said.

Sky's heart sank even further. What if it was bad news? What if her dad had cancer? Would she be able to stop her own pain from showing? She rested her head against the grimy window and took a slow, deep breath. There was no way she was going to chicken out this time. She was going to be there for Maali, even if it was bad news — *especially* if it was bad news.

"OK, the next stop's ours," Amber said, getting to her feet.

As Sky stood up her legs almost buckled. *Come on*, she told herself. *You can do this.* And somehow she made her way along the swaying bus, down the stairs and out onto the pavement.

"Here we are," Amber said, leading Sky into a large London square.

Sky, who'd been gazing at the ground, plucked up the courage to look up. She felt a slight twinge of relief. The grand old red-brick building in front of them didn't look very hospital-like. If it weren't for the blue and white sign over the door saying THE NATIONAL HOSPITAL FOR NEUROLOGY & NEUROSURGERY Sky would have thought it was a Hogwarts-style school.

"Sky, you came!" Rose exclaimed, running across from the communal garden in the centre of the square.

"Of course." Sky smiled at her weakly before Rose pulled her close for a hug.

"I'm so proud of you," she whispered in Sky's ear.

Sky nodded and looked back up at the hospital. She hadn't been with her mum when she'd received her cancer diagnosis. She'd been too young. The day it had happened, her teacher had given her a message that after school she was to go to her friend Claire's house for tea. At the time Sky had thought it a really fun surprise. She loved having tea at Claire's house. Sky shuddered as she remembered Claire's mum dropping her back home afterwards – the deathly expression on Liam's face as he'd opened the door. That day had turned out to be a cliff-hanger of a chapter-ending in her life story. Sky thought of Maali, somewhere inside the hospital. Was a chapter in her life about to come to an abrupt end too?

"How much longer are they going to be?" Maali hissed to her mum as they helped themselves to drinks from the water cooler at the end of the ward.

"I don't know," her mum whispered back. "But it can't be much longer. The day's almost over."

Maali stared angrily around the ward. She hated this place, with its hand-sanitizers and sick patients and strip-lighting. She wanted to be home. She wanted this nightmare to be over. She'd tried so hard to be patient and strong for her dad, spending all day playing stupid games and doing stupid word searches, but now she'd had enough. She felt like a piece of elastic, stretched to breaking point. Why was it taking the consultant so long? Had there been some kind of complication with the biopsy?

The ward door swished open and Maali spun around. But it was just a relative for one of the other patients, carrying a huge box of chocolates. *Where was the consultant? Why hadn't she come yet? Did this mean the news was going to be bad?* The ward door opened again and Maali's stomach lurched. The consultant was striding towards them holding a clipboard, her white hospital coat billowing out behind her like a cloak. Two more junior-looking doctors were running along behind her to keep up with her stride.

They hurried back to Maali's dad's bed, only just getting there before the doctors.

"Good evening," the consultant said, looking over her

half-moon glasses. She looked so stressed. *Why did she look so stressed?* She nodded to the curtain behind the bed and one of the other doctors pulled it round, so that they were partitioned off from the rest of the ward. *Why were they doing that? Why didn't she want anyone else to see? Was it because the news she had on her clipboard was bad? Was she worried they were all going to break down in tears?* Maali slumped into a chair beside the bed.

"I'm sorry to have taken so long to come and see you," the consultant said. "It's been a very busy day."

"That's OK," Maali's dad replied, smiling at her. *How was he able to stay so calm? How was he able to smile?*

"So, as you know, your surgery was a great success. As far as the scans show we seem to have removed all of the tumour."

Yes? And? Maali stared at her. *Was the tumour cancerous?* She shot a desperate glance at Kali. *Please. Please. Please.*

Amber stood in front of the bench that Rose and Sky were sitting on and stared up at the hospital. They'd been waiting in the garden for almost an hour now – Rose had texted Maali to say they were there – but they still hadn't heard anything.

"I think it must be bad news," she said grimly.

Sky got to her feet and started pacing up and down. "We need to be ready," she said. "We need to know what to say to her."

"What *do* you say to someone in that situation?"

Rose looked at Sky. "What should we do?"

"I suppose the only thing we can do is let her know we're here for her," Sky said. "And we need to be positive. Even if it is cancer, it doesn't mean that…" Maali was standing in the entrance to the hospital, silhouetted against the bright light inside. "Look."

The others turned to follow her gaze.

"Oh God," Rose whispered.

They all watched in silence as Maali made her way over to them.

"She's been crying," Rose whispered as Maali passed beneath the orange glow of a street light.

Sky's palms went clammy and her mouth dry.

Maali came and stood in front of them.

"He's OK," she whispered, tears spilling from her eyes. "The tumour was benign." Then her legs gave way.

Three pairs of arms reached out to catch her – and held on to her tightly in the silver moonlight.

Chapter Thirty-five

Maali placed a gingerbread-scented candle on her shrine, in between the statues of Kali and Lakshmi. It was Christmas Eve. Snow had started to fall softly outside, frosting the glass pane of her skylight. It was almost a year since she went downstairs to find her dad dizzy and confused in the living room and that whole nightmare was about to begin. So much had changed since then.

"Thank you," Maali whispered to the goddesses.

Her dad still had to go for regular check-ups but, apart from the scar running across the base of his skull, you would never know he'd been seriously ill. It was weird how, at the time, her dad's brain tumour had seemed like the worst thing in the world but, with hindsight, Maali could see there'd also been gifts in the experience. Having faced the prospect that she might be about to lose her dad meant that she no longer got stressed about the small stuff. And she appreciated her family more than ever. She knew her parents felt the same way too. They no longer put in such long shifts at the shop. They all spent more quality time together.

"Thank you for teaching me so much," Maali whispered as she picked up Kali and gave her a quick polish. She'd also learned that even in the darkest hour, there was always the hope of brighter days to come. Kali had helped her to see that although change could be painful and destructive, it was always possible to find love at the heart of it, in the eye of the storm. She put Kali down and picked up Lakshmi.

"Thank you for not giving up on me, even when I gave up on you. Thank you for helping me to still believe in love." She dusted the figurine, then placed her back on the shrine.

Rose saw a group of tourists approaching and walked out in front of the stall, holding a plate full of bite-sized pieces of cake.

"Get your fresh cupcakes here!" she cried. "Debuting today, the Minty Mistletoe."

"I taught her everything she knows, you know," Mel said with a proud grin.

"Why, thank you, kind sir," Rose said in a mock British accent. "Would you like a sample?" she said, offering the plate to the tourists. As one girl took a piece of cake, Rose had a sudden flashback to the day of the disastrous model casting, when she'd walked out on Matt and the others in the pub and bumped into Francesca outside her shop. It was a moment, Rose realized, that had gone on to change her life for ever. How awesome that on any given day, you could find yourself in a life-changing moment like that. She glanced across at Jet, who was inspecting the trays of jewellery on her own stall. The slogan on her t-shirt read F*** CHRISTMAS! over the picture of a skull clad in a black and white Santa hat.

"Whoa!" the tourist girl cried, putting her hand to her mouth. Rose watched her anxiously. Was it a good "whoa" or a bad one? The girl said something to her friends in what Rose thought was Italian. The next thing she knew they were all taking a piece of cake. Rose felt a wave of elation. She'd spent ages perfecting the recipe to get the balance of dark chocolate and peppermint just right.

Each of the tourists ended up buying a Minty Mistletoe, which meant they'd sold out before lunchtime. Success indeed. Rose couldn't wait to tell Francesca later, when she came to relieve her.

"Guess what?" Rose said, making her way over to Jet.

"What?" Jet looked at her and smiled. She smiled a lot these days – well, at least once a day – and when she did her whole face was transformed.

"I just sold out of Minty Mistletoes."

"I'm not surprised. They're delicious." Jet planted a kiss on Rose's lips. "I'm proud of you, babe."

Rose grinned and made her way back over to her stall. Yes, Jet was a pussy cat really, once you got to know her.

Amber typed the words THE END and gazed, startled, at the screen. She'd done it. She'd actually finished her first stage play. Well, the first draft of her first stage play, anyway.

There'd been many days, many *weeks*, when she thought she'd never see this moment. When her characters didn't seem to want to do what she told them and her plot took her down dead ends or tied itself in knots. But somehow she'd found the strength to keep going. Or rather, Oscar had given her the strength to keep going. She looked up at the quote she'd printed out and framed above her desk.

"Most people are other people. Their thoughts are someone else's opinions, their lives a mimicry, their passions a quotation."

In Amber's darkest moments of playwright's block she'd looked at that quote and willed herself on – to keep writing from the heart, to keep writing her truth – for Oscar. And now here it was – a whole ninety-three pages of script. She opened her desk drawer to get a memory stick to save a back-up version and caught sight of Gerald's sketch of her surrogate mum, buried beneath a pile of books. She took it out and stared at it. This time last year it had felt so loaded with meaning and now it was just a set of random lines on a page. To think that she'd invested so much hope in that sad gaze. To think that she'd been so wrong. Amber now knew that you'd never find your true identity inside another – even if you shared their DNA. Your true self was something you were born with – an original, unique you buried deep inside, like the smallest in a set of Russian dolls. And, even if you lost sight of it for a while, it was always there ... just like the moon. She took the sketch downstairs to the kitchen, where Gerald was standing red-faced at the stove, making his Christmas Eve paella.

"I think you should have this," she said, handing him the sketch. "I don't need it any more."

Sky stared at her laptop, then stared at Leon, who was lying sprawled across her bunk, jotting in his notepad.

"Oh my God, 'Free to Be's got a mention in the *Guardian* Online!"

Leon put his pad down and sat upright. "How come?"

"It's in a feature on the education system. It's only a mention – but it's a mention!"

"That's amazing!" Leon grinned at her. "Read it."

"'After a wave of recent protests by secondary school students, such as the Harlington High sit-in and the online *Free to Be* campaign, changes might be afoot in the education system.'" Sky sat down on the bunk next to Leon and continued to read. "'In a statement released by her office this week, the Education Secretary has outlined plans for an enquiry into the wave of unrest, to take place in the New Year.'" Sky stared at Leon. "Oh my God!"

Leon put his arm round her. "You did that, Sky-Blue."

"No, a lot of people did it."

"But you started it – putting the poem on YouTube and creating the hashtag and all the online campaigning."

Sky nodded but it felt impossible to comprehend. To

think that this time a year ago she'd been so terrified of starting school. And now, the government was taking notice of a campaign she'd started to make positive changes to the school system. "You started it, really," she said.

"How come?"

"With your poem 'Be the Change'. That night you read it in the Poetry Café – the night we met – you made me see that I didn't have to accept things I didn't like. You made me see that I could try to do something about it. I'm so glad you were there that night."

Leon smiled. "You and me both!" He kissed her, then checked the time on his phone. "I better get going and let you get ready for your Dreamers."

Sky leaned into him, soaking up the warmth for a few seconds more. One of the things she loved most about Leon – and there were a lot of things she loved most about Leon – was the way he was so understanding of her friendship with the Moonlight Dreamers and how he never tried to come between them. All of the girls loved him for it – even Rose, who had become even more understanding since she'd got together with Jet.

"Happy Christmas, Sky-Blue," Leon said, hugging her tight.

"Happy Christmas, Leon."

"OK, girls, I'm off to Savannah's," Liam said, coming out onto the deck of the houseboat. It was a couple of hours later.

Leon had gone home and the other Moonlight Dreamers had arrived.

"Good luck," Rose retorted. "When I left, she and Margot were making vagina vision boards."

"What?" Sky spluttered.

"It's to help them visualize how they're going to utilize the power of their sacred flower in the New Year, apparently," Rose explained.

"OK, I really don't want to know what that means," Amber said.

"I do," said Maali with a grin.

"It's basically just a *flowery* way – get it – of stating their dreams for the year," Rose explained. "Mom's got training to become a landscape gardener and doing a course in interior design on her list. Now that she's quit modelling the world's her oyster."

"It certainly is," Liam said. He'd barely stopped grinning since he and Savannah had got back together. But Sky was happy for him. He and Savannah had taken things much more slowly this time – going on dates like normal people and not moving in together. "I'll see you girls later, then," he said to Sky and Rose. "Don't forget to lock up when you're done here."

The girls watched him disappear into the darkness on the tow-path.

"Shall we go up on the roof?" Sky asked. "There's more room up there – and we'll be closer to the moon."

They instinctively looked up at the sky but it was too cloudy for any sight of the moon.

"Good plan," Rose said, grabbing a flask from the deck.

Once they were sitting in a circle on the roof Rose opened her flask and offered it around. "Home-made hot chocolate with a twist," she said.

"What's the twist?" Amber asked.

"Try it and see."

The other girls tried the drink and murmured their appreciation.

"Is there orange in it?" Maali asked.

"Yep. And a dash of cinnamon."

"It's lovely," Sky said and Rose grinned with pride.

"So, another year almost over," Amber said.

"Can you believe how much has happened since our meeting last New Year's Eve?" asked Maali.

"No!" Sky said. "Seriously, if someone had told me back then what was going to happen to me this year, I'd never have believed them."

The others nodded in agreement.

"Can you all remember what your dreams were?" Maali asked.

Amber laughed. "Yes. Well, mine certainly didn't come true."

"Yes, it did," Rose said. "Just not in the way you thought it would."

"You're right." Amber nodded.

"Same here," Maali said. "I thought meeting my soulmate meant meeting a boy, but now I know that soulmates aren't always a romantic thing." She looked around at them and smiled. "You guys are my soulmates and I wouldn't change that for the world."

"Amen, soul sister!" Rose raised her hand for a high-five.

"My dream didn't work out at all how I'd imagined either," Sky said. "When I dreamed of making poetry a bigger part of my life I had no idea that a poem I'd write would end up going viral!"

"Or that you'd fall in love with a poet," Maali said – slightly wistfully, Sky couldn't help noticing.

"Yes, that was definitely a bonus!" Sky grinned.

"And when I dreamed of properly kissing a girl I had no idea it would be with my arch nemesis," Rose said with a grin. "Or that I'd end up finding ragey chicks so attractive!"

"Do you think dreams ever turn out the way we plan?" Maali asked.

"Sometimes," Amber replied. "But it's the times when they don't that makes life so interesting."

"Yes." Maali smiled.

Amber sighed. "I wish it wasn't so cloudy."

Maali nodded. "I know. I want to see the moon."

Sky looked up and grinned. "Here she comes."

They all watched as a cloud scudded across the sky and an almost full moon began to appear.

Sky thought back to all the times earlier in the year when she'd looked up at the moon and begged it for help. And she wondered if maybe, when you told your fears to the moon, the moon heard and helped pull you towards the right decisions and the right people, just as she pulled the world's tides in and out, back and forth. As Sky looked around at the other Moonlight Dreamers, their faces glowing in the silvery light, she felt certain it was true.

ACKNOWLEDGEMENTS

A huge thank you to Mara Bergman, Emily McDonnell, Alex Spears, Kat Jovanovic and the rest of the team at Walker Books for all of your passion and enthusiasm for the Moonlight Dreamers ... not to mention the most beautiful covers! Ditto Walker Books Australia – it's a dream come true to be published Down Under. *Merci beaucoup* to Marie Hermet, Celine Vial and the team at Flammarion. A big shout out to K-Ci Williams for being the Moonlight Dreamers' number one cheerleader in New Zealand. And to Dubray Books in Ireland for all of your support. It's been such a thrill to see *The Moonlight Dreamers* being so well received around the world.

Thank you so much to Erzsi Deak at Hen & Ink and Jane Willis at United Agents.

Huge thanks also to all of the book bloggers, readers and reviewers who showed *The Moonlight Dreamers* so much love. I hope you enjoy catching up with Amber, Sky, Rose and Maali in their latest adventure.

Much gratitude as always to my family and friends.

Over the past few years I've been lucky enough to meet thousands of young adults from all around the world in my Dare to Dream workshops and talks. Every time I've come away feeling hopeful and inspired. YOU are the future. Your dreams matter. You have the power to make the world a much better place. I hope this book encourages you to be the change you want to see. Thank you for the great conversations, the lovely emails and for giving me so much hope for the future.

Siobhan Curham is an award-winning author and life coach. Her books for young adults are: *Dear Dylan* (winner of the Young Minds Book Award), *Finding Cherokee Brown*, *Shipwrecked*, *Dark of the Moon* and *True Face*. She loves helping other people achieve their writing dreams through her writing consultancy, Dare to Dream, and she was editorial consultant on Zoe Sugg's international bestseller *Girl Online*. You can find Siobhan online at:

www.siobhancurham.com
Twitter: @SiobhanCurham
Facebook: Siobhan Curham Author

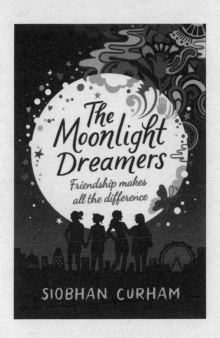

Amber, Maali, Sky and Rose may be very different, but they
all have one thing in common: they're fed up with being told
how to look, what to think and how to act.

They're not like everyone else
and they don't want to be.

An inspirational and heart-warming story
that celebrates friendship and finding
your place in the world.

#MoonlightDreamers